Nogglz

a novel

Tom Walsh

Nogglz
a novel
by Tom Walsh

Living Life Fully Publications

First Printing: 2015

ISBN: 978-1-329-19890-6

http://livinglifefully.com

To my colleagues at CVHS—
thank you for everything;
and to all students with whom
I've had the privilege of working
over the years—thank you, too!

hi anne-
thanks very much
for offering to help-
i hope you enjoy
the story!
tom

Prologue

Twenty-seven people. In the entire town. Twenty-seven souls living their lives in a tiny run-down mountain town filled with ramshackle houses that had seen some sixty winters and summers, almost all built within a three-year period back in the 30's when the coal mine was running full bore, when there were enough people around to fill all seventy-five houses with workers and their families.

Now, though, most of them stood empty, many falling apart, giving way to the ravages of time and weather. Several had collapsed over the years, but there was no one in town who had any reason to clear the debris. The town's location on a bluff a mile from the mine gave it a wonderful view from its southern edge, but it also put it in the way of severe weather all year long. From what Emily had been told, snowfall in July was not out of the ordinary. The average age of the people who lived there now had to be in the mid-60's. She had all the data she needed now, and she would just have to do the math to get the exact figures for her study.

She stood now next to her car on Main Street, the only paved street in town and the road that led off the bluff and down the mountain towards civilization. Just like the town, the pavement had seen better days. Some of its cracks ran a good fifty feet long, telling tales of passing time and reminding one of better days—the days before the cracks, when the road was new and whole, when children would ride their bikes on it and fall and scrape their knees, but then get up and cry it out and get on with their lives. Now, though, there was no reason at all to repair a road in a town like Canyon Bluff.

The November sky was brooding, grey and dismal. It threatened to start the season's snowfall, which surprisingly enough hadn't started yet just two weeks before Thanksgiving. She pulled the bag that held her notebooks up to her chest as she gazed at the houses that squatted there silently, enduring the cold and awaiting the onslaught of the season of wind and blizzards and frigid temperatures. Her notebooks were filled with the words of the townspeople, the ones who were still sticking it out in CB, the ones who had either tons of gumption or no other options, who lived on their Social Security checks and had nowhere else to go, no one else with whom to spend their last few years on this planet. She felt especially sorry for those who owned their houses and who could move only if they were able to sell them, which had been a virtual impossibility here for at least two decades.

No one was coming into town. There was no reason to do so and plenty of reasons not to. No school. No store. No restaurants. Even the Post Office had abandoned the place some fifteen years back.

When Professor Kiefer had suggested that she create a profile of the town for her master's thesis, she had loved the idea. It would be fascinating to find out all about the people who still hung on in a town with no future, with nothing to it but memories of better days behind. And in reality, the project so far had been a good one. Her research had taught her a great deal about how such towns come to be born and then die, how they can trip into a slow and agonizing descent into oblivion that can be avoided only if human beings make the decision to stay there, to contribute to the community, to stick out the bad times and the good.

For some towns, though, oblivion seems to be only a matter of time.

The good part was that the town made her feel young for a change. As a thirty-five-year-old graduate student, she almost always felt quite old on campus. Now the situation was turned around—except for a few younger people like Juan and Brad and Brian who were living in houses they had inherited from their parents, she was the youngest person within thirty miles.

Emily looked down at her car and smiled. It was eight years old and had just gone over one hundred thousand miles, but it was definitely the newest car she had seen anywhere in town over the last two days.

The people she had met had surprised her, though, for the most part. She had expected despair and hopelessness, but what she heard from the folks she had met was more in the line of resilience and orneriness. They were mostly good-natured folk—Emily made a special note to focus on the word *folk*, as it was so apt—who made the most of all that they had and where they were, even if most other people would see their situation as completely unbearable.

But it was the Nogglz that most perplexed her. Professor Kiefer had scribbled a note on her proposal: "Make sure to ask about the Nogglz," and then had refused to discuss the matter each time she asked about it.

"You're going to have to ask the people in the town," he told her. "I don't want to poison the well with my take on that."

And Emily had found that bringing up the Nogglz during her interviews was a sure way to kill conversations, a sure way to shut people up or to get them to change the topic immediately. A couple of people had dismissed the idea as an old wives' tale and had been willing to talk about them, but others seemed to take the idea very seriously. No matter what the response, though, there was no one who didn't know anything about them, and no one who was completely comfortable with the idea of them. She hoped that her last two interviews would be a bit more fruitful concerning them, but they would have to wait until the next day. It was close to dark now, and she had a half-hour drive ahead of her to get back to her daughter and her aunt's house for her last night there. Even though Pine was a tiny town itself, she was looking forward to getting to a place where they at least had someplace to eat and a few stores.

After her last interviews tomorrow, she would be able to head home so that she could get back to her classes on Monday.

One

Announcement

Sarah slowly closed her brother's leather-bound journal, then sat quietly gazing at it. The years had dried the brown covers so that they were rough and cracking, a fact that mattered not at all because no one ever opened it any more. She considered whether or not she would share it with the young woman who was coming to interview her the next day. Her project sounded interesting, but Sarah knew that she would be getting only a small portion of the story of Canyon Bluff by talking to the townspeople. There were certain things that no one wanted to talk about, that none of them discussed even among themselves these days. The journal would help her to understand what those things were and why no one was willing to discuss them.

On the other hand, was it any of her business? Should the story that Canyon Bluff had spent so long and worked so hard to keep to itself find life outside of the town? How many people's trust would she be violating by sharing this journal?

They were all getting old. What would happen if the last of them were to die—and those things were still there? And nobody knew what they were? She sighed as the thought stayed in her mind. She had never been able to shake the feeling that she was somehow responsible for them being there, that everyone who had ever lived in the town was responsible. It was a ridiculous thought, she knew, but one that would not leave her in peace.

The time had to be coming for some kind of change, she knew. But she knew it less than she felt it in her bones and her blood—change *was* coming. Perhaps the change was her own passing. She was certainly getting older.

She was looking forward to meeting somebody new, to having a guest in her home. It had been years since she had entertained her last visitor. When Emily had first come to her door two days earlier and asked for the interview, she had been hesitant at first. But once she had committed herself, she found herself getting more and more enthusiastic about spending time with another human being, about sharing her story, about telling someone else about the lifetime that she had been trapped in this town because of her father's legacy.

Her house was small, but more than roomy enough for her. Her décor was traditional and extremely unimaginative, from the paisley wallpaper to the uncomfortable blue couch that she never sat on, as she much preferred the even-less-comfortable matching chair where she sat to read or watch television. She paced now between her living room and the end of her dining room table, considering the choice she had to make about the journal. The dining room itself was almost a hallway, but wide enough for her small table against the wall and the three chairs that stood around it. A long shelf separated the area from the kitchen, which was also quite narrow. One end of the dining area opened up to the living room that had a small fireplace as its main focal point on the east wall. On the other end it led to a pair of doors on the left that led to two bedrooms, a very short hallway that led to the door to the basement, and a door on the right that opened up to the bathroom. Hers was a sparsely furnished home, a fact that she found fitting considering the sparseness of her existence her entire life long.

Suddenly she heard a sound from the basement, and she was immediately on edge. Adrenalin surged through her body, making her uncomfortable and edgy, as it always did when she heard unexplained noises in her house. She stopped dead in her tracks, just between the living room and the dining area. She stood motionless, listening, for at least two full minutes. And she wasn't motionless just to listen—if her greatest fears ever were to come to pass, she certainly didn't want to be heard, either.

She began to weary of the hyperattentiveness, and she slowly felt her body relaxing. Her mind started to pull back from listening, and she began to hear the night sounds again, the wind in the trees just outside the kitchen windows. She hadn't realized just how tense the sound had made her and she felt it fully in her shoulders and her back only as the tension ebbed from her body like a wave pulling back from the shore.

She looked around herself, counting the lights that were on, wondering if they'd be visible from the basement through any chinks in the floor. That's just paranoia, she told herself, but then silently chided herself for thinking such a thought. Anyone who had a door in her house like the one downstairs had every right in the world to feel tense and paranoid—even terrified—at any unexplained noises in the house. She had lived with tension for almost all of her 62 years in this town; it was as much a part of her as her hair or her fingernails. She had accepted it. She had no choice.

She finally shook her head and took a silent step towards the kitchen. At least four minutes had passed since the sound, and she was almost ready to chalk it up to a mouse or a chipmunk that had gotten into her basement and was searching for food and knocking something over.

These were the nights when she felt loneliest and the most helpless, when the burden of her years seemed heaviest. She had learned when she was still very young that hers wasn't to be a normal life, and that truth had dogged her every single day that she continued to breathe and her heart continued to beat. Husbandless, childless—even friendless in the strictest sense of the word, Sarah had made her way along a path through life that rarely intersected with the paths of others, that never took her through celebrations or joy or even grief. Her path always kept her in sight of life, but never let her step past its edges. There were times—many times, in fact—when she wished nothing more than that her path would come to an end, for she was tired of being alone, and tired of the burden her father and brother had tasked her with.

She forced herself to go through a mental checklist: the door downstairs was triple bolted shut, and the door itself and the locks were all made of reinforced steel. She had to be safe, she reassured herself, because nothing could get through that. At least, that's what her father had told her. The door to the basement was locked, though if anything managed to get through the steel door, it would be nothing for it to get through the one at the top of the stairs.

The journal. It had to stay safe. She grabbed it and quickly went into her bedroom, where she put it into the small portable safe in her closet. This she considered to be the most important thing she could do, because if her worst fears ever came true someone had to know what had happened to her. She closed the safe and made sure that it was securely latched. She was feeling extremely nervous now, almost to the point of being nauseous.

It seemed that this happened at least once a week. Living on her own up in the mountains wasn't bad enough, being far from everyone and everything. She had to be tied to her family's history, one that she didn't completely understand—she had to be the one who kept watch at the house, the dark house on the north edge of town that most of the other people in town regarded as an ominous, horrifying place that they wouldn't visit even on a drunken dare. The stories were bad, but they were stupid. Nobody really knew at all what they were talking about when they talked about the house's history. Sarah had done fairly well with the house. She had used the trust fund quite effectively to fix it up and at least make it as livable as possible. But no matter how livable she tried to make it, the house still had her under its control, demanding her time and attention and presence forever and always.

Tonight was different than the other nights, though, for just as Sarah turned on the water in the sink so that she could start washing the plate and fork and glass that she had used for dinner, she heard another sound from the basement, and it was no mouse. It was a loud thud, like something slamming against a wall—or a heavy door. In moments she heard the sound as a continuous pounding, a drumbeat that terrified her to the very core of her being. She was on high alert again; the adrenalin rushed through her body again; a chill fell over her heart.

She really didn't know what to do. Should she go downstairs and investigate? Should she hide? Should she get the hell out of the house?

Before she could make a decision, a loud screech from metal on metal—reinforced steel on reinforced steel, she was sure—forced her to cover her ears with both hands, an effort that didn't help to block the sound very much at all. She suddenly couldn't think straight, and she found herself paralyzed with fear. This was it, was all she could think; this was what Dad warned me about all those years ago. What did he say I was supposed to do?

The question crashed through her fear and brought her to her senses. Warn people! That's what she was supposed to do. But warn them of what? About all the stuff in the journal? But everything in there was from fifty or sixty years ago—who in the world would possibly take her seriously?

She turned, intending to go back to her bedroom and grab the safe, but the screeching sound forced her to start immediately for the front door. To hell with the journal. She didn't have time to grab anything, and the journal at least was safe. She suddenly knew that she had to find Jackson—he would know what to do. He'd been in CB forever. The sound was now constant, like someone rubbing metal on metal. Or trying to open a metal door that hadn't quite given yet.

And suddenly, after one last loud crash, all was silent.

She stopped in her tracks, just as she was reaching for the doorknob. A feeling of horror started to overwhelm her just as she noticed the horrible stench that now filled her small clean living room. She started to gag, and she watched in terrified fascination as the roses in the vase on the end table—a birthday gift to herself just two days ago—began to wither in front of her. She heard the pounding of feet on the stairs to the basement, and then the sound of the door at the top of the stairs being smashed open.

Sarah grabbed the doorknob and turned it, only to find that she had already locked the deadbolt. The two seconds that it took for her to unlock it with her shaking hands were enough for the creature that had crashed through the basement door and appeared in the living room behind her to strike. It looked human—shriveled and bent and wiry—but human nonetheless.

But looks can be deceiving, because what it did to Sarah, few humans could have done. She was fortunate that its first savage and ruthless blow to her head killed her.

Two
Discovery

Taylor was out walking Fritz early the next morning when she passed Sarah's house. It was odd that Sarah's door wasn't open yet, as she was usually the first one up every day, out for a long brisk walk followed by breakfast on that wonderful porch she had added to the house—even when it was this cold. It usually pissed Taylor off that Sarah was so cheerful, because there wasn't a single other person in town who was any sort of cheerful at all. Taylor was stuck there at the age of 72 because she didn't have anywhere else to go. That fool of a husband of hers had bought their house in town with the promise that "one day, when people see how beautiful this area is, this house is gonna make us rich as hell."

As hell was right—just as the coal had died fifty years earlier and her husband had died thirty years back, her hope had died as the popularity that Jessie had promised her had never come to be. And with the sparseness of the Social Security payments that she got and her complete lack of any family anywhere else, moving just wasn't in the plans. He hadn't made her rich, he had never given her any kids, he had gone and died early and left her stuck in a hellhole that was shrinking before her very eyes every year. She used her morning walk with Fritz to ruminate over the past and blame her dead husband for pretty much everything, and it usually made her feel a bit better. As a matter of fact, she usually felt fine for the rest of the day.

But never so damned cheerful as Sarah.

Something was wrong—Taylor could feel it. She had already passed Sarah's house, but she turned slowly and regarded the house closely. There didn't appear to be anything out of place or missing. But the front door was closed, that was for sure.

Taylor decided just for her own peace of mind to go find out if Sarah was okay; she knew that it would eat at her all morning if she didn't. Fritz the Yorkshire Terrier, though, wasn't nearly as sure that such a thing was a good idea. As soon as Taylor started up the walkway to the house, the dog started whining and pulling back on his leash, trying to set his tiny feet in defiance but just being dragged along in spite of his efforts.

"What the hell's wrong with you, Fritz?" Taylor demanded, dragging the dog along behind her. "It's just a little social call."

Fritz wasn't convinced, and his whining grew louder as they climbed the three steps to the porch.

"Oh, just shut up," Taylor said impatiently, trying to decide if she should look in the window first or ring the doorbell. Since the blinds were still down, she decided on the doorbell.

She waited for about thirty seconds after she rang it to call out Sarah's name. "Sarah, honey, where are you?" she yelled. When there was no answer to her call, she reached for the doorknob. It was just what neighbors in tiny isolated communities did in their efforts to help each other out when help was needed. What would happen if Sarah were sick and she couldn't come to the door? Someone had to do something. Not trying the door was almost a crime.

The door was unlocked, which didn't surprise Taylor a bit, especially since she hadn't locked her own door ever. She pushed it open slowly. Before she had a chance to look inside, Fritz started up such a howling that she had to turn around to shut him up. He would have none of that, though, and he pulled so hard on the leash that Taylor just let him go—she knew he'd go straight home, so there was no need to worry. "Stupid mutt!" she called after him, then turned back to the door which had swung open in the meantime.

The first thing to hit here was the smell, and she quickly covered her nose with her hand. Then she was astonished to see that someone seemed to have sprayed red paint all over the walls of Sarah's living room, and she surveyed the walls in stunned fascination for just a few moments until an uneasy realization started to creep into the back of her mind. The thought was confirmed a few seconds later when she dropped her gaze to the floor and saw an arm—it had to be Sarah's arm, she thought deliriously as she started to lose everything—lying on the throw rug in front of the TV.

And then she did lose everything, and she collapsed on the porch of Sarah's house. It was good that she lost consciousness when she did, or she would have seen much, much worse than a severed arm.

Three
Facing Demons

Ray was pissing in the river when he got the call. He was on his way to what the sheriff generously called the station when the third cup of coffee that morning forced him to pull over and relieve himself. Six months on the job in the mountains had made him take things much easier and much more slowly, especially since Bill the sheriff encouraged that approach. It doesn't do much good, he always said, to be working at a high level of intensity when the people you're working for and with generally function at no level of intensity at all. And while for the most part Ray had always been a go-getter who tried to excel, he found that the sheriff was right: taking things easy was absolutely necessary in the Colorado mountains if he didn't want to be ridden out on a rail or shot in the back at some random moment by some random poacher or thief or drug addict.

It wasn't that the people who lived there were lazy or mean or anything like that; it was just that they had the pace and style of life that they had chosen, and they didn't appreciate it when someone came along and told them they had to change, whatever the reason. When in Rome, Bill always said, though Ray wasn't completely sure what the connection was between Rome and Richardson County.

The call was a relay from the sheriff, who told him to get up to Canyon Bluff as soon as he could. CB's location made it impossible for them to have radio contact when they were up there. Any calls had to be phoned to the station, where Janet would then relay the message on the radio. If the call came at an odd hour, they just called Janet at home. This call came with no details at all—just a sense of urgency.

Since Ray was a good thirty miles away, he had at least forty minutes in the car to wonder what the hell was going on. Bill usually at least gave more details about what was going on if he called for Ray. And Bill was extremely capable and had years of experience, so a call like this had to make Ray wonder. Did one of the loners up there in the middle of nowhere finally lose it and blow himself away? Or blow away someone else?

A light mid-November rain fell softly but steadily as he made his way up the mountain to the old coal-mining town. From what Bill had told him, the town was full of miners' descendants who never had moved away, or people from anywhere who were just looking for a place where they wouldn't be bothered. Ray wasn't really looking forward to spending time amongst a bunch of old geezers who didn't have anything going for them. And they were well armed old geezers, too. Bill said that the number of guns per person up there was among the highest in the country, but he almost never had any problems from anyone other than minor disturbances. Ray guessed that with that many guns and probably everyone carrying a concealed weapon, people would be too afraid to get on anyone else's bad side. Or maybe there was just no reason to get on anyone's bad side.

He was surprised that the rain wasn't snow yet—the fall had been mild so far, with temperatures reaching the low 40's almost every day. It wasn't normal, but it did make driving easier. Other than the large pothole that he had to swerve to avoid and that he normally would call in, he made good time to CB. When he crested the small ridge that looked down over the town, he saw Bill's car with the lights still flashing in front of a modest dark red house next to the small cliff that worked its way up higher to become part of the mountainside. The house was set back at least thirty yards from the street, unlike all of the others that had been built almost right on the street in an obvious attempt to cram as many living quarters as possible into the available space.

Ray hadn't spent much time in Canyon Bluff, given the size of the sheriff's jurisdiction. The county included at least 12 other small mountain towns that had been established decades earlier at the height of the coal mining boom. Wherever coal was discovered, a town went up quickly, and the mining companies added to their profits by building all the houses and renting them out to the miners and their families, not to mention building the only stores and saloons in the towns. And when the mines had petered out, the people of the towns found themselves with nothing to do except leave, or stay on and subsist in whatever ways they could find. When Ray really thought about it, he wondered how the hell most of the people actually were able to get by.

There were more than fifty houses in CB, he guessed, but most of them stood empty, silent memorials of days gone by, better times when they were filled with families and kids played on the streets and men dreamed of days when they could get out of the mines and give their families a better life. Most of the empty ones were in bad shape, with unstable foundations and rotting beams and broken windows and sagging roofs. Some of the occupied buildings weren't in much better shape.

Ray parked behind Bill's cruiser, a modified SUV that allowed him to drive over some of the roads that a normal car couldn't handle. He saw Bill sitting on the top of the steps leading up to the porch; there was no tape put up, given where they were—crime scene tape seemed a bit silly sometimes.

Ray started to worry as he approached Bill. The sheriff didn't even look at him approaching; it was like he hadn't noticed that he had pulled up. Bill just kept staring straight ahead, as if he were pondering something that had his mind completely occupied. Ray slowed his pace when he smelled the acrid odor of stomach acid, and he glanced at the ground next to the steps and saw a puddle of vomit—someone had had bacon for breakfast and hadn't chewed all that well, he noticed.

"What the hell's up, Bill?" he asked quietly. "Is that your breakfast?"

The sheriff looked up at him with surprise. Bill really hadn't noticed him arrive. He glanced behind himself at the house, as if to reassure himself that he was where he was, then looked back at Ray.

"Hey, Ray," he said quietly. Then he paused for several long moments. Ray waited. The sheriff was big and stout—he had to be six-three and at least 210—but at that moment he looked weak and frail. Bill turned back towards the house. "I suppose you're gonna have to have a look inside," he drawled, revealing his Southern origin. "It ain't pretty."

Ray didn't say anything. There was a tension in the air that was almost tangible, and it didn't feel good. He slowly but resolutely started up the stairs. A little voice inside was telling him not to go, but another voice told him that this was his job and he had to go.

When a bird suddenly burst out in song from the fence separating Sarah's yard from the neighbor's, Ray suddenly realized that he was still in the world—his mind had become so focused on Bill and on wondering what was going on that he had lost sight of that fact. He was suddenly very aware of the creaking of the wooden stairs under his feet and the peaceful breeze that blew across his face. Visually, the door and the small outside part of the peephole became clearer, more distinct, and he didn't even need to turn his head to see the rest of the porch because he could see everything there in his peripheral vision. He had entered a zone the likes of which he hadn't felt since his high school football days, and he didn't know why—but he guessed quickly that it had to do with adrenaline and the danger that he thought he would reveal as soon as he opened the door.

He paused only the slightest of moments once his hand touched the doorknob and he looked back at the sheriff, who was back to staring straight ahead. Not a good sign, he told himself, then turned the knob and pushed the door open.

His eyes were first captured by the splashes of deep dark color on the walls—it looked as if someone had gone crazy with a can of spray paint or had just dipped a brush into the paint and stood in the middle of the room and swung the brush, creating random patterns everywhere. He knew immediately that it was blood that had darkened almost to black by now, and he felt a lightheadedness wash over him quickly. He dropped his gaze to the living room couch just below the blood, where he saw a woman's head lying carelessly among the pillows and the throw that had been there; the head was facing him, staring at him accusingly with the one eye that was left. He felt the bile rise in his throat and he slammed the door shut, turned and bolted down the stairs and fell to his knees and threw up in the middle of the lawn.

His mind wouldn't leave the image of the head, no matter how hard he tried to banish the picture. He looked helplessly at the sheriff, who was now regarding him almost curiously.

"Two for two," Bill said quietly. "What'd you see?"

Ray stood, feeling queasy and not trusting his legs. He was right not to trust them, and he almost immediately sat down hard on the grass.

"I made it to the head," he managed to say, choking back the retching that was trying to make its way through his throat again.

The sheriff nodded. "I didn't get much further," he said. "I ain't never seen anything like that before."

"What do we do?" Ray asked, completely at a loss about how to proceed. "What are we supposed to do?" Bill didn't answer immediately, and Ray looked around the scene, almost surprised to notice the trees and the flowers in the narrow garden that bordered the street. He realized that something was missing.

"Where is everyone?" he asked. Crime scenes were usually interesting to onlookers, who hung around to try to be the first to learn anything so that they could pass it on to everyone else.

"Chased 'em off," Bill said. "There were only a couple of people, anyway." He let out a long, labored sigh and then slowly got to his feet. "My legs weren't working either after I looked in there," he said. "There ain't nothing can prepare you for something like that. I already called the state police—they should be here in half an hour or so. What we gotta do is go inside and make sure the immediate danger has passed."

"Go in there?" Ray asked, as if he didn't believe what he had heard. He knew even as he asked, though, that Bill was right. "Holy shit," he muttered.

Bill smiled wryly. "This is where we earn those huge paychecks they give us every couple of weeks." He reached to his holster and unsnapped it, then drew his pistol and made sure that there was a bullet in the chamber. Its weight in his hand was reassuring, and he felt a sudden confidence from being armed. "Make damned sure you're ready to fire and that you've got a full clip," he ordered Ray, who stood again unsteadily and drew his weapon.

"You sure we can't wait for the troopers?" Ray asked.

Bill gave him the look that told him that he already knew the answer to his own question, then turned and slowly ascended the stairs. Ray followed.

Four
Awakening

Killing the woman had been satisfying—no, more than satisfying, it had be[illegible] act that he had waited sixty years to commit. Sixty years of dark, of anger [illegible] resentment and the desire for revenge had come to a head so quickly. Sixty years of searching for the way out, the escape route that had been blocked off by the explosion.

But he knew nothing of sixty years. In fact, it could be said that he knew nothing at all. His brain had long ago stopped processing information on the level of thought. Rather, it served as a host for instincts and forgotten feelings—the anger and the desire for revenge were no longer conscious elements but simply integral parts of who—or what—he had become. He felt the bloodlust that filled him, and he knew instinctively that his companions felt the same thing through every bit of their shriveled, wasted bodies that somehow possessed incredible strength and speed.

The killing had been good in a visceral way, and they felt the urge to do more of it. He was satisfied with the killing, though satisfaction was a concept that he no longer understood. For some reason he had kept on after she had died—kept on attacking her as if she were fighting back, as if with every pull and tear and rip he were exacting deeper revenge, making her hurt even more. He had felt almost as if he had been an observer of the carnage that his body was creating, and that was a feeling that he had had often over the last six decades. He had no idea who she was or why it was her that he found on the other side of the door, and he really didn't care.

He was beyond caring.

They even tried to feed off of her—for so long they had eaten nothing but the glowing moss and worms—but their teeth were almost completely gone, and there was no way they could bite into the flesh.

The world under the surface was nothing but dark. It felt good to escape the pain of the lights, but they really had no conscious realization why they felt drawn to return to the depths after the killing. He and the other four had simply made their way back down into the darkness before the sun came up. Not that he knew when it would rise—or even that it would rise—but their instincts were stronger now than they had been before their time below. They had finally made their way out, and they could be patient—they had waited this long, after all.

They didn't use language to communicate—their larynxes had long since ceased to function normally to give them voices. But their connection to each other was much stronger than it ever had been on the surface. They had been together so long down there that they seemed to think as one at times; they knew what they needed to do and when to do it. He had made sure that they went back down—his gestures made it clear that they had to leave, and none of them were happy about that choice. But he was still somehow in charge of them after so much time, and the others were used to following his directions, like them or not. So they went back down into their prison, feeling that this time, they would be back out whenever they wanted to leave, In a matter of hours rather than decades.

And they would be back.

* * *

Emily drove slowly up the mountain, not wanting to take the curves too quickly on the wet road. This was her last day in Canyon Bluff, and she wanted it to be over soon. She had agreed to meet with Sarah at ten-thirty, but she wanted to arrive early just in case she might get started before then.

She was starting to feel antsy, wanting to get home, and it took all her effort not to simply turn around and drive back down to Pine and then to the highway that would take her back to her nice, comfortable house. These interviews were interesting enough, but she was pretty sure that she wasn't going to hear anything new today. Though talking to Sarah did seem to be a promising prospect, based on what she had heard about her from others.

She almost stopped when she hit a large pothole in the road, one that shook her car violently as the right front wheel dropped into the hole and hit its opposite side straight on. She didn't remember it from her previous two trips up. She was able to swerve just enough to avoid hitting it with the rear wheel also. It surprised her and forced her to slow down, but when she couldn't notice anything different with the way her car drove, she decided to continue on to CB and her interviews. It wasn't like she had much of a choice.

She was more than a little surprised to crest the hill where Main Street started and see two police cars on Main Street in front of Sarah's house, one of them with its lights still flashing. She slowed down and pulled over to the other side of the street just short of the vehicles and saw the word "Sheriff" on the door, then she looked up to Sarah's house. There was no one there, but the door stood wide open. She looked at her watch; she was supposed to meet with Sarah in about forty minutes. It didn't look like that was going to happen, though. She looked down the street and noticed Taylor standing in the garden before her house. It would probably be her best bet to see if Taylor could tell her what was going on before she bothered the sheriff with any questions. She pulled back onto the street and slowly drove the extra fifty yards that brought her to Taylor's house. She smiled and waved as she caught Taylor's eye, but though Taylor weakly returned the wave, there was no smile in return.

Five
Hidden Features

In a speech class in college, Ray's instructor had suggested that students look at the wall in the back of the room if they got nervous and needed to avoid making eye contact with other students. Ray remembered that strategy now and tried to make full use of it, staring at the corners where the walls met the ceiling so that he didn't look directly at anything on the floor or anywhere else as he followed the sheriff into Sarah's home. He supposed that as a law enforcement officer he should be examining the crime scene carefully, but he wasn't up to that yet.

"We're in here quick, and then we're out," Bill told him. "We go together and we don't split up. You got that?"

"Absolutely," Ray responded gratefully—the last thing in the world he wanted to do was to go around checking out rooms on his own.

"We're looking only for imminent danger," the sheriff continued. "We can look for everything else later. If the perp is still here—which I seriously doubt—he's probably hiding in a closet or in the basement. If you see any movement at all, don't hesitate to shoot. Sarah didn't have any family that anyone knows of, and no pets neither, so there's no reason at all for anyone or anything else to be in this house."

"Gotcha." The word sounded strange to Ray as soon as he said it. This didn't feel like a "gotcha" situation.

They moved swiftly through the living room, where Ray's peripheral vision betrayed him and allowed him to see the body parts that were strewn about. Fortunately, he couldn't make out any details unless he looked straight at them, something that he was avoiding. He did know that the victim's torso was under the window in the corner of the living room, and Ray could make out the legs and arms in various spots in the room. There was something that he couldn't quite identify under the dining table, but he had no intention of examining it more closely to figure out what it was.

The stench in the room was awful. It reminded him of the smell of rotting meat, but it was different.

"The smell is horrible," he said suddenly.

"Sure is," Bill agreed. "At first I thought it was from the body, but it hasn't been here long enough to start smelling."

"Maybe she was just a bad housekeeper?"

"Yeah, right. If you feel light-headed again, warn me if you're leaving because I'll be coming with you. I ain't about to be left alone here in this house."

"I'm okay."

"Good. Living room and kitchen are clear. Looks like we've got a bedroom over here to the left. The door's open. I'll lead."

That was one of the things that Ray liked about working with Bill—Bill never would ask one of his deputies to do something he wouldn't do himself.

And in this situation, given the many more years of experience that Bill had, Ray was glad that he was on point.

The bedroom was untouched. None of the attack had happened here. Bill led the way over to a door in the corner, behind the queen-size bed, and pushed it open with his foot. The bathroom also was empty and clean.

Bill turned and looked around, and Ray could tell that he, too, was glad that they could look about in the room without seeing blood and entrails and body parts. Bill pointed his pistol at the closet door. "Go open that door," he said quietly.

Ray moved quickly to the wall beside the door, then reached over and turned the doorknob and pulled the door open, leaving Bill a clear shot in case he needed it.

There was nothing dangerous. Clothes on hangers, shoes on the floor, a small safe on the shelf above the clothes.

"Reach in and push on those clothes," Bill said, and Ray caught his drift. He stayed to the side and reached in and shook the dresses and coats, then pulled them to one side as far as he could. "Looks clear," Bill sighed. "Come on, we've still got the rest of the house to go."

"Shouldn't we take the safe?" Ray asked half-heartedly. He didn't really want to carry it around with them while they were clearing the house.

"Grab it," Bill replied tersely. "And put it on the dining room table. Let's go."

It took them only another minute to be sure that the main floor was clear. After they checked what looked to be a spare bedroom, both of them eyed what looked to be a door to the basement.

"I hope that's a closet," Ray said quietly, "because I sure as hell don't want to go down into any basement."

"Only one way to find out," Bill replied. "Flashlight?"

"Yeah." He reached to his belt and pulled off the light.

"Cover," Bill said, then reached and opened the door as Ray backed up and took aim. Ray felt his heart drop as he saw the top step of a stairway leading downward. The door came open without any effort on Bill's part, and they both saw immediately how the wood had been torn apart where the latch had been—the door had been smashed outward.

"Look," Bill whispered, pointing with his flashlight, even though the top few steps were lit by weak sunlight. Ray looked where he was pointing and saw a large smudge of red on the top step, then trained his light downward—every step had blood on it, and most steps had several smudges. He looked straight down at the floor beneath his feet and saw Sarah's blood all over it—spread by what seemed to be footsteps.

"What the hell?" he asked aloud. "Why didn't I notice these before?"

Bill grinned without humor. "When you're looking at the ceiling the whole time, you don't see much on the floor, now do you?"

Ray sighed. "Yeah," he replied, "but you don't throw up all over the place, either. Now do you?"

Bill chuckled, but said nothing.

"This looks like more than one set of footsteps," Ray said. "What the hell is up with that?"

"Don't know," Bill said. "But it don't look good."

"Whoever killed her went down there afterwards."

"Most likely."

"And is probably still there."

"Could be."

"And we've got to go down there and check it out."

Ray felt a bit of hope grow in him when Bill didn't reply immediately, and he hoped to hear words to the effect of waiting for the state police to arrive. His hope was quickly dashed.

"Yeah. Let's get this over with." And with those words, the sheriff reached out and flipped the light switch in front of him. He smiled wryly as the light came on. "Looks like we don't need these," he said. He put his flashlight back on his belt, then started down the steps. "Don't know what I was thinking." Ray followed closely.

The basement was small and simple. It consisted of four walls of cinder block, and the north wall—the wall that was built up against the mountainside—had a doorway built into it. On the cement floor lay what looked to be a solid steel door, one that Ray guessed easily could have been used as the door to some sort of vault, it was that thick and heavy. The footprints were less obvious here, but there were still a few splotches of blood on the floor. There was enough for them to know that the footsteps led through the doorway and out of the basement.

"What the hell?" Ray whispered. "Is that a cave?"

"Mine shaft," Bill said, looking over the door. "This thing's solid steel, and something's knocked it right off its hinges." Ray saw his eyes grow wide for just a moment. "And if I ain't crazy, whatever did it, did so from inside the shaft." Bill reached down and tried to lift one end of the door, but he was able to lift it only about a fraction of an inch before he let it back down again. "It's solid something," he said quietly.

Ray took his flashlight back out of its slot on his belt and turned it on, moving over to the shaft entrance and playing the light into the dark, where it diminished quickly into nothingness.

"What the hell is she doing with a mine shaft in her basement?" Ray asked.

"Don't rightly know," the sheriff replied. "But for now we're just getting the hell out of here."

"You mean you don't want to head into a dark, narrow mine shaft to go after something that ripped a woman apart, armed only with a pair of flashlights and a couple of pistols?"

"You could put it that way," Bill said. He turned and started for the stairs.

"Works for me," Ray said, with one last glance down the shaft, which ran level for as long as the light lasted. He followed Bill up the stairs; the horrid scene in the living room brought him back to reality and ripped his mind away from the mine shaft for the moment. He would never know that if his flashlight had been a bit stronger, he might have caught a bit of movement as something scurried away from the light, something that felt pain when the light hit its eyes, and something that wanted more than anything else to rush out of the shaft and kill these new people.

Six
Hints

Ray and Bill stood quietly on the lawn, both of them looking down at the grass, deep in thought. They both knew that one or the other would have to say something soon, but neither of them had any clue what to say. As he looked down at the dying grass, Bill realized that he could practically count the blades. He felt hyper-aware, and his mind was racing in a thousand different directions, none of which he liked. "Okay, breathe," he told himself, hoping to calm his nerves and slow his brain. As he focused on breathing slowly and deeply, he felt himself relaxing. Soon, given his position as sheriff, he found the need to speak overwhelming.

"All right," he said finally, "what do we do now?"

Ray made a sound that sounded almost like a laugh. "Hell, I was hoping you'd be able to tell me, Bill."

Bill shook his head. "I've never come across anything like this. What's in there just ain't right, and there's no way for me to believe that it actually happened."

"But there it is."

"But there it is. We have to assume that whatever it was that did this came up from the basement, out of that mine shaft. We have no idea if that door's been knocked down for some time, or if that also happened last night."

"Whatever? Not whoever?"

"I don't know of too many whos who can bust their way through a door like that. Maybe a large bear could have knocked it down, but how the hell would a bear come up from a mine, knock down a steel door, dismember a woman, and then head back down into the mine? Not to mention the fact that the footprints in there look to be from a human being. Or beings. Or something close."

"What could that door be for?" Ray demanded. "Who builds their house right over a mine shaft, anyway? And then closes it off with a door like that? Do you think that door was there before they built the house? Was the mine there before they built the house?"

"I've got nothing but a whole lot of I-don't-knows for you. This is an old mining town, and trust me, the mining towns had secrets that the rest of the world never wanted to know. People lived by their own rules, and the mining companies ruled however the hell they wanted—there wasn't anyone who would dare challenge their laws. Miners were mostly decent folks, but they were pretty much trapped where they were. The company owned everything, and the miners and their families had no real say in how anything was done. And a town like this was the worst of all because it was so far away from the nearest law."

"But what does that have to do with the shaft downstairs?"

Bill looked at Ray as if he couldn't believe the question. "Just told you, Ray—I have no idea. Sarah could've told us, but she's kind of dead right now.

I'm sure someone in this town knows something, but I also know that gettin' someone to talk won't be easy.

"The whole situation sure could lead to a lot more speculation. The main coal mine was a mile up the hill. Someone could've started their own mine in their own basement, though they would've had a helluva time getting rid of the dirt and rocks they pulled out as they went along. There could be lots of reasons for someone to want to keep something like that secret. Could be someone was after some gold or silver on the side."

"We aren't going to have to go down in there, are we?" Ray asked.

Bill shook his head. "Not until we have a whole army to go down there with us. When the state police get here, we'll come up with some kind of a plan then. Right now, the best thing we can probably do is talk to the woman who found her this morning. She was pretty hysterical when I first got here, but could be that she's calmed down a bit since then. Think you could go talk to her?"

"Sure," Ray replied, glad for any excuse to get away from the house. "Anything in particular you want to find out?"

Bill shook his head. "The usual. Everything you can. I'll hold down the fort until the troopers get here."

Better you than me, Ray wanted to say, but he stayed silent.

"She's in that blue house over there," Bill said, pointing across the street. "White shutters, nasty little Yorkie in the yard, if it's still out. Number 24, I think. Her name's Taylor. Taylor Humphrey, if I'm not mistaken."

"I can do that," Ray assured him. "'Nasty little Yorkie'?"

Bill gave him a stern look. "Any dog smaller than a golden retriever is a nasty little something."

Ray laughed in spite of himself. "You sure we should split up?"

"Ray, I'm not sure of anything right now. But I figure the best we can do is do *something* rather than just standing here twiddling our thumbs and going over and over in our minds what we just saw in there. There's a lot to be said for keeping yourself busy sometimes."

"I guess you're right. See you soon, then." Ray walked to the street and headed towards the house that Bill had pointed out. He had to fight to notice details as he walked now; his mind was so completely overwhelmed that nothing appeared normal to him. He focused first on the pine tree to his right, then on the first house on his left, and in a few moments he started to notice details of the street, the pavement that was severely aged and falling apart in places, the dirt that passed for sidewalks on either edge of the street, the lack of a center stripe, the cookie-cutter houses that lined the south side of the road. Over the years they might have been painted different colors, but there was no hiding the fact that they all came from the same basic design. At a different time he might have tried to imagine what it would have been like to try to raise a family of five or six in one of these tiny boxes, but today wasn't a day for imaginative thinking.

There was a part of him that knew that as a sheriff's deputy, he eventually would have to be exposed to unpleasant crime scenes. He had hoped that it would come later rather than sooner, though. He was only 23, and he had many more years to give to his career. A dismembered body could have come years later, like it did for Bill. Bill was only a couple of years from retirement and he hadn't seen anything like this, but for Ray it had come early.

He was a bit surprised by the lack of people. Anywhere else, curious people would have congregated quickly and stayed together until they got answers. He didn't notice any signs of life, though, even though he knew that there were some people in the town. Not even a curtain falling back into place after someone looked out at him. Nothing.

There was no dog in the tiny yard of Taylor's house, so he opened the gate and followed the walkway five steps to the door and pushed the doorbell. He wasn't surprised when there was no sound; he had been half-expecting to have to knock anyway. He did, immediately sparking an outburst of annoying little-dog barking.

As he waited for a reply, he looked up at a few blue patches in the sky. The rain had stopped, but the day wasn't about to become pleasant—they were deep into autumn, and he knew that days like this usually turned into snowstorms eventually. The air just smelled of snow. He took a deep breath in and held it for a few moments, then let it out slowly. Then he knocked on the door again.

"I'm coming," came a weak-sounding voice from inside. A few moments later, he heard someone working the locks from inside, then the door swung open to reveal a frightened old woman pointing a very large pistol directly at him.

Ray stepped quickly to the side, out of the path of the pistol's aim, but her wavering hand followed his motion. "Hold on there, ma'am," he said quickly. "Be careful with that thing!"

Taylor didn't reply immediately. He could see the fear in her eyes, and even more the confusion that had to result when she had seen something so unexplainable. Ray knew that he was having trouble himself getting a grip on reality, and this was his job. But for an older woman who had accidentally happened upon a scene like that. . . .

"Oh, deputy," Taylor mumbled. "Come in, please forgive me, come in." Ray reached out and took the gun from her without a word, then stepped past her into the house. She immediately closed the door behind him and locked it with both the lock on the knob and the deadbolt. Ray watched, realizing suddenly that if the steel door that he and Bill had seen was any indication, those locks would do absolutely nothing to protect anyone inside the house.

Taylor reminded him immediately of his Aunt Karol. She only came up to his chin, and her silver hair fell straight to her shoulders. Her face was deeply wrinkled, a fact that gave it a look of character and wisdom. Despite her current state, she seemed to be an energetic person, and her green eyes looked friendly enough, though also somewhat challenging.

"Ms. Humphrey," Ray said quietly, "I know you've been through a lot, and I'm really sorry but I do have to ask you a few questions, if you don't mind."

Taylor looked him in the eyes, and it was as if she were suddenly seeing him for the first time. She shook her head to clear it, then looked back at him.

"Mind?" she said. "Hell no, I don't mind. I need to talk to someone, even if it is a deputy." She stopped. "No offense, I'm sure you know."

Ray managed to smile. "None taken," he said. "Is there somewhere we can sit down?"

"Right here, in the kitchen," she said, motioning to a table that was covered with books and papers. Another woman, younger, was sitting at the table, holding a coffee cup in her hands, looking at him with curiosity. This woman was in her thirties, with jet black hair and soft brown eyes that smiled at him even though there was no smile on her lips.

"This is Emily," Taylor said. "She's been in town to interview us all the last couple of days. I think she's trying to figure out why we're all crazy enough to stay up here in this charming *ville* of ours."

Emily stood up and shook Ray's hand. "Emily Ramirez," she said. "Actually, I'm doing a master's thesis on the people of this town."

"You must be studying psychology," Ray said as he reached out and put Taylor's pistol on the table. "Lots of craziness in this town, that's for sure." He surprised himself with his own sense of humor, though Emily didn't seem to get the joke.

She shook her head. "Anthropology, actually," she replied. "It's nice to meet you, deputy."

It was Ray's turn to shake his head. "I'd normally say the same thing," he said, "but under the circumstances, I'm not sure what to say."

Emily nodded. "Taylor told me a bit of what she saw over there. I made her stop, though. It's really bad, isn't it?"

"It is." Ray pulled out a chair and sat, and Taylor and Emily both sat, too. Just as they did so, though, there was a loud knock at the door and Taylor jumped right back up to her feet as her dog started barking once more. Ray stood, too. "I'll get the door, Ms. Humphrey," he said calmly. "Please, have a seat and keep that pistol put away."

He went to the door and opened it to find a man he had never seen before. "Hello?" he said, looking the man up and down. He looked to be in his late sixties, but Ray could tell immediately that he wouldn't want to mess with him, no matter what his age. He was thin and wiry and looked to be strong for his size—Ray had seen plenty of skinny guys easily take care of guys twice their size when they needed to do so.

"Deputy," the man said, nodding. "Taylor in?"

"Yes, she is," Ray told him. "She and I were just sitting down so that I could ask her some questions."

"Without a lawyer present?" the man demanded, narrowing his eyes.

Ray was taken aback. "Lawyer? She doesn't need a lawyer. I'm just—"

The man suddenly laughed and slapped Ray on the shoulder. "I'm just shittin' with you, deputy. You won't mind if I join you?" the man said, not really asking and stepping into the house past him. "Taylor?" he called out as he passed Ray. "You okay, Taylor?"

"Jackson!" Taylor replied. "I'm so glad you're here!"

Jackson looked at Emily. "You're still here?" he asked with a smile. "We haven't run you out of town with our tales of woe yet?"

Emily smiled slightly. "Not yet," she said. "This may do it, though."

Ray locked the door and came back to the kitchen and joined the other three at the table. The first thing that he noticed was that the pistol had been placed on the table where its edge met the wall.

"How are you holding up, Taylor?" Jackson asked her.

"I'm better now," she said with a faint smile. "With two strong men in the house, I feel safer, anyway."

"What the hell happened?" Jackson said, turning to Ray. "What's going on with Sarah?"

"Oh, Jackson, it was terrible!" Taylor cried out. "There was blood all over the walls, and I looked down at the floor, and all I saw was an—an—" she couldn't finish, and her voice trailed off into silence.

"If she looked at the floor," Ray said as matter-of-factly as he could, "then she probably saw an arm." His thought was verified when Taylor let out a sob and covered her eyes with her hands.

Jackson regarded him with a look that he couldn't decipher, started to say something and then stopped. Emily paled a bit more, and she looked queasy. Jackson looked at Taylor, then back at Ray.

"We don't know who or what," Ray told him, pulling over another chair from against the wall and sitting down, "but someone or something killed Sarah last night, and. . . well. . . basically ripped the body apart."

"Who the hell would do something like that?" Jackson demanded. Ray saw that he suddenly looked thoughtful. His face was as thin as the rest of his body was, and his grey hair reached his shoulders—it looked like he still had as much hair now as he ever had. His skin was tanned, even this late in autumn, which told Ray that he spent a lot of time outdoors. His eyes were blue—a cold, piercing blue that Ray imagined could make the strongest person tell the truth if Jackson were to demand it. They were eyes that you couldn't resist. Jackson wore a red wool shirt and jeans, with no jacket. He looked like someone who belonged in Canyon Bluff, someone who had been there an awfully long time.

"We have no idea, really," Ray replied. "We only had time to go through the house and secure it. Once the state troopers get here, we'll be able to find some more answers, I'm sure. Ms. Humphrey, here, was the one who discovered the body this morning. As far as I know, she's the only other person who's seen anything."

"I passed right out on that porch," Taylor said, lifting her head. "I saw that arm, and I passed right out. I'm lucky that whoever did it wasn't still there, or I would have been an easy target. I came to a few minutes later and I came home as fast as I could, locked every door and every window, and called the sheriff. Fritz was the smart one—Fritz wouldn't go anywhere near that house. I wish I would have listened to that damned dog, and hadn't opened that door. I don't know if I'll ever be able to sleep again without nightmares, I'll tell you. It was horrible. Horrible!"

Jackson reached out and took her hand.

"Ms. Humphrey," Ray started, but Jackson interrupted him.

"Call her Taylor," he said. "Her name's Taylor. Call her Taylor."

Ray lifted his eyebrows, more out of surprise than anything else. "Fine," he said. "Taylor, did you notice anything different about the house this morning, anything out of the ordinary?"

Taylor looked at him as if he had just asked a stupid question. "Well, of course I did—that's why I went to the door in the first place. Sarah is usually the first person up around here, and by that time of the morning, rain or shine, her front door is usually open. Even when it's cold, mind you. She likes the fresh air. This morning, the door was closed. I figured she might be sick, or need help or something, but I never imagined. . . ." Her voice trailed off.

"Was there anyone else around, anyone that you didn't recognize, anyone that seemed out of place?"

"Deputy, in this town, everyone is out of place. Even most of the people who live here. When we see outsiders, we know immediately. There was no one like that this morning."

"Other than the door not being open, did you notice anything different?"

She shook her head, looking tired. Tired and scared.

"Deputy, I appreciate the fact that you and the sheriff need information," she said, "but tell me this—if we don't find who did this today, what's going to happen tonight?"

The question surprised Ray, mostly because it was something that he hadn't had time yet to consider. He had been thinking about the carnage as a matter of law enforcement, of figuring out what had happened and who did what, but all of a sudden he saw the personal stake that everyone in the town held. What would happen that night? Or the next night? In the case of killers, he had learned that they rarely if ever struck two nights in a row, but since they had no idea what they were dealing with here, could they be sure of that? All of a sudden he realized the public safety issues involved, and he felt even more unsure of himself.

"I don't know," he said simply. "I honestly don't know. We're going to do everything we can to make sure this doesn't happen again, but we really have no idea what we're up against at this point."

"You're up against evil, deputy," Jackson told him.

Ray was puzzled, and he was sure that Jackson could see that in the way he was looking at him.

"What do you mean?" Ray asked finally.

"I mean that Sarah's house has always been marked by evil, ever since it was built. And now that evil has freed itself. I'd be willing to bet you found something in there that you didn't expect to find, something that kept that evil at bay. But now it's got loose, and it's killed the gatekeeper. And if you haven't found that something, you aren't looking hard enough."

Ray cleared his throat. He was unwilling to tell Jackson that he was crazy, but he was also unwilling to believe that something evil could have come from that house. As much as he didn't want to believe it, though, his mind leaped suddenly to the door that had been covering up the hidden mine shaft. "Umm—gatekeeper? I don't get you," he said, trying to sound nonchalant.

"Look, Sarah never wanted to live here in this town. She lived here because her brother set up a trust fund for her that made her comfortable enough to stay without working, without any real responsibility. Her only responsibility has been that house. Now I knew her brother—he was a bastard, and he was the son of a bastard. They've always kept that house completely off-limits to anyone else. They've been hiding something in there, and none of us know what it is. There have been plenty of rumors, but no one really knows anything at all for sure. The only thing that is sure is that there's something wrong over there." Jackson spoke sincerely, and he spoke forcefully, and Ray found himself believing him. But all in all, there was nothing specific to believe, nothing that would give him any clues as to what had happened.

"Could you be more specific?" Ray asked Jackson.

"No, I can't. I've never been in the house. And Sarah never talked. At times she'd run her mouth a bit and say something she probably shouldn't have said, but that was pretty rare. All we know here in town is that she has never stepped foot out of this town for the last twelve years, and that she rarely even leaves the house. That woman was ecstatic when satellite TV finally got here because she finally had some contact with the outside world. Cable companies never would run cable all the way up here for so few people. Not that TV did her any good at all. But that trust has kept her going ever since Wayne died, and I don't think she's worked a day in her life. She definitely hasn't worked a day in the last thirty years, which is when he croaked."

"Wayne?"

"Wayne. Her brother. Like I said, he was a real bastard, and he had complete control over his sister. She hated him, she said after he was gone, but there she was, still doing his bidding by living in that house and living off that trust. That was the main stipulation of the trust—that she continue to live there and never leave the property for more than twelve hours at a time."

"Never? How do you know all this?"

"Never. My wife used to work in the bank down in Pine, and they administered the trust. She wasn't supposed to tell me some of this stuff, but she did anyway. Not a whole lot more to talk about up here."

"So you're saying that the reason that Sarah stayed in the house all day every day was whatever it was that killed her? But what would that be?"

"I have no clue," Jackson said, slowly and deliberately. "And I'm pretty damned sure that I don't want to know. What I do know is that it had something to do with her father, David, and her brother, Wayne. I think it's mostly her father, and her brother just picked up where he left off. Read up on the Naugles, and I think you'll start to get an idea of what evil sons of bitches those people were. How the old man ended up with a sweetheart of a daughter like Sarah, I'll never know."

"Are those the Nogglz I was supposed to ask about?" Emily asked, looking up from the notes that she had been taking.

Jackson looked at her as if he were suddenly seeing her for the first time. Then he smiled wryly. "Looks like you're getting a hell of a lot more than you bargained for up here, aren't you?" Emily and Ray exchanged a glance as they realized that Jackson had evaded her question.

Ray's radio suddenly came to life with a loud series of high-pitched beeps, startling all four of them. Taylor put her hand over her heart when she saw where the sound came from, relief that it was something known showing through her fear.

"Sorry," Ray muttered, pulling the radio from his belt and responding. "This is Ray. Go ahead."

"Need you down here, Deputy," came Bill's voice, loud and clear. "Troopers are here." His voice sounded more natural to Ray than it had when he had left Bill twenty minutes earlier.

"Gotta go," he said to Taylor and Jackson. "Look, I'd like to hear more about these Naugles. Are you going to be here in town all day?"

"Looks that way," Jackson replied. "I had planned on going into Pine, but today doesn't seem to be the best of days for that. But don't count on any of us telling you more about Naugle's boys. Only person could've done that is having lunch with God right about now. Or breakfast. I don't know the time difference."

"Would I be able to talk to you later, anyway?"

Jackson looked from Ray to Taylor. Then he nodded. "I'll probably be here, watching after Taylor. She's been through a lot."

He saw Emily sitting quietly, an intent look on her face. He felt that he wanted to say something to her, but he had no idea what. She just looked completely out of place, just as he felt.

"She certainly has," he replied. "Then I will see you later, once we're through at the house." Ray shook hands with Jackson, then took his leave of the trio to walk back to Sarah's house. Outside, the soft rain had once more begun to fall, and there were no more breaks of blue in the clouds. He noticed a beat-up blue pickup in front of Taylor's house; it had to be Jackson's. It looked like it had been around forever, and he guessed it would probably last forever, too. Just like Jackson seemed that he could.

Seven
Troopers

"This is Sergeant Mike Fogel," Bill told Ray a few minutes later. "That's his partner over there, Corporal Alejandra Lopez. This is Deputy Ray Lerner."

"I'm very pleased to meet you, Ray," Fogel said formally, reaching out to shake his hand. Ray immediately disliked him—something about the way that he carried himself and the way that he spoke made Ray uneasy. He was instantly glad he didn't have to work with him regularly. They stood in the middle of Sarah's lawn, while Lopez was over by the house, too far away to hear them.

"I understand that you've just interrogated the witness who discovered the body?" The question was spoken more as a command than as an inquiry.

Ray paused before he spoke. "I don't really interrogate witnesses, especially old ladies who just saw what she just saw. Yes, I talked to her." He turned to Bill. "And I talked to a man named Jackson, too, who was there with her."

Bill nodded. "Good man, Jackson. He's a good one to have on your side if you ever need anything up here."

"He seemed pretty straightforward."

"Absolutely. Like I said, get on his good side."

"Gentlemen, if we could stay focused here," Fogel interrupted, "I think it's time that we go inside and survey the crime scene."

Bill looked at Fogel as if he didn't believe what he had just heard, then looked back at Ray and lifted an eyebrow, as if to ask "Is this guy for real?" On another day, Ray might have laughed. Today there seemed to be nothing funny.

The sheriff looked Fogel straight in the eye. "I know you've got to go in there, but you'd better prepare yourself for what you're going to see. It's not just that it ain't pretty, but that it's a worse thing than most people could ever even imagine."

Fogel looked towards the house, then back at Ray, then at Bill, like he was trying to read their faces. "I think we'll be fine, Sheriff," he said with a hint of derision in his voice.

"I'm sure you will be," Bill replied. Ray knew he wasn't sure at all. Fogel looked soft, like a loaf of squishy white bread that you couldn't cover with peanut butter without ripping it apart. His face was a bit rounded because he was somewhat overweight, and Ray found himself wondering if that got him into any trouble with his commanding officer. He was just a tad taller than Ray's five-eleven, but he was a good thirty pounds heavier than Ray's 170. Fogel's dark eyes darted from place to place, and it made Ray uncomfortable that he never made eye contact for more than a couple of seconds. In Ray's book, that meant that he couldn't trust the man.

They were some fifty feet from the house, and Fogel turned without another word and started walking towards the steps. "Lopez!" he snapped as if he were talking to a misbehaving child, and Ray liked him even less. He glanced in bewilderment at Bill, who was stifling a smile.

"Major asshole," Bill mouthed, and Ray nodded in reply.

Lopez had been studying the outside of the house along the west side, looking carefully at the walls and the ground, but when she saw the three men move, she came over to them.

"Find anything?" Bill asked her, knowing her answer before she said anything.

"Not a thing," Lopez replied. "You were right." Ray was impressed—that kind of line would go a long way towards getting her in Bill's good graces. Lopez was very dark-skinned and quite pretty; she carried herself with pride and dignity, providing a sharp contrast to Fogel, who was just kind of there, the kind of person you wouldn't even notice as you walked by him in the supermarket candy aisle. She definitely had quite a bit of the Central American Indian blood in her, he guessed, given the dark eyes, the straight nose, the strong brow and cheekbones. She stepped up to Ray and held out her hand. "My name is Lopez," she said.

"Ray. Nice to meet you."

"So, are you two coming in with us?" Fogel demanded.

"Depends on where you're going," Bill replied. "We're going to need someone outside, and that'll be Ray here, if you don't mind. Then we're going to need someone to stay at the top of the basement stairs. I nominate Lopez. And no one's going into that shaft. We'll look at it and then we'll get the hell out."

Fogel regarded Bill carefully, and Ray could tell that he was weighing his words, deciding what to say and what not to say. Ray felt that Fogel had every intention of going into that mine shaft—he seemed just idiot enough to do it—and no intention of telling Bill that he planned to do so.

"That works for me," Fogel said, then climbed the stairs and went to the door.

Bill turned to Ray. "You good with staying out here?"

"Good? Hell, I would have paid for the chance." Lopez overheard him, and she smiled slightly, completely without malice. Smile now, Ray thought to himself, because you won't be smiling for the rest of the day after you go in there. He took a post between the door and the living room window, and Fogel opened the door.

He took three steps into the room and then stopped, completely overwhelmed. Bill was behind him, and he stepped up quickly as Fogel started swaying and tried to catch him before he fell to the floor in a dead faint. He failed, though, and Fogel hit the floor with a rather pathetic thud. Ray smiled, and he couldn't help but think about how wrong his thoughts about smiles had been just a few seconds earlier.

Lopez' face had gone pale, and when Bill looked back at her, she seemed not to have noticed at all that Fogel had passed out. He could see her struggling to maintain control, to keep her wits and her consciousness. It took about fifteen seconds before she, too was overwhelmed, and she turned and ran out the front door and lost her breakfast over the railing of the porch.

"Should we drag him out of there?" Ray asked, looking in at Fogel's prone figure.

"Drag him out?" Bill asked in surprise. "That sounds like a helluva lot more work than it's worth, don't you think?"

Bill put Fogel's hat over his eyes in a kind gesture, to keep him from seeing the scene when he first regained consciousness. Then he turned and took the four steps out of the house to where Ray was waiting.

"Four for four," he said drily.

"We're all pretty much wimps, I would say," Ray added.

"You gonna be okay there, trooper?" Bill asked, and Lopez nodded.

"You guys too?" she asked, wiping her mouth with a handkerchief she had fished out of her pocket.

"Oh, yeah," Bill said. "It's gonna take someone a hell of a lot more used to that kind of thing not to puke their guts up when they see it. It's a shame, too. That poor woman in there—or what used to be a woman, anyway—is going to have lots of people remember her as just pieces scattered about a room."

Lopez looked like she was going to reply, then seemed to think better of it. There really wasn't much anyone could say.

"Once your macho partner in there wakes up, we'll give it a go. The trick is to try not to look directly at anything. I think we all made the mistake of fixing our eyes on something specific, like that head on the couch, and our brains aren't made for processing that sort of thing."

"Head on the couch?" Lopez asked, appalled. "Oh, God. I didn't even see that."

"I would try not to look at the couch, then, if I were you," Ray offered.

"Of course, now that you tell me that, guess what'll be the first thing I look at." Lopez' voice sounded resigned.

"Your partner said the coroner is on his way up here?" Bill asked.

She nodded. "Should be here in an hour or so. Maybe he'll be able to walk in there without losing it."

Bill grunted. "Could be. But I wouldn't put any money on it, personally." He heard a groan from inside the house. "Sounds like birdman's awake," he said simply.

"Birdman?" Ray asked. "Why do you call him that?"

"That's his name, Ray. 'Fogel' means 'bird' in German. Except they spell it with a 'v.' Still pronounce it like an 'f,' though. Don't they teach you nothing in school anymore?"

Ray chuckled. "Not German, in any case. They do touch on double negatives, though." He watched Bill turn around and head back in the house, then heard him ask Fogel if he was going to make it. He heard only a groan in response.

He looked at Lopez, who seemed to be struggling with whether or not she was going to go back into the house.

"If I can do it," he told her, "you sure can. Like Bill said, though—just don't look straight at anything. Keep your eyes moving on neutral targets, like the ceiling. The blood on the wall's not nearly as bad as the other stuff." He almost added a repeat of the warning not to go into the mine shaft in the basement, but she looked smart enough not to do that. Besides, Bill had said he wanted her at the top of the stairs.

Lopez didn't reply, but he could see the thanks in her eyes. He could tell that her mind was too focused on just getting back in there to be able to handle much of anything else. He heard Bill inside—"Alright, let's try to stay on your feet this time. Here's your partner. Good. Let's get this over with."

Ray looked out to the street, where a group of four people stood quietly on the lawn just across from Sarah's house, looking over towards him, seeming as uneasy as he would expect a group of people who had just heard the news they had heard to be. Finally something that seemed normal. Onlookers. He raised his hand in a weak wave, but none of them waved back.

Eight
Lost Thoughts

The light at the end of the tunnel didn't look nearly as bright any more, and he found that he could move closer to it without it hurting him. Something in his memory told him that if he suffered the pain for the moment, it wouldn't hurt for long. He no longer had words with which to form thoughts—he was all feeling, and all of his feeling was malevolence. All of his feeling was anger, and all of his feeling was of revenge.

He was one of five. They all felt the same way. They had lost everything, though they had long since forgotten just what it was that they had lost. It had taken them so, so long to find their way out of the darkness, so long to dig through the rubble where the cave had exploded so many years ago, so long to reach the world where they had once lived.

If he had any true thought processes any more, he would ask himself why he was still alive, why he and his companions hadn't long since died there in the darkness and the silence and the horrible nothingness. He would have wondered how they could be surviving just as skin and tendons and bones with so very little muscle or flesh on their bodies. And he would have wondered how they could be so incredibly strong and fast, even without the body mass that anyone on the surface would have considered to be absolutely necessary for someone just to keep on living.

Not that he would have considered what they were doing to be living. In the depths of what mind he had left, he felt the emptiness, the helplessness, the anger of a person who had suffered the ultimate betrayal of being sent unsuspecting to his own death. He and the other four had trusted, and they had been betrayed. And they wanted everyone, anyone to pay for it.

He crept closer to the light. He hadn't heard any sounds for a while, but he was wary nonetheless. The light burned into his head, but it wasn't as bad as it had been before. He backed up just a bit until the pain subsided, but he could still see the light.

Behind him, the other four were somewhere down in the caverns, instinctively waiting for the hours of darkness when they knew that there would be no problems with the lights.

This new part of the tunnel, the part they had just discovered when they had made it through ten feet of rubble, was wider and even had a few spots behind beams where he could hide if he needed to. His instinct for self-preservation paired with a mind that had once been able to think and to reason told him that he might need to hide, like a dog that runs under the bed at the first sign of thunder and lightning.

He backed off a bit more when he heard voices coming from the direction of the light. All was instinct, and all was hatred, and all was staying alive so that he could avenge all that he had lost.

Nine
The Idiot and the Mine Shaft

Fogel and Bill made their way carefully down the steps to the basement, their guns in one hand and flashlights in the other. The sheriff had left the basement light on earlier that day, a decision that he had no idea had helped him immensely, keeping at bay an evil that he couldn't even begin to comprehend.

"We are not going into that shaft, Fogel," Bill said quietly. "Not until we have a frickin' army here to back us up. And that's the army that you're going to call in."

"I can't call in anyone until I know what's going on," Fogel said, but his bravado sounded strained, like he was trying to impress someone more than he was saying what he really felt. Bill had the sudden impression that he was with someone who was still functioning as a 14-year-old in some respects, especially where ego was concerned.

"If you go in there, you're an idiot, plain and simple," Bill said, immediately regretting his words. He realized that Fogel would probably take them as a challenge just to prove that Bill was wrong, whether he actually was wrong or not. "Look at all the footprints on these steps," he continued, trying to appeal to Fogel's reason. "There's got to be more than one of whoever—or whatever—it was that did this. And there's a damned good chance that they'll be waiting for anyone stupid enough to go into that mine." He cursed himself silently for that last sentence, knowing that he had just added fuel to the fire. They were in the basement by then, standing next to the steel door that was lying on the ground.

The air was cold and damp, and Bill was thankful for his jacket. The basement was tiny, just some twelve feet by twelve feet, and there was nothing else down there but the stairs and the door on the floor. There wasn't even a furnace; that must have been somewhere upstairs. Which meant that the only purpose for this particular basement was to have access to the mine.

Fogel didn't say a word. He just stood looking into the shaft, and Bill found it impossible to read what he might have been thinking.

"Look, Fogel," he tried again. "I've got a wife at home and two kids away at college, and the last thing they need in their lives is to find out that I got ripped to shreds even though I could have avoided it. We wait." He pointed to the door at their feet. "That door there, they had to break through that thing to get out of there, it looks like. Whatever it was or they were, they're strong as hell."

Fogel didn't answer—his attention was riveted to the shaft that stood beckoning before him. He turned on his flashlight and pointed it down the tunnel, peering closely to see if he could see anything that this sheriff and his deputy might have missed.

"I'm going down to that first beam there," he said quietly. "No further."

Bill was aggravated. "Why?" he demanded. "What can you possibly hope to accomplish?"

"I'm examining a crime scene," Fogel responded, though he didn't sound at all confident. "If the perpetrators escaped down this mine shaft, then it's our responsibility to investigate this shaft."

"Yeah? Well, if what you saw they did to that woman upstairs made you faint, just imagine how it's going to make you feel when they do the same thing to you."

Fogel turned and looked Bill in the eyes, his own eyes widening at the thought. I hope he's smart enough not to do this, Bill said to himself.

Fogel turned back to the tunnel. "Cover me," he said quietly.

"Fucking idiot," Bill muttered, watching the ample body disappear slowly into the opening. If he was going to cover him, he was going to do so from the stairs where he could make a quick escape if he needed to.

"Lopez," he called up the stairs.

"Yeah," she called back.

"Your partner's in the mine shaft. Be ready to make a very quick exit if we need to."

"Shit," he heard her say, not at all quietly.

Fogel walked slowly into the darkness, his flashlight illuminating not nearly as much area as he had thought it would. He was overwhelmed by the silence that surrounded him, that pressed in on him, that told him in no uncertain terms that he was out of his element. The horrible smell didn't help matters. But he knew that when he walked out of there, he would have something over this hick sheriff, for he would have at least had the guts to face something that the sheriff was afraid of. He trusted his pistol, and he told himself that he wasn't afraid to use it, even though he had never yet done so in the line of duty.

The walls of the tunnel were dark, and they were rough. The floor, too, was uneven, bumpy, hard to walk on. This hadn't been a regular mine—it was wider than one person, but not quite wide enough for two, and it didn't seem possible that anyone would be able to pull a load of coal out easily. Fogel shook his head as these thoughts ran through his mind—the last thing he needed to do was distract himself by analyzing his surroundings.

The first support beams were some forty feet from the entrance, he guessed, and it took him a good minute, step by step, to reach them. He ran the light over them, up and down on the left, back and forth above, up and down on the right. Nothing. He turned to call out to the sheriff when he heard the slightest of noises and he froze. It had come from above, from behind the beam, he thought. "Sheriff. . ." he called out, his voice unsteady and much, much quieter and higher-pitched than he had intended. "Sheriff!" he yelled, keeping his light trained on the beam, not having any idea what might be on the other side of it.

"Get your ass out of there!" the sheriff yelled, moving closer to the mouth of the tunnel. "Now!"

That was just what Fogel needed; he turned and started moving back towards the basement just as an arm reached down from behind the crossbeam and tried to grab him by the neck. Because Fogel had just moved, the hand only grazed the back of his head, but the long, sharp fingernails still were able to dig into the skin and draw blood. Fogel screamed and started running, not making it far before he fell to the ground, bashing his right knee against a chunk of rock that was sticking out of the ground.

"Move it, Fogel!" Bill yelled. He was now at the entrance, pointing both his gun and flashlight in the trooper's direction. Fogel got to his feet quickly and rushed the rest of the way out, then straight up the stairs, past Lopez, past what was left of Sarah, and past Ray out onto the lawn, where he collapsed onto the grass.

Bill turned and started after the trooper as soon as he ran by him. He hadn't seen anything in the tunnel, but he had noticed the blood in Fogel's hair as he ran by. He took the stairs three at a time and yelled a quick "Let's go" to Lopez, who looked unsure as to what she should be doing. She was still holding the small safe that Bill had asked her to carry, and he pushed her ahead of him and followed her out the door to the porch, where Ray was waiting, holding his pistol ready as the two other officers went by. When everything looked clear Ray turned and moved out onto the lawn.

"Happy, Fogel?" Bill asked wearily. Then he turned to Ray. "You know what?" he asked rhetorically. "I think we're screwed."

Ray was looking back at Sarah's house. "Shouldn't we be guarding that door in the basement?" he asked.

Bill followed his gaze. "Absolutely. We need to get our act together and come up with some sort of strategy, because we have absolutely no idea what we're up against here."

Ten
Spreading the News

As if on cue, one of the men who had been standing across the street approached. "What the hell's going on, Sheriff?" he asked, with no touch of challenge in his voice—just concern. "You guys look like you've just been attacked by the devil himself."

Bill turned towards him. "You could say that, Henry," he said. "How ya doin'?"

Henry kept his steady gaze on the sheriff. He was a tall man and husky, who still had a full head of black hair though he looked to be at least in his sixties. "Don't rightly know, Bill," he replied. "I thought I was doing fine, but now it looks like things may not be going so well."

"You got that right, Henry. What do you know about Sarah and that house? Things are all sorts of screwed up over here, and it looks like they're going to be getting worse rather than better. Something just attacked that trooper down in the shaft, and I have no idea what it was."

Henry smiled slightly. "Shaft? That's news to me. Sounds like the old stories were true. But what I know about the house and what I've heard about the house are two different things, Bill. That's the way it is with everyone around here. We've heard lots of stories, but we haven't seen any proof of anything."

Lopez approached from the direction of the State Police vehicle, where she had gone to grab a first-aid kit. "Sheriff," she said, "we've got another problem."

"Now how did you know that those were just the words I was longing to hear right about now?" Bill asked. "What the hell else is going wrong?"

"That woman over there told me that the road is out about five miles down the canyon." She pointed to an elderly woman who was getting into a blue pickup. "Said she tried to go down to Pine but couldn't get there."

"The road is out? How the hell can the damned road be out? Now that doesn't make any sense at all." He turned back to Henry. "You see what I mean? Worse before they get better. Although that one was completely off my radar."

"Did she say what happened to the road?" Ray asked Lopez. "We all just came up that way."

She shook her head. "She just said that it was washed out. That she had to turn around and come back here."

"Okay," Bill said, "the road's a problem, but right here and right now, we need to find out who or what killed Sarah and who or what took a swipe at this moron's head." Fogel was still on the ground, muttering to himself about the pain while he applied the antibacterial ointment Lopez had brought him. The cut on his neck was fairly deep, but the blood seemed to have stopped flowing. Fogel's right pants leg was ripped at the knee, and blood had soaked into his uniform there, too. In short, Bill thought, the man was a pretty pathetic sight.

"Sheriff," Henry ventured, "you asked what I know about Sarah and that house. I knew Sarah pretty well, and I've been in that house just as much as anyone else over the years—which is maybe ten times, just to do some maintenance. She did mention some strange things to me. You didn't happen to find a journal in there, did you?"

"A journal? No, why?"

"She told me a few times that if anything ever happened to her, she had a journal that would explain everything. Now, I've got no idea what 'everything' means, but it sounds like this might be the situation she was talking about."

Another woman from the group had joined them, and now stood listening to the conversation. "My guess is that it has something to do with the miners that disappeared years back," she said.

"Hello, Rita," Bill said. "You know something about this, too?"

"Know something? No." Rita looked to be Henry's age, though her hair was silver through and through. "But I do know that I grew up listening to stories about how they'd be back someday, and when they did come back, there'd be hell to pay."

"What do you mean?"

"Well, it was kind of folklore of the town. Just a group of miners who had been sent down into the mines and never came back out. But that was sixty years ago. Or so. They'd certainly be dead by now."

Bill turned to Lopez. "What did you do with that safe?" he asked her.

"Right there," she replied, pointing to a small box that sat next to Ray's vehicle. Ray walked over and picked it up and brought it to Bill. Bill looked it over—it wasn't the highest of quality, and he was pretty sure that a bullet or two could open it up. It was more like a strongbox than a safe, designed more for protecting against fire than anything else.

"You think she might have kept that journal in here?" he asked Henry, who simply shrugged. "Well, once we get this opened we'll find out. Anyone in town know how to open this thing? Other than searching her entire house for a key?"

Henry shook his head.

"Ray, you think you could take this over there to that pile of sand and put a couple of rounds into it?"

"I'll give it a shot," Ray said, then got a pained expression on his face. "Sorry," he said, taking it from Bill. "Didn't mean it that way."

"It sure is a damned poor time for throwing around puns like that," Bill told him. "Once you get that thing open, I'm going to have to send you and Lopez back in there to guard that door. Whoever or whatever we're dealing with is down there in that shaft, and we've got to keep him or it from coming out again. Or them—I keep forgetting all those footprints." He turned back to Henry.

"How many people you guys got here in this town?" he asked.

"This time of year, twenty, thirty maybe."

"We're going to have to let all of them know that they may be in danger. Most of them got guns?"

Henry smiled slightly.

"Of course they've all got guns," Bill muttered. "I hope to hell they've all got a lot of guns. How long you think it would take you and Rita here to let everyone know to stay indoors and to get all their guns ready? And possibly to get ready to have everyone meet in one place? I've got a thought in my head that daylight is keeping those things in that mineshaft, but daylight ain't gonna be sticking around forever." He looked at his watch—it was already past eleven. "In fact, we may have just about five hours or so before it starts getting dark. We need to get everyone notified as quick as we can. You think you can do that?"

Suddenly a shot rang out, and everyone looked over at Ray, who was half a block away at the pile of gravel that was used on the streets in the winter. He was kneeling over, trying the box. They watched him put it back in the sand, take three steps back, and fire again. When he reached down to check the box, he looked back at the group. "Got it!" he yelled, and reached down and opened the box. He pulled out a couple of articles and came back to the group.

"Looks like you were right, Sheriff," he said. "That is, if this is actually a journal. Just this and about five hundred in cash. Nothing else." He started counting the twenties that he had been carrying in his other hand, then handed the bills to Lopez. "I got 520," he said.

She quickly counted. "Five-twenty," she said, handing them back to Ray. He folded the bills and put them into the inside pocket of his coat.

Bill was looking through the journal. "This ain't even hers," he exclaimed. "Look at this—'The Journal of Wayne Naugle.' First entry's 1934. What the hell good is a journal from sixty years ago going to do us?"

"Don't rightly know," Henry said, holding his hand out to Bill, who gave him the journal, "but if Sarah said it's important, then my guess is that it's pretty important."

"I don't doubt that you're right," Bill replied. "But how in hell are we going to read that thing? We've got enough on our hands as it is."

"Let me," Henry offered. "I'll read it for you and mark all the important parts, and you can keep on doing what you're doing. Which as far as I can see," he said almost playfully, "is standing around on the street talking."

Bill started to look angry until he realized that Henry was joking. "Piss off, Hank. Go read. I'm surprised you can, to tell you the truth. And Rita, you and the others over there, you guys go around and make sure everyone's up to speed with the little that we know so far."

"Aye, aye, captain," she said, and turned and left. Bill looked after her like he wanted to say something else, but he thought better of it. He turned to Ray and Lopez.

"We've got to get back to work, such as it is. Hey Fogel, you ready to get back on the clock?"

Fogel looked up from where he sat on the ground. "I'm good," he said. "What do you want me to do?" He sounded a bit humbler than he had sounded twenty minutes earlier.

Bill pointed to Sarah's house. "Porch duty for now. Set yourself down in one of those comfortable chairs and make sure nothing comes or goes without your blessing. And be backup for these two in case they need it."

Ray knew what that meant. "Mine shaft?"

Bill looked apologetic. "Take the shotguns from both our vehicles, and make sure that you're both fully loaded. "I want one of you at the top of the stairs at all times, and the other at the entrance to the shaft. Keep the lights on—I'll see if I can get a flood lamp somewhere to point down that tunnel. Don't be heroes—anything looks or sounds wrong or dangerous, get the hell out. You saw what happened to Birdman here. I'm going to drive down and see what's up with the road."

Lopez turned to Ray. "Looks like we just got the shaft," she said with a half-smile, and Ray rolled his eyes.

"I deserved that," he said.

Lopez laughed. "You ready?"

"What if I say no?"

She didn't reply, just turned and started walking slowly toward the house. Ray went to his vehicle to grab his own shotgun, then to Bill's to get his.

Bill stood alone in the street, not quite sure where he should start. "You'd better be a fast damned reader, Henry," he muttered, then jumped in his vehicle.

Eleven
The Shaft

Ray followed Lopez up the stairs to the porch. Fogel was already sitting there on the swinging bench that looked out over the front yard. "How you feeling, Fogel?" she asked.

"I'm okay, I guess," Fogel replied. "I feel like an idiot, though. I never should have gone into that stupid mine."

"That's true," Lopez replied, "but you'd better leave it behind you right now. We need you to be focused up here. We can't have you watching our back if you're not on."

Fogel looked up at her. "You're right," he said. "I'll be fine. I'm just a bit groggy right now, but that will pass."

"Let's hope so." Lopez looked back at Ray. "You ready?"

"To go back in there? Hell, no. But since I've got to, we might as well get to it." He didn't relish the idea of walking back through that living room, and he liked even less the idea of going down to the basement where there was only one way out—heading outdoors, at least. There were actually two ways out of the house, but he didn't want to consider the mine shaft as a possible escape route. Ray handed her Bill's shotgun; she checked to make sure it was loaded. Ray felt more comfortable as soon as he saw her do that—she paid attention to details, which was a trait that could end up saving their lives.

"We're going to have to be careful," Lopez said as she moved to the door. "We've been out of there for twenty minutes now. There's no telling what's been going on in the meantime."

"Do you want to clear the whole house again?" Ray asked.

She thought for a moment. "No, I guess there's no need for that. But we've got to keep our eyes and ears open."

"You don't have to tell me that twice," Ray agreed. "Let's go."

Lopez opened the door and took a deep breath, and Ray noticed that she fixed her gaze on the ceiling as she walked in. She carried the shotgun in her left hand and her pistol in her right, and she walked slowly and carefully towards the far end of the room, past the kitchen to the door to the basement.

Ray followed her closely, also keeping his eyes off the lower parts of the room. He wasn't nearly as horrified as he had been less than two hours ago, but he still wasn't ready to treat the room as if it were a normal crime scene.

"So we're not going to get a coroner in here to take care of things?" he asked, disappointment in his voice.

"Looks like not," Lopez said quietly. "It's going to be creepy, leaving this room as it is. Doesn't seem right, especially for her. It's like a mockery of her memory."

"Yeah," Ray said. He hadn't thought about it that way, but she made sense. They reached the door to the basement, and Lopez reached out and opened it very slowly and quietly. They both listened carefully, but they heard nothing from downstairs.

"You take the stairs," Lopez whispered. "I'll take the floor. And let's prop this door open."

"Yes, ma'am," Ray whispered back, and she stopped.

"I'm sorry," she said. "I'm really not trying to order you around or anything."

Ray smiled. "Don't worry—I'm not taking it that way. We're working together—that's all. So let's get to work."

"Good," she said, and started slowly down the stairs. The opening to the shaft stood menacingly in the far wall, and they both fixed their gazes on it as they climbed lower. The light in the basement was still on, but it did next to nothing to illuminate the interior of the tunnel. When they both reached their positions, they stood motionless for several long moments, not sure of what to do from there. Finally, Ray said in his normal voice, "I really don't think it's necessary to be quiet and sneak around. I'd bet everything I have that whatever they are, they know that we're here right now."

Lopez paused before answering, then she spoke at a normal volume, too. "You're probably right," she acknowledged. "Maybe letting them know that we're here and that we're well armed is the best thing we can do."

"Bill must be right about there being more than one. Did you see all those footprints up there? All those bloody footprints?"

"So either there's a lot of them, or one of them went up and down the stairs twenty times. The feet are so small—they look human, but they're so much smaller than an adult's foot. What could have made prints like this?"

"You've got me. Whatever it is, it's capable of extreme brutality. I don't know if I even want to guess." Even though they were talking, neither of them were able to take their eyes off the mine shaft for more than a moment or two at a time.

"None of this seems real," Lopez said quietly. "Two hours ago, Fogel and I were at HQ, just getting ready for our day, and now here we are. He's hurt and we're guarding the opening of a mine that was sealed up with a steel door that something didn't have all that hard of a time getting through. This wasn't how my day was supposed to be going."

"Tell me about it," Ray said. "Two hours ago all I was thinking about was what I was going to have for lunch."

"At nine o'clock in the morning?"

Ray smiled. "Slow day. But now I keep thinking about that poor old woman up there. Twenty-four hours ago, she didn't have any idea that she was going to be dead so soon."

"With her body ripped apart and her blood all over the walls and floors," Lopez added. She thought for a moment. "Do you think the same thing could happen to us?"

Ray looked at her in surprise. "Holy crap," he said slowly. "I hadn't even thought about that as a possibility." He paused and thought a moment. "I guess our job now is to do everything we can to make sure it doesn't."

Lopez nodded. "That sounds like a sensible plan to me."

"You know, as big and heavy as that door is," Ray suddenly changed the topic, "a door's only as strong as its hinges. Look at the frame—it's cement.

And if the cement wasn't allowed to set properly when it was poured, there's a good chance that it's been weakened over the years. It's still a hell of a feat to break that door down, but it's not like they broke through solid steel—they just forced the steel hinges out of the cement."

"Huh," Lopez replied, sounding completely unimpressed. "And you could do that?"

Ray laughed lightly and humorlessly. "Hell, no," he said. "I'm just trying to be perceptive."

"I wonder how long we're going to be down here?" Lopez asked.

"At least until Bill comes back," Ray said. "Damn. I want to sit down, but not on all this blood. I've got a feeling we're in for a long, long day."

"And night," Lopez added. "Don't forget that if the road is out, we're stuck here."

"Wow—there's a pleasant thought," Ray muttered. Neither spoke for several long moments until the silence became too oppressive. There seemed to be a tangible danger present, and neither of them wanted to allow their thoughts to focus on it.

"So, are you from around here?" Lopez asked.

"From Pine, actually. I went to college in Denver, though, then came back. You?"

"Texas originally. My family moved here when I was sixteen. Now we live in Montrose, my son and I. He's six. And no, my husband didn't take off. He died in a car accident about three years ago."

"Oh, man. I'm sorry." Ray didn't know what else to say.

Lopez shrugged. "Thanks. I've gotten used to it, though. I live close to my parents still, so Danny has someone to be with when I'm not there. It helps. How about you? I don't see any rings on your fingers."

Ray looked down at his left hand, which was holding the shotgun. "Nope—nobody else in my life right now. My last girlfriend and I broke up about a year ago. It's probably a good thing. This job keeps me pretty busy."

"She move off to college?"

"Nah. She found someone else while I was away at college. They're married now."

"That was quick if she broke up with you a year ago."

"Yeah, but I think they'd been seeing each other for a while before she broke it off with me."

"Ouch. Sucks, doesn't it?" Lopez said. "How's that sheriff of yours to work with? He seems like a pretty good guy."

"Bill? Bill's great. Lets me work on my own and doesn't meddle, but he's always there when I need help. I rode with him my first month, and I learned more from him in those four weeks than I ever did in school."

"I like people who are down-to-earth and practical."

"You mean like that partner of yours?"

Lopez laughed. "Fogel's not my partner. I'm with him this week because no one else wants to ride with the guy."

"So you volunteered out of the goodness of your heart?"

"Short straw, more like."

"Why doesn't that surprise me?"

"Well, he comes off as an arrogant prick, but that's just because. . . ." Lopez' voice trailed off, and she thought for a moment. "I guess it's because he *is* an arrogant prick," she said, laughing again.

"Gee, I hadn't noticed," Ray said. "I wanted to deck the s.o.b. for the way he was talking to Bill."

"Yeah, that's pretty much the prevailing sentiment concerning Fogel. He is definitely not well liked. But he has stripes, so he's still around."

"That's a shame. A job like this, you don't want to be working with assholes you can't trust."

"And yet, here I am."

"Hey, thanks a lot," Ray protested, pretending to be hurt.

Lopez looked at him quickly and saw by his smirk that he was joking.

"You're welcome," she said simply, then smiled and turned back to watch the mine shaft.

Twelve
Washout

Bill drove as fast as he dared on the rain-slicked road that headed down the mountain, winding his way through the pines that grew thick as soon as he left the CB town limits. The rain was falling a bit heavier now, but it still wasn't anything more than a heavy sprinkle. And he wasn't sure, but the air felt colder to him—he wouldn't be surprised if the rain turned to snow by evening. It would be about time.

Five miles out of town he came around a curve and had to slam on his brakes to avoid driving his vehicle over the edge of what used to be the road. He stepped out of the car, looking down in amazement at the huge chunks of pavement that now sat in pieces some ten feet below road level. A good one hundred feet of the road was gone. He could see right off how it had happened—a small section of the river had started flowing under the road itself, chewing away at the ground beneath.

"Holy shit," he muttered, and he looked up at the cliffs on either side of the canyon. He'd have no radio signal here, either, he knew. He went to his car and got out an emergency marker, a reflective red triangle, and he walked a quarter mile back around the last curve, and set it up in the southbound lane. There was enough of an inner edge on the road that he could cross over the washout on foot, so he took another marker and set it up down the road a piece on the other side. Ten minutes later, he was driving back up to Canyon Bluff. He hoped that someone would notify the sheriff's office about the road, but the fact that he hadn't seen anything posted on the other side wasn't a good sign. He couldn't know that he had missed the "Road Closed" sign that his other deputy already had set up by about a hundred yards, just around the next bend in the road.

It looked like they were stuck in CB, which was pretty much what he had expected since he had heard about the road. There was no way out of town—most of the other mountain towns had dirt roads leading in and out that provided pretty reliable access, but CB had been built on a small level section over a valley with steep walls, and it was completely inaccessible without the road.

So they were cut off. They would have to fend for themselves against this threat, without any sort of backup. He supposed that they could bring people in by helicopter, but since copters were scarce and expensive, and they still really didn't have any reason to do so, that wasn't going to happen. Hell, they had four law enforcement officers on site already in a town with thirty people in it. That should be enough. He'd call the office by phone as soon as he got back to town.

When that thought hit him, he slammed on his brakes and looked at the telephone poles on the side of the road. They were on the cliff side of the road here, but. . . .

He turned the vehicle around quickly and sped back to the damaged section of the road. Just before he got there he saw that the phone lines crossed the road to the river side, exactly what he had feared. He stopped and got out of the car and noticed a fallen pole just downriver from him. The cliffs had been too close to the road here to put the telephone poles on the inside of the road, so they were there on the outside. He hadn't noticed it before because the pole had fallen among the pines and the broken wire had dropped into the river.

He got back into his car and hit the gas. Now they were completely cut off. He knew that the power lines came up a different route, but the phone lines had come along a couple of decades later, and they had followed the road. They would still have electricity in town, but no way to contact the world outside.

This changed things.

He suddenly had the urge to call his wife, to talk to her and hear the reassurance in her voice. He liked working with Ray, and Lopez seemed okay, but no one knew Bill like his wife knew him. And they certainly didn't know the things to say to make him feel better during difficult times. He'd been with his wife for forty years, and he had always been able to discuss his difficulties with her. She saw the world in a completely different way than he did, and that fact helped him greatly to find perspective.

The thought suddenly struck him that he might not see her again. How would she deal with that? he wondered. She'd be okay after a while, he knew, but he had to do everything he could to make sure he got back home safely. And that might be a challenge today.

He crested the last hill before town and the road started descending towards the group of ramshackle houses. He took several deep breaths—a trick he had learned from his father—to center himself so that he could get focused immediately on the task at hand, trying to eliminate the threat from this town.

Thirteen
Into the Light

When he felt the contact between what used to be his fingernails—but which now more closely resembled claws—and the back of the man's head, he felt a keen sense of pleasure; but as the man ran out of the tunnel toward the light, the feeling turned into something bitter, more of a sense of loss and frustration.

His companions had withdrawn back behind the rubble that they had dug through to finally reach the door. There they waited for the light to go away. He had no such intention—his instinct told him to remain as close to freedom as he could, as close to the outside, as close to an escape from this darkness and this claustrophobia as he could.

He stayed clinging to the crossbeam long after the heavy man disappeared into the light, long after the sounds of others stopped coming from outside the shaft. He hung in the darkness patiently, for there was nothing else for him to do but wait. He could reason no more, so there were no plans to make, no decisions to reach. Right now he could feel only that his freedom lay right before him, and he didn't want to let it out of his sight or his hearing.

After a while, he became aware of a sensation on his back, something that he couldn't describe and could feel only barely. He looked back, annoyed, but saw nothing touching him. He became curious—there was no way that nothing could be there if something was indeed touching him.

His eyes over the years had actually become useful. He didn't see things exactly as he had when he was a human being living above ground, for in the darkness in which he lived such a thing was simply impossible. Now that there was a bit of light reaching where he was, he actually saw what he was looking at for the first time since he didn't know when. This was something that he experienced only in the feeding rooms, but this light had no green tint. But he wasn't reacting to what he saw. He felt something other than the damp still air of the mine, and he wasn't sure what it was.

There was a time when he had been a much different being, when he had been a man able to lift his two daughters in his arms and hear their laughter and feel the softness of their cheeks when he kissed them tenderly, when he would have recognized the feeling as a breeze blowing over his skin. He reached back and suddenly felt the same thing, ever so slightly, on his hand. His mind told him nothing about what it was, but his instinct told him to find its source. He scoured the surface of the ceiling of the mine and saw, just a foot from where he was clinging to the rocks behind the crossbeam, a hole about as wide as the one they had squeezed through the night before to finally escape the mine. He reached his hand next to the hole and felt the moving air more strongly. He shifted and put his face there, looking up but seeing even less light; nonetheless he reached up into the hole, which seemed to be big enough for him, and pulled himself up into it.

He didn't think about danger; he didn't think about getting stuck or not being able to get back out. Not being able to think, it appeared, was an advantage for him in some ways.

The space through which he moved was tight, but not tight enough to stop him. After four feet or so it even broadened some, giving him room to move about more easily. After about ten feet, it became a small cave of its own, and the air there was different—drier and slightly warmer than the caverns had ever been.

As he held out his hand to search for the moving air once more, he suddenly realized that again he was in the presence of light—ever so little light, but light nonetheless. He let out a low sound like a growl once his hand felt the stream of air once more, and he almost moved ahead when the thought of his companions crept into his mind. He stayed unbalanced for several long moments—rejoin his friends and bring them here? Or keep going?

He reached out and touched the surface of the cave above him, near where the air was coming from. It was soil here, not solid rock, and he scraped his claws through it, feeling it give easily beneath his touch. His instinct for movement took over, and he continued scraping away at the soil.

Fourteen
Bye Bye, Birdy

Bill pulled his vehicle up in front of Sarah's house as the rain was strengthening, something that didn't sit well with him. Rain was an equalizer that made it very difficult to create any sort of advantage on either side of a conflict, and he wanted an advantage.

He got out of the car and put on his hat for the first time since he had gotten there this morning—with the rain growing heavier, he'd need to stay dry, especially if he wasn't going to be able to get home and change clothes.

He looked across the street at Taylor's house, then back at Sarah's, where Fogel was now standing at the railing of the porch, looking out over the lawn towards him.

"What's the news, Sheriff?" he heard Fogel yell to him. Bill was surprised—Fogel sounded almost friendly. He waved in reply, then decided to go check in with Ray and Lopez before he visited Henry to find out what he had learned from the journal.

He had just taken his first step towards the house when the creature came around the corner of the porch, quickly and without a sound that he could hear. It jumped to the railing from the lawn side of the house, then actually jumped to the top of the window sill behind Fogel, where it clung to the window frame for just a moment before it launched itself at the unsuspecting trooper.

Bill had just enough time to lift his arm and point, but the creature was on Fogel even as the man's name left Bill's lips. Fogel's throat was ripped out before the words "behind you" ever found the air. Fogel's body fell to the ground, the creature still perched on his shoulders as he went down. It landed atop the trooper's body, holding on to the collar of his shirt, its arm raised and ready to deliver another blow. Then the creature looked up at Bill.

Bill was a good shot, but his hand wasn't completely steady and his shot was rushed, so it went wide of the mark, through the picture window of the living room. The creature looked behind itself at the broken window, then simply stood up straight, turned, jumped and disappeared with a hideous, blood-freezing growl that sounded more animal than human, back the exact same way it had come.

"Coming out!" Bill heard Lopez yell from inside the house. She couldn't come out to see what was going on right after a bullet had gone through the window.

"It's clear!" he yelled back, and he started running to the corner of the house where the creature had disappeared. When he got there, though, there was nothing to see but a couple of trees and the side of the house.

"Shit!" he yelled, and he heard Lopez yell Fogel's name. He came back around the corner of the house to see her holding his wrist in her hand, feeling for a pulse. Her eyes were averted from Fogel and she looked at Bill with wide, frightened eyes.

"What the hell did this?" she asked, a serious catch in her voice.

"I have no fucking idea!" he growled. "I watched it attack him, and I have no idea what the hell it was. Ray!" he yelled, and listened for Ray's reply, which came immediately.

"Get out here!" he yelled again. Then he said to Lopez, "No damned reason to be in there if whatever we're looking for is out here now."

Ray burst out through the door and took a quick look at Fogel's body. "Damn!" he muttered, then took a closer look. "His whole throat's been ripped out," he said, looking away quickly and feeling sick. "What in the hell could do something like that?"

"And with one rip, too," Bill added. "That's all it took—one swipe and he was dead. Whatever it was, it's strong as hell and twice as mean."

"You saw it all?" Lopez asked.

"I had just gotten out of the car. Whatever it was, it wasn't a person. Not like we know people. It was all shriveled up, and it looked like it was crouching as it ran. It was about a foot shorter than Fogel, and it didn't have a bit of meat on its bones. And it was fast—that was the fastest thing I've ever seen. And nimble—it hung on the window frame there like some sort of monkey. That thing could take any one of us whenever it wanted to if we let our guard down."

"Oh my God," Lopez muttered. "Where did it go?"

"Came from around this corner of the house, then went right back where it came from. And believe me, it moved like it had a purpose."

"So watching the entrance to the mine shaft isn't going to be all that helpful," Ray said.

"You got that right. Look, let's get this body indoors and go find Jackson. We've got to get these people grouped. If people are alone, this thing can pick them off one by one at will. And if there's more than one of 'em, we may be completely screwed here."

Ray looked at Lopez, who looked down at the body and then looked quickly away. Neither of them looked interested in moving the corpse. "There's so much blood," Lopez murmured.

"Just grab a leg each and drag," Bill said impatiently. "He's dead—he don't give a damn any more. And we've got too much work to get done." He turned and stalked back to the side of the house. "And once you finish, get down here with me," he yelled back.

"God," Lopez said to Ray as they dragged Fogel's body into the house, "this is so wrong."

"It sure is," Ray agreed, "but right now we're pretty short on choices between right and wrong." He dropped Fogel's leg when they got the body inside, and Lopez followed his lead. Ray reached to close the door. "Crap," he muttered when he heard the dull thud of the door hitting Fogel's head.

"What's wrong?" Lopez asked.

"I can't close the door," Ray sighed. "He's not far enough in. And I just looked over at the couch again."

"This isn't going well at all so far," Lopez muttered. "Not well at all."

Ray moved to Fogel's feet and reached down and pulled, bringing the body in another foot. "And I don't see any signs that things are going to improve," he said when he was done. He closed the door and the two of them joined Bill.

Fifteen
Rules

"He came from over here," Bill said quietly when the three of them were together. He had used the few moments that he was waiting to calm himself down. "He jumped onto the porch railing there," he pointed, "then onto the window frame, then on to Fogel. Then he came back this way. I couldn't see where he went once he reached the corner of the house. Let's start here, twenty feet apart, and check the yard. It's small enough that we should be able to find something. If there's anything to find." He started to move away, then stopped. "And just so you know, the road's completely washed out a couple miles down. Looks like water's been running under it for a while now. We won't be getting any help up here for the time being."

"Well, that's good news," Lopez said with mock cheerfulness. "Today's just full of warm and fuzzy moments, isn't it?" Neither Ray nor Bill had a reply for her.

They spread themselves out and started walking towards the back edge of the yard where it met the cliff.

"What are we looking for specifically?" Lopez asked.

"If this thing did come from the mine shaft," Bill replied, "then the chances are that it came out of another entrance, possibly just some sort of hole in the ground. Look for scuffed grass, a hole, blood, anything out of the ordinary. It had to come from somewhere."

"Downstairs," Ray replied, "the shaft goes northwest. If it came out of a hole from the shaft, then the chances are that it would be in that direction." He pointed towards the cliff that made up the boundary of the side yard, and up against which the house had been built. "If it's up high at all, it could be pretty difficult to spot."

"I just hope that it didn't circle back around the house," Lopez added. "It could be back out front looking for another victim."

"Or sneaking up behind us," Bill said, looking dubiously behind himself. "That's not too comfortable a thought. Not that it really matters, anyway—we don't have the entrance to the mine shaft guarded, either. They can definitely make their way out of there."

"But that should be okay with all the lights on, right?" Ray asked, and all three of them stopped and looked at each other as they all realized the same thing at the same time.

"This one was out in the daylight," Lopez said with a hint of despair in her voice. "That means the rules have changed. It's cloudy and rainy, but it's daylight still."

"I guess those were just what we thought were the rules," Bill said, turning and continuing his sweep of the yard. "I don't see anything here, and I don't think we're going to find anything. If those things are going to have the run of the town, then we need to get everyone together and armed, not necessarily in that order. Running after these things isn't going to keep anyone safe unless we kill 'em, and I'm not sure we're going to be able to do that."

"What's our plan, Bill?" Ray asked. He was nervous, as they all were. Things were not going well, and they knew it.

"Plan? Hell, Ray, I don't know," Bill replied. "These things have the upper hand right now, and that is definitely not good. The first thing that we have to try to do is get the advantage back on our side. We have the numbers and we have the firepower, so that shouldn't be too hard to accomplish. But until we do, we're pretty much at their mercy, guns or no."

"So what do we do?" Lopez inquired. "We don't even know how many of these things we're dealing with—one or seven? Or fifty?" She herself was at a complete loss, and she was sure the others were, too—this wasn't something that any of them had any experience in.

"Right now we have to assume we're pretty much under siege. I don't care if there's two of them or a hundred of them—there's something coming up from that mine and killing people. We have to assume they're going to keep doing that because they certainly aren't coming up to introduce themselves to us and start a reading club. We've got to get ourselves ready for anything, and get the people in this town ready, too. Hell, some of them will probably have much better ideas about what to do than we would. They aren't exactly shackled by SOP's and protocol. They'll have their own ways of thinking about things. And maybe Henry will have learned something from that journal that will help us out. Let's get over to Taylor's and at least figure out where we are and what we need to do."

They had reached the short cliff at the back of the yard, and they still hadn't seen any sign of a hole from which the creature might have come. "It could've come from up there," Bill said, pointing up to the top of the cliff some twelve feet above their heads. "It looks like flat ground there, but I'd rather get a few more people out here before we start trying to find these things and engage them." They turned and started back across the lawn.

"Do you want me to stay here and keep looking?" Ray asked. "Or do you want me to start rounding people up?"

"No and not yet. I don't want anyone alone right now. We'll start gathering people as soon as we know where to put 'em. And I'm willing to bet that not everyone's going to come, either. They'd rather trust their doors and their locks and their pistols and rifles than the sheriff and a deputy and a trooper."

They were halfway across the lawn towards Taylor's. The sound of the rain hitting his hat and jacket was loud in his ears, and Bill looked over once more at Sarah's porch as they went by. The image of the creature clinging to the window frame and then leaping so gracefully and quickly onto Fogel lay heavily on his mind—this was something that none of them had ever heard of before, much less faced head-on.

He wasn't too sure that they were going to be able to fight it in any ways that they were used to. The blood on the porch and the two dead bodies in the house told him that regular rules of engagement were moot, that he'd better be trying to think up something new and different, and quick. And he still wanted to call his wife. He looked at his watch. It wasn't even one o'clock yet.

Sixteen
Stories

Taylor's house was starting to feel cramped when they got there. In addition to Jackson and Emily, Henry and Rita had come, and with Bill and Ray and Lopez, the living room was more than full.

"What was that shot we heard, sheriff?" Taylor asked anxiously as they took off their coats.

"One of those things got the other trooper on Sarah's porch," Bill replied. "I got off a shot, but I missed it. The son of a bitch was fast. Real fast."

"Oh my God," Taylor said, suddenly looking even more frightened. "Is he dead, then?"

"Yes, ma'am," Lopez said quietly.

"I'm so sorry," Taylor said to Lopez.

"You mean you actually saw what killed Sarah?" Jackson sounded fascinated. "Was it a person, then?"

"I couldn't rightly tell you, to be honest. It looked like a man, basically, but it was all shriveled up like, small and skinny but strong and fast. It looked like it was literally skin and bones."

"You mean like Henry?"

"Piss off, Jackson," Henry said loudly from the kitchen. "I'll take on your sorry ass any day."

"Boys," Taylor protested, "behave." She turned to Bill. "What are we going to do?"

"That's what we need to figure out. And we're not going to be getting any more help because the damned road's out. And I'm assuming the phones are out, too?"

"Yep," Jackson confirmed. "Tried to call my daughter about half an hour ago."

"So it looks like the only luck that we have is that the power lines come up a different route than the phones. Otherwise we wouldn't have any electricity, either."

"So we're completely isolated up here," Emily said quietly. "And there's no way out."

Bill was grim. "Looks like you got a bit more than you bargained for."

"Now that's exactly what I told her, Bill," Jackson said.

"Kind of like a perfect storm, isn't it?" Henry asked, coming into the room. "Kind of like all the circumstances are working in favor of someone else. Or something else."

"What are you talking about, Henry?" Bill demanded.

"You all ought to take a seat. That journal has quite a fascinating story to tell."

The three law enforcement officers exchanged glances, the kind of glance that asked what they were in for, curiosity mixed with dread and a bit of fear. None of them had fully processed Fogel's death yet, but the realization that one of their own had just been brutally killed was starting to seep into their consciousnesses. And the question "who's next" still hadn't begun to run around in their brains.

Bill noticed that the grad student also looked afraid and concerned. On the other hand, Taylor, Jackson, and Henry all looked as if they had almost been half-expecting what was going on. They seemed resigned to learning what they were about to hear.

"Can we get the condensed version?" Bill asked. "We've got a lot of work to do, and not a lot of time to do it in."

"Ten, fifteen minutes, tops," Henry assured him. "But I'm pretty sure you'll want to know who you're up against. Or what."

"Go ahead then."

"All right. The journal belonged to Wayne Naugle, the son of David Wayne Naugle, one of the biggest bastards this town has ever seen. No—the biggest bastard. Easily. David was around when all of these houses were full of miners' families—he spent about three years in charge of the coal mine up the hill. He came from back east—I'm not sure where, but his son mentions family in Boston quite often. The dad was well known for being a hardass, someone who cared only about the bottom line rather than the safety of his workers. He was universally hated, but no one could do anything about him. Twenty-five people died in the mines during his tenure here, which lasted about 32 months, all in all, if his son's figures are accurate.

"Wayne was only about ten years old when the family came here, and he could never figure out why all of the other kids in town hated him so much. Sins of the father, so to speak. He started this journal when he was in his teens, said he needed to write it down so people would know.

"Anyways, D. Wayne, the father, wasn't satisfied with his salary and the power he had over the miners and their families—he wanted more, and all the rumors of gold in these hills had worked their charm on him. He was sure there was gold, and he was going to be the first to find it.

"To give you an idea of just what a bastard this guy was, his son talks about one time when a group of eight miners were trapped by a cave-in. Naugle told everyone that the company was doing everything it could to rescue them, of course, but behind closed doors he was telling his people to write them off as lost and figure out a way that they wouldn't have to pay the full amount of compensation to the survivors. And since most of the miners and their families were immigrants, most who spoke little or no English, they were able to get away with it.

"Now here's where it starts to be relevant to us, maybe."

"Maybe?" Bill raised his eyebrows.

"Maybe. It was so long ago that even though it makes sense, it doesn't seem at all possible. In any case, Naugle had a team—'Naugle's Boys,' they were called. Seven tough sons of bitches who were more or less his enforcement squad. If someone caused problems, complained, didn't do what they were supposed to, they were pretty much guaranteed an ass-kicking. Sometimes they even beat the families of the miners. Especially oldest sons. They were not good people. Broken arms and legs were not unheard of.

"In any case, Naugle's boys also served another purpose. Naugle had taken over this old mine shaft here in town because he kept hearing rumors that there was gold to be found in it. The interesting thing about this mine is that whoever had dug the original shaft years earlier had stumbled upon a huge system of caves that just seemed to go down and down and down, with no way out except the shaft that had been dug into the caves in the side of the mountain here."

"That's the shaft in Sarah's basement?" Ray asked. "The one that was blocked off?"

"I don't know about the 'blocked off' part, but that sounds about right. Naugle was convinced that those caves were full of gold ore, but he didn't want his secret leaking out. So twice a week he had his boys explore—three of them one day, two another, in addition to their other work at the mine. They were excited about it and willing to keep it secret because they were promised a percentage of whatever they pulled out of there. In retrospect, that was obviously wishful thinking, but how were they to know that?

"Now here's where it seems to get sketchy. They kept going deeper and deeper into those caves, and Wayne writes that it was easy going—it seems that he was allowed to stay in his father's office whenever he met with the boys. For half a year they were exploring twice a week, but they never came up with any gold and old Naugle's getting suspicious. They keep telling him there's nothing there, and they're getting tired of going down into these caves every week, but Naugle not only doesn't flinch, but he starts to get suspicious that his boys are holding out on him."

"So Wayne is the son?" Ray asked. "The one writing?"

"Right, and David Wayne—D. Wayne, as he liked to be called—was the father.

"Now his son says that he's not completely sure about things that happened after a certain point because his dad started being extremely secretive. During this time, his dad had even built a house over the mine shaft, with the tunnel itself in the basement so that it wasn't in the public eye. He wasn't fooling anyone in town, of course—everyone knew what was going on—but he did what he could to cover his tracks, basically.

"One day, one of Naugle's boys doesn't come back with the others. The others are spooked, and they don't want anything to do with going back down in there. David wasn't allowed in his dad's office any more, but when you have grown men yelling at each other, it isn't hard to hear through the walls. They said that their companion had been dragged off screaming by something, but they had no idea what. Their lights weren't strong enough to help them see what was happening, and they just turned around and high-tailed it out of there. Naugle calls them cowards for having left their friend behind, and they get pissed. When they get pissed and start threatening Naugle, he gets defensive and starts threatening them back. When everything finally gets calmed down, Naugle convinces them to go down one more time to rescue their companion, and he gets all of them to go together for safety's sake. He promises them he'll shut down the mine for good once they bring back their companion—or his body—and that they'll never have to go down there again.

"In the meantime, though, he arranges for another guy, someone who is completely beholden to him because of debt or whatever, to rig some charges some hundred yards down the mine shaft, which he does. The day the group of Naugle's Boys heads down into the mine—all six of them together—they wait until the men are far enough into the caves and they blow the charges, collapsing the shaft and blocking off their escape. So basically, he kills them."

"So how is that relevant to us?" Bill asked. "Are you saying that we're dealing with those people who went down into that mine some sixty years ago? That was back in the 30's, wasn't it?"

"Well, I'd be pretty crazy to say something like that, wouldn't I? And yes, mid-30's. But consider this—the Naugle family moves into that house, because the old man doesn't want anyone messing around in the mine. And the guy who set the charges and blew the shaft, he dies a couple weeks later in an accident that's obviously more than a bit suspicious. What the son figures is that his dad was up to something even more horrible than just trying to get hold of some gold, and that he was trying to cover up his tracks because his boys—his enforcement squad—knew more than the old man wanted them to.

"After this, the old man basically loses control of the mines—he tries to recruit a new enforcement team, but no one will have anything to do with him. Three months later, he's history, but he refuses to move out of the house. And he brings in someone to build some sort of covering over the mine shaft, and he just stays in that house with his wife and his son."

"That would be the steel door that was ripped off its hinges."

"That would make sense. But the father only lasts a year or two. He catches pneumonia and dies, much to the pleasure of the residents of the town. As the years go by, his son gets kind of spooky. Once the journal goes from telling about what he remembered from when he was a kid to his own life, he's still living in the place, refusing to leave. His father had made him promise to be a guardian, sort of, a keeper of the gate. He gets married and lives on in that place with his wife and little sister, named Sarah. And Wayne, he sets up a trust so that his sister will have plenty to live on while she stays in the house herself, never leaving, never going on vacation."

"That's why she never went anywhere," Taylor said quietly. "I always used to think there was something odd about that. Except for a trip into town every other week or so, she pretty much never left that house."

"No, she didn't. She was the next gatekeeper. She was supposed to warn people if anything ever happened. Wayne wanted to tell people what had happened; he wrote that he was extremely frustrated because he knew that no one would ever believe him that there was any sort of danger after so much time. But something made him think that there was a danger, something that caused him to forfeit his sister's whole life watching a door in a basement, causing her to give up any chance that she had to get something out of life. By the time he dies, the coal mine is history. The price is down and it's just too expensive to keep pulling the stuff out of the mountain when there's no place to sell it nearby."

"This doesn't make a whole lot of sense, Hank," Bill protested. "Those guys would be long dead."

"That's what I thought," Henry said thoughtfully. "But then I realized that I had kind of glossed over something when I was reading."

"What was that?" Lopez asked.

"The other one of Naugle's boys. The first one to disappear. Naugle thought that he had run off with gold or something like that, but the men who had been down there with him said that he was 'dragged off screaming.' Which would mean that there had to be someone or something else down there with them. Before them. And he doesn't say at all that the man was killed down there—just dragged off screaming. I'm not completely sure, but it sounds like some of their trips down into the mine near the end were taking two days, there was so much to explore, so much distance to cover. Naugle thought they were just making it up to hide something from him. Put yourself in his position. They could have found gold and have been taking it out of another entrance somewhere else, for all he knew. And since he was a bastard himself, he would expect them to be doing something underhanded and dishonest—basically betraying him as he would do to them as soon as he had the chance."

"But that would leave a question still, assuming that I'm going to believe that any of this is possible. Is that thing that I saw one of Naugle's boys, or is it the something that dragged the first guy off?"

"I don't know," Henry said. "But it seems to me that it would be the men who were trapped down there, assuming they were able to survive this long. Seems like they'd be pretty hell-bent on revenge. I would be. Maybe." He didn't sound completely sure of himself.

"But they'd all be in their eighties," Lopez protested. "Are you telling me that a bunch of eighty-year-olds somehow knocked that door down, killed Sarah, and killed Fogel? After having been shut off in an abandoned mine for the last sixty years?"

Bill looked at Henry. "What do you think?"

Henry shrugged. "It all seems pretty far-fetched to me, but the way you described that thing, it looked human, but it didn't. If there were something down there before those guys went, it had plenty of chances to attack people on the surface, but didn't do so. Naugle's boys would do everything they could to get back to the surface, and they'd be pretty pissed when they did. You've got to wonder, though, just what that much time underground would do to a brain. They can't be anything like what they were when they were trapped down there. I mean, they would have lost all sense of time, all sense of direction, pretty much everything that we use to gauge our lives. No sunrise, no sunset. They would have had to adapt physically to be able to function down there—if there's no light, their eyes would have become useless fairly quickly, and they would have had to develop another way of sensing where they were and what was around them. Or their eyes became much more sensitive, much more able to see in the dark. I don't know what they would have maintained from their lives up here."

"I know that eighty sounds old," Jackson pitched in, "but how does the human body age when most of the stresses of the lives we lead are taken away? If they *have* been down there and they *do* have some sort of food source, they certainly haven't been worrying about work and family and paying bills and such. And who knows what kinds of food sources might be down there, what kinds of effects they might have?"

There was a moment of silence as his words sunk in.

"Sounds pretty far-fetched to me," Lopez finally said, "but something came up from that mine shaft and killed two people. It had to be something, didn't it?"

“Something pretty nasty," Taylor said. "And if it is them, it seems like they've pretty much held on to their anger. Their desire for revenge."

“Okay, so let’s say these are Naugle’s boys," Bill said. "What do we do now? What’s our plan? We just spent fifteen minutes listening to you tell us this, and that’s fifteen minutes they could have been surrounding this house or going after someone else in this town.”

“Come on, Sheriff,” Jackson said. “Any decision that we make right now is going to have possibly negative—hell, possibly fatal—outcomes. If we decide to guard against one thing, they could easily do something else. It’s not like there are rules here.”

Bill sighed. “You got that right. Let’s think this through. Where are we going to put all of the people? Do we want everyone together, or everyone in their own homes?”

“We’ve got to get everyone together, Bill,” Ray said. “Keeping people on their own is just asking for trouble.”

“I agree.” Bill turned to Jackson. “Now, the people up here, are you all going to be okay with having everyone in the same houses? Do you think people will go for that? And which houses are we going to put everyone in?”

“Everyone’s been hearing stories about something like this for as long as anyone can remember, so I don’t know that getting people together is going to go over well. I think this one’s a good one,” Jackson replied. “We can keep an eye on Sarah's house from here. My house would work pretty well, too. I live right at the end of the street here. And Lyle's house, if he’ll let people in. He’s pretty much as much of a loner as anyone gets up here—he may not be all too hot for company. I’m not exactly sure how many people we’ve got.”

“Twenty-seven,” Emily pitched in. “I counted. Well, twenty-six now. . . .” Her voice trailed off. “But with me here, that makes twenty-seven again,” she added.

“Well, we’ll try to convince Lyle and the other twenty-some," Bill said. "Since the road’s out, we’re going to have to make do with what we’ve got for now. And with the phones out, too. Damn me if all this doesn’t seem a little too coincidental to be true.

“We’ve got to get a lookout set up for across the street. We can do that two ways. We can park one of the cruisers on the lawn and set that up as a lookout, or we can do it from in here, since there seems to be a pretty good view from this window here.”

“I’m for here,” Lopez said quietly. “Those things broke through a steel door—there’s no way the glass windows in the cars are going to protect us. And you're not exactly mobile when you’re in a vehicle that you’re not driving. Anyone we put out there in a cruiser is going to be our next body.”

"You're probably right there," the sheriff replied. "So we'll set up a watch from right here. You willing to take first shift, Lopez?"

"I can do that. I'd like to bring everything in from the vehicle, though."

"That's a good idea. Let's empty all three vehicles into this house. Taylor, I'm sorry, but your house is going to be our Command Post."

"That's fine by me, Bill," Taylor said. "There's nothing to apologize for if you want to make this the safest place around."

Bill smiled. "Thank you. Ray, we're going to need to canvas the neighborhoods and get everyone moving. If we can get hold of a list of everyone in town, you can use that as a checklist. We've got to make sure we hit everyone. They already know what's happened, right, Rita?" Rita nodded.

"What do I tell them?"

Bill looked Ray in the eye. "Tell them that if they don't get into one of these houses with a lot of people, that they're probably going to die."

Ray shrugged. "Sounds fair."

Taylor stood. "I have a list of everyone for you. It's kind of like our phone book, but it's only about half a sheet of paper." She handed it to Ray, who quickly scanned the names on the list.

"And where are we asking these people to go?" Ray asked.

"Have them come here," Bill said. "We'll start assigning people to homes so we can kind of keep it even, and we'll send them on to the proper place when they get here. Taylor, do you think you could do that? You know everyone just as well as anyone else. Make sure we don't put any mortal enemies into the same house." Taylor nodded, and he turned back to Ray. "Have them start coming in an hour. It's almost one now, so one thirty should be good. Tell them we'll explain everything once everyone's grouped together. Oh, yeah—and tell them to come armed. Jackson, do you have any more weapons at home?"

Jackson smiled. "Depends, Sheriff. Do you mean the legal ones? 'Cause the illegal ones, those I don't have."

"Yeah, right. Listen, today's an amnesty day. I don't see anything, I don't take action on anything. Once we get through this thing, I forget everything I didn't see. Is that okay with you, Lopez?"

Lopez looked surprised that he had asked her. "That's fine with me," she said. "I don't know that I have any say in that."

"You and I don't work together. The people here need to be sure that once this is over, you're not going to bring the state troopers up here to check for weapons."

"That's not going to happen. They can bring machine guns, for all I care. After what that thing did to that woman and to Fogel. . . ." She shuddered.

Bill noticed the shudder and realized that he was going to have to keep an eye on both her and Ray. Neither of them had seen before the kinds of things they had seen already today, and once some of the day's events started sinking in, they were both liable to lose their focus, even if only momentarily. Things had been happening too fast for anyone's mind to process anything. If things slowed down, the processing would begin quickly. And what was going on threatened to be completely overwhelming.

"We'll set up three houses. We don't need to worry about having enough beds to start with—let's just get people there. And we'll make sure that every house has someone who can handle weapons well. I think we should stay together here in case we need to head out and take care of any emergency situations. We should have everyone in place by three or three-thirty. Once we have that done, we can come up with a plan and go after those damned things."

"That sounds good," Lopez said, sounding relieved. "I was afraid we were just going to sit around waiting for something to happen."

"If we do that," Bill said, "then we've lost already. So let's get to work." He turned and looked out the window just in time to see three men walking by, well armed and heading for Sarah's house.

"Looks like our plans just got changed for us," he muttered.

"Hey, wait up!"Bill yelled as he and Lopez and Ray reached the street. The trio of men ahead of them stopped just short of Sarah's yard and turned, regarding the three officers with interest.

"Never fear, sheriff!" one of them said loudly and happily, in a friendly tone. "The calvary is here!"

"That's what I'm afraid of, Juan," Bill replied.

"You mean 'cavalry,'" Lopez said. "Calvary's a hill near Jerusalem."

Juan turned and regarded Lopez with interest. "You don't say?" he asked. "And who might you be? *¿Y qué haces p'acá, guapita?*"

"This is Lopez, and I guarantee you that if you talk to her like that again, she'll kick your ass, Aguiar. And let's keep it in a language that we all understand. And the first question in that language is just where are you gentlemen off to?"

Juan smiled. "No offense meant, ma'am," he said politely. "And isn't it obvious what we're doing, sheriff? We're just gonna go kill us some Nogglz."

Bill looked down at the ground and thought for a moment. "I'm afraid I can't let you do that," he said, but his tone of voice said that he knew he couldn't stop them. "I've got to maintain public safety here."

"My ass, sheriff," the taller of the men said. "You know as well as I do that's a load of shit." His voice was friendly, as if he were chastising Bill for playing a bad bluff in a poker game.

"Nice to see you, too, Xavier," Bill said without a hint of anger. "You know, you may be right there. But put yourself in my shoes for a moment or two. You see three people with a shitload of guns about to go down into a mine where they're probably going to get themselves killed, and what would you do?"

Xavier laughed. "Hell, I don't know. Maybe deputize them?" He was the youngest of the group, still in his thirties, and Bill knew him mostly because of his tendency to hunt out of season. It was something that Bill never caught him at, but his hunting habits were common knowledge. He was one of the few Navajo in the entire county—his father had worked the mine when it was open and then stuck around after it closed down. Xavier had a great smile and was one of the people who always watched other people's backs, and did so well. He was like most of the people up in these mountains, Bill figured—decent people who over the years had learned to do things their own way, laws or rules be damned. As long as they weren't hurting anyone else, Bill was inclined to see only what he needed to see. Hell, if he didn't give them some leeway, they'd all be spending time in the jail in Pine from time to time. It just wasn't worth it.

Bill raised his eyebrows and smiled slightly. "You fellows want to give me two minutes, please? I know you're in a hurry, but two minutes, okay?"

"I'm timin' you, sheriff," Juan said, looking at his bare wrist as if there were a watch on it.

Bill motioned to Ray and Lopez, and they stepped away from the men.

"We don't have time to stand and argue with these guys," he said quietly.

"Do you think we can actually stop them?" Ray asked. "That could get ugly."

"But we've got to do something," Lopez said. "We can't just let them go down in there and get killed."

"Oh, there's something we can do," Bill said. "Like Ray said, this can get very ugly for no reason at all. That's why I think I'm going to let them go."

"You can't be serious," Lopez protested. "They'll get killed down there."

Bill smiled. "Lopez, those guys are better with their guns than we'll ever be. The quiet guy over there is Larry. He was Special Forces, three tours in 'Nam. I don't care if he is in his fifties—he's still better than I'll ever be. Juan was over in 'Nam a couple of times himself. And all three of them hunt and track extensively around here, mostly in season, I think. These aren't some punk kids with a bunch of guns and a boatload of bravado. They know what they're doing."

Neither Ray nor Lopez replied immediately. "It makes sense," Lopez said finally, "but it just seems wrong. What if. . . ." her voice trailed off.

"What if they die? Should we make them sit around in their houses just waiting for us to do something even though they're more likely to be successful than we are? And what if we go down there, and we die? Then they might have lost the chance to actually do something about those creatures. This is the only thing that makes sense. And we got it served to us on a silver platter. I am not going to look this gift horse in the mouth." He turned around and walked back to the men.

"As soon as you set foot on Sarah's lawn, consider yourselves deputized. You'll get an idea of what you're up against when you pass through Sarah's living room. The basement door is straight to the back, and the mine shaft is in the basement. Do you have lights?"

"We've each got a headlamp," Juan said. "And a flashlight."

"So we're deputies?" Xavier asked. "Cool! What does it pay?"

"We don't get paid, dipshit," Juan said, then turned to Bill. "Do we?"

"No pay. You don't even get one of these cool hats. Though if you take care of those things, I'll see what I can do about getting you each one." He saw Larry smile slightly, which he knew was a good sign.

"Uh—I don't mean any disrespect there, sheriff," Xavier said, "but I think I'll pass on the hat. If you could scrounge up another one of those vehicles that you drive, though. . . ."

"Okay, no hat. And you don't get to arrest anyone, either. And once you're out of her house, consider yourselves un-deputized."

Juan hit Xavier on the shoulder. "You're lucky, man. I was going to arrest your ass as soon as we hit that lawn."

Larry spoke up for the first time. "How many are we looking at, sheriff?"

"Don't rightly know, Larry. Judging from what Naugle's journal and the footprints in Sarah's house tell us, anywhere from two or three to seven. And we haven't been down there, but supposedly they blew the shaft sixty years ago to trap them down there, so there's no telling what you'll have to go through to get anywhere. They were trying to block off the exit, keep these things—they were men, then—from coming out. And they're fast and strong. The one that I saw appeared, took out the trooper, and disappeared in a matter of fifteen or twenty seconds."

"How'd it take him out?"Xavier asked.

"Ripped out his throat. You'll see him in Sarah's house."

"Damn." Xavier felt his own throat with his fingertips.

"Yeah. Damn. So don't go down there thinking this is going to be a cake walk. If you do that, we'll be burying you next week. The parts that we can find, anyway."

"Thanks, sheriff," Larry said, then turned and started away. "Come on. We've got a job to do."

Juan and Xavier turned to follow him, and Bill was sure that they felt a bit less cocky than they had a few minutes earlier.

"Just a moment, men," Bill called after them. "Did I forget to mention that I'm coming with you?"

Lopez and Ray looked at each other in surprise; neither of them had seen this coming. He turned to them.

"This may be our best hope of taking care of these things before they bring it to us out here," he said. "If anything happens to me, Lopez, you're in charge. Experience over jurisdiction."

Juan turned around and smiled. "That's not necessary, sheriff. We're fine."

Larry spoke up. "I was wondering when that was coming. Let's get going then." He put a hand on Juan's shoulder. "He's the sheriff. He's gotta do what he's gotta do." He turned and started walking away once more. "Let's do this."

Bill followed them, walking backwards for a few moments to talk to Ray and Lopez. "You guys guard the yard. Position yourselves on the lawn so that you can see the back of the yard and the front door. And don't come in, no matter what you hear." Then he turned and followed the others across the lawn.

"Just one question, sheriff," Juan said as they reached the steps to the porch.

"What's that, Juan?"

"What the hell is a cake walk?"

Seventeen
Gratification

His last kill had felt even better than the first. The feel of the contact between his hand and the man's throat was somehow fulfilling, gratifying. Feeling the body slump to the ground as he clung to it gave him a rush that he no longer had words to describe, a feeling of power and a feeling of finally being able to do what he had spent so long being unable to do. The frustration was gone. Before his conscious brain functions had ceased, before the ability to reason and plan and comprehend had faded away, his mind had been on one thing—revenge—and that was the thing that most strongly affected him now, the drive that rose above all other drives. Even the freedom that he had felt out in the open, under the grey sky with the raindrops falling down upon him, even that didn't give him the gratification that he received from his violent action.

But even though it had affected him so strongly, there was something odd about it. It wasn't the same as it had been with the first one. As he made his way through the darkness to where he knew the other four would be gathered, something gnawed at his mind, telling him that the killing hadn't been as good as his instincts told him it should have been. Since he had no ability to think things through, though, there was no way for that something to become more than just an uneasiness, undefined and useless. There was no way for him to realize that killing an outsider, someone who had no ties at all to the town and its past, really meant nothing compared to killing someone from the town, someone with such a connection. His inability to reason kept him from ever coming close to understanding such an idea.

All he knew was that it was time to go above. It was time for the five of them finally to leave these caves, these tunnels, for good. It was time for them to have the revenge about which they had fantasized for so long until they could no longer fantasize, the revenge that became their basis for being after their minds had faded away decades ago. It was time for them to kill.

Eighteen
Hospitality

Taylor heaved a huge sigh and stood up from the dining room table. "If we're going to have extra company for a while, it would probably be best to get some food made. You think you could give me a hand, Emily?"

Emily looked surprised. "Absolutely," she said quickly and got up. She had been overwhelmed for the last two hours, trying to understand and get a feeling for what was going on. It wasn't easy. The sheriff and his deputy seemed on edge and unsure, the trooper seemed overwhelmed and a bit confused—but still very capable—and the townsfolk seemed to be resigned to something that they might not have understood completely, but that didn't seem to surprise them as much as it should have.

"So are these the Nogglz that I heard about?" she asked as Taylor started to pull pots and pans from her cupboards. The question stopped Taylor for a moment, and she paused before answering.

"I'm guessing they are," she replied, "but I sure as hell never expected that they were real. They were just something our parents used to scare us—'You'd better not do that again, or Naugle's boys will get you,' they'd say. It became part of the folklore of the town, and when we were kids, we didn't even know how to spell 'Naugle's'—we spelled it like it sounded to us." She pulled a pot now full of water from the sink and put it on the stove, and looked at Emily. "I like our spelling better. I remember one time when I was about ten, me and my brother decided to go hunting for the Nogglz—they weren't 'Naugle's Boys' to us—and he left a note on his bed that said 'Went looking for Nogglz'—he said just in case we got killed, our parents would want to know what had happened to us. Boy, did we get a lickin' that day."

Emily smiled. "It sounds like this story has been a part of the culture of this town for a very long time."

Taylor looked down at Emily's hands. "You don't have anything to write with," she noted.

"What do you mean?" Emily asked.

"Just what I said. Think about it for a moment. You're in the middle of something incredible, and we're in the middle of something that we've been dreading for decades. By the end of the night, we may all be dead, if these things really are what we think they are. I'm old enough to know that sitting here denying that they exist isn't going to make them go away. I'd feel a hell of a lot better if I knew that someone was recording all of this for posterity's sake. And you may just have a story that could make you famous. Or a lot of money. Or both."

"That's assuming that I don't die, too, isn't it?" Emily was surprised at her own words, and she suddenly realized that this was something that she hadn't wanted to think was possible.

Taylor stopped. "Now I have to admit," she said, "I hadn't even thought of that as a possibility. The Nogglz want us, I think—I never thought of them wanting to kill you."

"Why do they want you?" Emily asked. "That doesn't make a lot of sense—you aren't the ones who sent them down into that mine. Why would they want to kill you?"

"That was the thirties, honey—this is the nineties. I have no idea how those monsters have stayed alive this long, but don't you think that if it really is them, they're going to want to take their revenge on whomever they find here?"

Emily shrugged. "That makes sense, I guess. Except for the part about them still being alive, of course. And when you say 'whomever they find here,' doesn't that include me? I'm in the wrong place at the wrong time, it seems."

"Or the right place at the right time."

"You are right, though. Let me go get my notebook. If we all die, at least I can warn whoever finds us about what they may be facing." She went back out to the living room and was back in less than a minute.

"So what do you think about the idea of Sarah being some sort of gatekeeper?" she asked Taylor.

"To tell you the truth," Taylor replied, "it's the first thing I've heard about Sarah that's made sense. I never could figure that woman out. She's a nice enough person—was a nice enough person—but why the hell she stayed up here in that house never made any sense to me. And she wouldn't tell anyone. She was one of the most secretive people I've ever known. I guess she was afraid of not being able to make her own way if she lost that trust money.

"I used to sit with her on her porch many an evening, and we would just talk. She never mentioned the trust at all, and she never mentioned any sort of mine shaft in her house. She also never invited people in, and she didn't do much visiting herself. I asked her a few times why she didn't just get the hell out of town. . . ." her voice trailed off as she thought.

Emily waited a few moments before prodding her. "And what did she say?"

Taylor looked up, a bit startled, and she smiled. "All she would do was ask me why I didn't do so myself. Could you hand me that can opener there?"

"And why haven't you?"

Taylor shrugged as she lifted the lid of a pot to check the water. "I honestly don't know, Emily. There's one side of me that says that it's my husband's fault, that it's just because I own this house outright and I wouldn't be able to sell it even if I tried. That side of me likes to blame him and be pissed off. But there's another part of me that knows that I'm tied to this town just as strongly as Sarah was. That there's no way I could ever leave. For so long this was all I ever knew, and all I ever wanted to know. When I was young, the sense of community here was incredibly strong—we all knew everyone else, and we knew that no matter what happened, someone would have our backs and take care of us. Of course, there's always been the bad mixed up with the good, plenty of drinking and hitting and fighting, but there always is, I think. I grew up loving this town—or at least, the people who made it what it was—and I couldn't bear the idea of leaving.

"If I go into Pine now, or God forbid over to the Springs or to someplace like Denver, then I feel completely out of place, lost. I know I could die on a street in Denver and no one would care the slightest bit. Even though this town is close to closing up and calling it over and done with, there's still the feeling between those of us that are left that we belong, that it's a place that we can call home for the rest of the time that we have left on this planet."

"It sounds kind of nice, to have that kind of attachment to a place," Emily said. "These days, it seems like very few people have much of a connection with other people. No one stays in one place all that long anymore."

"It does have its down sides, that's for sure. Like now, for example. I feel like I might die here for the sins of someone else's fathers—I never did anything to those men. Hell, I was barely born when they were trapped down in that mine or those caves or wherever. But it's my ties to the town that will make me a target, if what seems to be happening is what's actually happening. But I've given it a good run. I can't say that I'm disappointed with my life. If it were to end today somehow, that wouldn't be such a tragedy. I've had my share of time here. But you, that's another story. I'm hoping that whatever happens here in the next day or two, you and the sheriff and the deputy and that trooper make it out of here in one piece." She stopped and looked up at Emily. "I didn't mean it that way," she said.

Emily smiled. "I know," she said. "But if I do write a book or something about this, I can guarantee you that line is going to be in there."

Taylor smiled, too. "As well it should be, I suppose. We've got to keep our sense of humor about us, don't we?"

"We sure don't have a whole lot else right now," Emily said. "Especially with the road out. It's a good thing there's enough food and shelter for everyone. And that we still have electricity."

Taylor looked up at the light in the ceiling. "Can you imagine what this would be like without electricity?" She shook her head. "I think that the light is keeping us sane. We will take care of each other, as well as we can. We are family here, even though almost none of us were born to the same parents. And I think that's what's always held me back when I thought about leaving—I don't have family anywhere else, so there's never been any reason to go anywhere else. Even though we're facing something pretty horrible right now, at least we're facing it together."

Emily didn't reply. She heard an incredible strength in Taylor's words, but she also heard a vulnerable woman sharing her thoughts and her life in a way she probably never had before. And Emily felt almost overwhelmed that Taylor was sharing the story with her, someone she hadn't ever met until two days earlier. Could she live up to the trust that Taylor was showing her?

Nineteen
Down the Throat of the Dragon

It was a silent group of four men who mounted the stairs of Sarah's porch and stopped at the door. Bill looked back to make sure that Lopez and Ray were moving towards their spots. He paused to consider warning the others about what they were going to see. He decided against it; they probably knew what had happened in there, and more words weren't going to do anyone any good.

He pushed open the door and moved in quickly, his pistol in his right hand, making his way towards the basement door. He glanced at Fogel only to avoid the body, as the idea of tripping over him wasn't one of his more pleasant thoughts. He heard the others swear behind him as they got their first look at what had happened to Sarah, and Bill suddenly felt a surge of pity for her—by all accounts, they should have been able to at least move her body parts from where they were lying. It just seemed damn disrespectful not to have done so yet.

"You weren't kidding, Sheriff," Juan said quietly as he joined Bill at the door to the basement. "This is a frickin' mess." Larry and Xavier were there quickly also, and the four men grouped to get ready to go downstairs. They all had headlamps on, and all were carrying an extra flashlight in their belts.

"Okay," Bill said. "Headlamps on, and they stay on. Flashlights only if necessary—let's save all the light we can. We shouldn't be more than twenty minutes, whether it goes good or it goes bad, so we should have plenty of light. We'll alternate point—one man move up, twenty-foot maximum, last man ten steps past everyone, all the way in. Be careful of your shooting—if you're on point and you see something, shoot away and ask questions later. But if you're in the rear, be damned careful that you don't hit one of our own.

"Questions?"

"With all due respect, Sheriff," Larry said quietly, "we're going to be in a narrow tunnel with almost no light. With all that moving past each other, we're gonna find ourselves in a pretty major clusterfuck in about two minutes."

As soon as he spoke, Bill knew that he was right. "What would you suggest, Larry?"

"We pair up. Juan and I take point. You and Xavier cover from behind. That way no one's on their own and we don't worry about who's coming up running from behind." Larry spoke matter-of-factly, with no trace of judgment in his voice, even though they all knew Bill's plan had been seriously flawed.

Bill appreciated Larry's objectivity. He looked at the others. "That sound good to you?" he asked, knowing what their answer would be. They both nodded, and Bill saw in their eyes that he had just passed a test. "All right," he said. "Let's go."

"Uh, Sheriff?" Xavier said. Bill looked at him, and Xavier tapped on a piece of plastic that was in his ear. "You don't want to be in a mine with guns going off without plugs."

"Damn," Bill muttered. "They're in my vehicle."

Juan quickly stepped into the bathroom and pulled two sheets of toilet paper from the roll. Bill quickly rolled them up into ear plugs, and they were ready.

Larry led the way into the basement, which was dark. "This isn't a good sign," Bill muttered to Xavier. "We left the lights on." He looked towards the light bulb in the ceiling, which was already in the beam of Juan's headlamp and which had been broken since he had last seen it. "Let's be careful, men," he said. "This basement was our turf, but I think it's theirs now."

"Look at all these damned footprints," Juan said quietly. "There has to be more than a couple of these things." They look human, but not. Too small, too narrow. It looks to me like five or six of them."

Bill thought about that for a moment. "I was hoping two or three. Five or six changes the odds—if that's true, then we're heading in there outnumbered."

"Two blasts from my shotgun and we're even or we outnumber them," Juan said confidently. Bill liked Juan's attitude. He was confident, but Bill saw it as a cautious confidence.

"And if they get one of us, they're up two to one," Xavier said.

"Then let's make sure they don't get one of us," Larry said. "We've got to do what we've got to do and think about it later." There seemed to be silent assent among the others.

"Let's go," Larry said, and he and Juan moved slowly into the mine. Bill and Xavier took up positions at the entrance, Xavier kneeling just inside the shaft and Bill standing just outside, still in the basement. They watched Larry and Juan move away from them down the narrow, straight corridor, and Bill couldn't help but think about Fogel doing exactly the same thing just a few hours earlier.

Larry moved quietly into the tunnel, keeping close to the dark rocky wall beside him. He was glad that Juan was with him—the sheriff was a good enough guy, but Larry had no idea how he'd handle himself if things hit the fan, and he didn't want to have to do any babysitting in a situation like this.

He let Juan take the lead by about five feet, and the light from their headlamps showed them a very narrow shaft that obviously hadn't been meant for more than one person at a time to pass through. Larry found himself wondering who might have had the time or energy or equipment—or reason—to create such a tunnel, but he quickly stifled that line of thought and brought himself back to the present moment. He needed to be fully here, and he knew it.

Juan suddenly held up his left fist and stopped, as did Larry. They were almost a hundred yards into the mine, Larry guessed, and he saw just ahead what had caused Juan to stop. The tunnel was filled with rubble, large chunks of rock that had caved in. Almost chest-high in the rubble, though, he saw a hole that looked just big enough for a person to squeeze through.

He looked back to see lights about fifty yards behind him. Bill and Xavier had followed them in, keeping them in sight.

"Hold up!" he said simply, then turned back to the situation at hand.

"That don't look good," Juan said quietly.

Larry said nothing. He hadn't considered this possibility. He had been thinking of the mine shaft as he saw it in the basement—something that they could easily make their way through without anything impeding them. But he suddenly saw how vulnerable they would be if they were to go through that hole one by one, completely exposed and unable to maneuver or defend themselves.

"No, it doesn't," he said quietly, turning his head so that the light was pointing to the hole in the rubble.

"First man through's a sitting duck," Juan said softly.

"Or a dead duck," Larry added. "But it could be that there's nothing there on the other side, and then we've got nothing to worry about."

"And it could be that they're all just sitting there on the other side, waiting for us."

"Either or," Larry said. "What are you thinking?"

"I'm thinking we go in. We're down here for a reason."

Larry didn't reply.

"Let me check out the hole," Juan said. "It could be bigger than it looks." He moved forward and slowly approached the rocks and dirt that filled the passageway. He heard nothing, which he took for a good sign until he thought about it a moment. Then he realized that if he were waiting for someone to step into a trap, he would be as quiet as he possibly could. So the silence told him nothing.

Larry watched him move closer to the hole, and he felt more uneasy with each step that Juan took. His gut was telling him to call Juan back, that something was wrong. But he also knew that the entire situation was wrong, and his instincts could be reacting to that fact. They had to check out as much as they could of the tunnel. It was virtually a no-win situation. He watched as Juan stopped short of the hole, which was just at the level of his head. Juan moved his head around, playing the light from his headlamp around the edges of the hole, and then through the hole, trying to see as far in as he could. The rubble formed a steep slope from the hole to the ground, and Juan took three slow and careful steps up the rubble, moving his head and the light closer. The silence was overwhelming—each pebble or rock that he dislodged sounded like a boulder rolling down a mountain to Larry, and he suddenly realized that he was holding his breath.

He watched Juan take one step backwards from the hole and turn back towards him, shining his headlamp straight into Larry's eyes. In his sudden near-blindness from the light, Larry caught a flash of movement in the hole. He yelled Juan's name, and the light that had been shining in his eyes was suddenly jerked back until it was shining straight at the ceiling for one quick moment. He heard Juan scream, and then he heard a deafening gunshot and saw a flash from Juan's pistol. There was no telling if the shot had hit home because Juan was being dragged, head-first, directly into the hole. Juan screamed again, and Larry watched in horror as Juan's body was pulled unceremoniously and quickly out of sight. Juan was gone before Larry was even able to react, but he wasn't dead yet—Larry heard Juan scream again from somewhere beyond the hole, but only once until suddenly the sound stopped.

"Sheriff!" Larry yelled back into the darkness. "Up here!"

He saw one of the lights moving towards him. A moment later Larry saw that Xavier was following the sheriff, an unforgivable tactical blunder in Larry's eyes, but there was nothing he could do about it right now.

"What the hell happened?" the sheriff asked loudly as he came quickly towards Larry. "Where's Juan?" He stopped and kneeled some ten feet short of Larry's position.

"Get back to the basement, Xavier!" Larry yelled, then in his normal voice that showed no evidence of stress or distress, he addressed the sheriff. "Juan's gone. He was standing next to that hole there when something reached out and dragged him in. I'm going after him."

"Through that hole? Are you insane?"

"Some would say. And they may be right. But we leave no one, sheriff. He was still alive and screaming on the other side, so there's a good chance he's still not dead. I've got at least five hours of batteries left, so I'm going in."

"Larry, we need you up here."

"Right now, Sheriff, Juan needs me a hell of a lot more than you do. Get out of this tunnel. If I'm not back by midnight, go to my house. There's a small trap door in the closet in my bedroom. Open it and you'll find five grenades. Five-second fuse. Two of you can get all five in there for one blast, but you may bring this whole shaft down. Otherwise, one at a time, first one furthest, then closer."

"Are you serious? And trap you in there?"

"If I ain't back in five hours, sheriff, I'm not coming back. And neither is Juan. Now get your asses out of here—I've got to get going." Larry turned back towards the hole and moved forward. He couldn't let Juan go after he had failed him—even though Juan had been in the way, Larry couldn't help but feel that he should have gotten off at least one shot. He reached the hole and peered into it, half expecting something to appear and try to grab him. It looked like a tight fit, but if Juan had made it through, he could too.

Larry took a deep breath and reached up into the hole, pulling himself up and in. Then he started crawling, pulling his body forward as quickly as he could. He couldn't see ahead because he didn't have enough room to lift his head to look. He watched the rocks beneath him come into view and then slide away as he moved.

"Let's get out of here!" Bill yelled to Xavier, turning around as Larry disappeared into the hole. He started out of the tunnel and he saw that Xavier was only some thirty feet behind him.

"What happened?" Xavier asked, and Bill heard fear in his voice.

"Something got Juan, and Larry's going after him," Bill replied quickly. "Come on, let's move!"

He kept moving, his head down so that his headlamp illuminated the ground for him. Xavier stood still for a moment, then he too turned to leave. His head was down, too, so that he could see the ground.

Because they were looking down, neither of them noticed the figure that was once again clinging completely still to the crossbeam nearest to the basement. Xavier started to run under it, but just as he reached it the figure dropped in the darkness and grabbed his head; in one smooth motion, almost before its feet even hit the ground, it twisted Xavier's head violently, breaking his neck immediately. But Xavier's instincts were quick—as soon as he felt the touch of something on his head, he pulled his pistol around and squeezed off a desperate shot.

Bill saw the flash and felt more than heard the report of the pistol, which was amplified to an almost painful level in the shaft, even with the toilet paper in his ears. At the same moment he heard the high-pitched sounds of ricochets, and he saw two sets of sparks almost simultaneously. He had lifted his pistol instinctively also, and he was ready to pull the trigger when he felt an impact in his left side, just under his chest. "Shit," he thought even as he was pulling the trigger twice.

He fell to his knees, not seeing that one of his bullets had hit home. He heard a fierce and horrible shriek come from what seemed to be a very far distance, and the thought immediately entered his mind that he had to get out of the tunnel. He forced himself to his feet; with his right hand he applied as much pressure as he could to his wound, and he held his pistol with his left. He started staggering towards the basement.

"One at a time, Bill," he muttered aloud as he moved. "One step at a time."

He felt no sense of satisfaction when he saw the dead creature on the ground, especially since it had fallen partly atop Xavier's body. Nor did he even feel any curiosity about what it was like. "Damn," he muttered as he looked at Xavier—his eyes were open and staring.

"Ray!" he yelled, but not nearly as loudly as he'd hoped. He had no idea if Ray would be able to hear him from outside.

He was having a hard time staying on his feet. The shock was overwhelming him and he had almost given up and was about to allow his body to crumple to the floor when Ray appeared in the entrance to the basement, just ten feet away.

"Okay, Bill, I've got you," he heard Ray say, and in a moment he felt Ray's strength as Ray took the pistol from Bill's hand and pulled Bill's left arm over his shoulder and around his neck.

"Hang in there, Bill," he heard, and he felt a surge of energy that came with Ray's help. He was going to make it out of the mine, which was all that he wanted at the moment.

Twenty
The Bastard

Their companion was still outside, still in the new part of the cave, the part they had discovered when they had cleared enough rocks and made a hole that they could climb through. They didn't know why he was out there or what he was doing, but the other four were nervous and fidgety. They wanted to move, they wanted to do something, but even after finding their freedom after so many years, they were held in place by the most primal of all feelings: fear.

Their companion seemed to avoid nothing that their instincts told them to avoid, and that made them uneasy. When they were all still trapped in the never-ending caves, when they could still speak and think and they were all on equal terms, at first making plans to find the way out without light, he was fearless. Later, when they had developed the ability to move in the dark but lost the ability to think and to reason, he still took risks that none of the others would take. Even so, they always had done things on equal terms—there was no leader, there was no alpha. They helped each other, they learned from each other's mistakes, they did all they did for the sake of all.

But now there he was, apart from them, doing something different. He hadn't come back inside since long ago, but they all could smell new blood. He had killed again, something that riled up their instincts and caused their bloodlust to renew even more strongly.

They spent most of the day near the hole, waiting for the other to come back in. They weren't able to think of other possibilities. He was out there and they were in here, and since they no longer were able to communicate with words, they would have to wait until they saw him so they could "decide" as a group what to do next.

Suddenly they heard voices, something that they hadn't heard for decades. They couldn't know what the voices meant, but their instincts told them to be on guard. One of them put himself directly under their escape hole, where he kneeled and listened. There was silence for a time, then the voices came again, much closer. Suddenly they saw light coming through the hole, and they all shrank back, not sure what the light meant, remembering the pain the light had caused them earlier.

The one nearest the hole suddenly scrambled up into it, moving towards the light. Just as he moved, though, the light dimmed to almost nothing. There was still light there, but it wasn't nearly as strong as it just had been. He reached the end of the tiny tunnel and saw the closest light, but it wasn't shining on him. The light was on a man's head, and another, brighter light was shining directly on him from farther away. He would get rid of the closer light first. He reached out his arm and grabbed, but instead of a light he grasped a handful of hair. He pulled.

His strength was incredible, and he was able to pull the full-grown man through the small hole by the hair with almost no effort at all. The whole time he was dragging the man into the cave with them, the man was screaming. As they came out of the other side of the hole the one who had grabbed and dragged Juan took the light that was on his head and threw it against the tunnel wall and broke it. Then he delivered a backhanded blow to Juan's head that immediately knocked him unconscious.

They worked quickly and well together. One of them lifted the man's legs and put them on his shoulders at the knees, while another grabbed his arms and put them over his shoulders, the man's head pushed down into his back. When they had him, the two started running, carrying the body between them, dragging it over the ground and allowing it to hit any protruding rocks. It didn't matter to them. They just had to get it somewhere and then get back here. They ran quickly, following routes that would have been invisible to anyone else in the darkness, but which they knew by rote. The fact that they could carry a full-grown man over this route was extraordinary.

The two carrying the body heard the faint report of the gunshots up higher, but the two who had stayed heard them loud and clear. When they heard their companion howl in pain, they returned the howls—his agony caused them agony. They knew they had to get out there and do something.

But that would have to wait. Right now, they heard a noise and saw a light in their escape tunnel—someone else was coming through. They drew back thirty feet to a spot where they knew there was a hiding place, a deep recess in the ceiling of the tunnel they were in. There they waited until they heard soft footsteps approaching.

It might have been because they were just two without the others; it might have been because they felt a deeper impulse to go to their companion outside. Whatever the reason, they let Larry walk by, and they watched the light grow stronger, then dimmer. Then they dropped once more into the passage and hurried to the exit.

By the time they made it through the hole and stopped at the body of their companion, though, there was no one else there in the tunnel. There were two bodies on the ground, one of their companion, and the other of a person they saw as their enemy.

They looked at each other. They were outside the hole once more, and the feeling was a good one, not a frightening one. They knew they had something they had to do. They picked up their companion, one holding the ankles and one the wrists. He had to be moved. He had to go to the stream. He had to be in the water. They didn't know why and they weren't able to understand their own actions, but they didn't need to. They just moved.

That's why all four of them were at the stream with their loads thirty minutes later, deeper into the caverns than anyone above imagined they even stretched. They stopped in a room that actually glowed brightly in the darkness with a light that no other human eyes had ever seen before. The light from the walls was exquisite, a shade of green that had a peacefulness about it that belied its location two miles deep under the surface of the earth. All four of them dropped the bodies they carried next to a shallow indenture through which flowed a small stream some eight inches deep. They pushed the two bodies into the stream, face up, just as another creature, larger and much stronger, entered the chamber from the other side.

The four sat down, obviously subservient to this new being. They lowered their heads, looking down at the ground as the new creature approached them slowly. It was larger but it was just as thin, and its body was as shriveled and hideous as those of the others. Somehow, though, it carried itself with power and strength, and it was obvious that it would be able to overpower any of the others with little problem. It came to the stream and looked at the body of Juan in the water, then reached out and touched Juan's face. . . tenderly? It seemed to have the gentleness of a rancher who had just seen a new foal, glad to see the newest addition to his stock.

Sixty years earlier, after the blast, Naugle's boys had followed the caverns deep into the ground, knowing that if there were an escape route, it would have to lie in a direction other than the one they knew. When they first saw this creature, all five of them knew that they had found the thing that had dragged away their companion. They had "met" it one by one, as that was how it took them from each other, twice as they all slept, the other times as they made their way slowly through the darkness. They each had woken up with a headache caused by a vicious blow to the head, shivering in the almost-frozen waters of the stream in the glowing room. And each had started to eat of the glowing moss and the glowing worms that covered the walls of this chamber and three others, not having any clue that this food source would doom them to long lives and extremely diminished mental powers. Their thoughts started escaping them almost immediately, and were completely gone within months.

They had called this one "The Bastard" during their first few weeks in the caverns, during the time when they were still able to speak. After they lost their ability to speak to each other, their cognitive abilities started to fail them. They had no idea that they lost their ability to think because of chemical interactions between their brains and their extremely addicting food source, the only food available to them. At first, they constantly tried to think of ways to escape, but The Bastard had other plans for them—he was brutal and merciless when they disappeared for any amount of time at first, though he became much more tolerant of their activities as they lost their minds. They had simply traded one merciless master for another, without having any choice in the matter.

Eventually, one of them had started moving rubble from the only exit they had ever known, but it was very slow going. It was especially slow because they would sometimes forget about it for days and weeks at a time, returning to their work sometimes by accident as they wandered through the caverns. Sometimes a spark of instinct would strike one of them, leading him up to where the caverns ended and the mine shaft began.

The Bastard didn't seem to care about them moving rocks. Sometimes he would disappear, too, deeper into the caverns than they ever went because he kept them from going there. They tried, but they learned very quickly that when The Bastard was angry, he could cause a great deal of pain.

Then it looked to the body of the creature in the water, and it touched its face, too. This time there was no tenderness, for it could feel the absence of living essence in the body. It growled softly and pulled the body from the river, holding it aloft in one hand while he turned to face the others. It could sense something in them and on them; he could smell and feel the surface. These five had been out of the caves, among people—this it knew from the smell of human blood, something it hadn't perceived in decades of life away from the humans.

It was impossible to tell if it felt any emotion tied to what it now knew. It did nothing to the other four. . . it merely strode off carrying the body, which it took to the edge of a pit on the other side of the chamber and threw into it. Then it shuffled back to the group and sat before them, reaching out to a rock near him and scraping off a piece of glowing moss that was growing on it. This he ate, feeling the strength of the plant immediately. He stared at the four, who still looked down at the ground, and he grunted. His instinct wasn't telling him what to do. Yet. But it would.

Twenty-One
Down and In

Ray and Lopez had set themselves up to watch the yard next to the house. Ray stood on the lawn at the corner of the porch, while Lopez waited next to the small pine that stood some twenty yards from the house, where the forest began about halfway back to the cliff that the house was built into.

Ray stood quietly, feeling nervous and antsy. He knew that if the second opening were in the cliff above, there was a good chance they would never find it unless they saw something actually coming out of it. He knew there was nothing they could do about that, but he wanted to be doing something rather than nothing at all. His mind always started running far too quickly when he was standing around waiting for something to happen.

Ray glanced now and then at Lopez, but they both stayed silent. He wanted to talk, but he couldn't think of anything that seemed worth saying.

Suddenly, he heard a muffled scream come from the ground somewhere near the cliff, followed quickly by a shot. Another scream came quickly after the first, a man's voice but he couldn't tell whose. Then the yells started growing fainter, and they suddenly stopped. Ray looked around frantically, trying to locate the source of the sound, knowing that it had to be coming from the opening they had been looking for. Suddenly another shot rang out, and Ray was able to get a better sense of direction, but he was unwilling to approach the hole and leave his post. Almost immediately two more quick shots sounded. Then came an unearthly howling that seemed to be a cross of pain and anger, a sound that couldn't be attributed to anything with which Ray was familiar. Then came silence. Silence was the worst possible thing for Ray.

He had just decided to move towards the sounds to find the opening when he heard Bill faintly yell out his name. The sound came from the lawn, from the same direction from which the shots seemed to have come from.

He looked over at Lopez, who was looking at him. She looked as confused as he felt.

"I'm going in there," Ray said.

"Go," was all she said in reply.

He was on the porch in two steps, through the living room and on the stairs to the basement in seconds. He saw a moving light coming from the mine entrance, and he reached it just as Bill got there—the sheriff was weak and staggering. The only light was from Bill's headlamp, and it partially blinded Ray. He was still able to notice, though, that Bill was holding his left side with his right hand, and that there was a lot of blood there.

"Okay, Bill, I've got you," Ray said, taking Bill's gun from his left hand and pulling Bill's arm over his own shoulders. He knew they had to move quickly as long as Bill was still able to stand—having him pass out in the basement would have been a disaster, given the circumstances.

"Xavier's dead," Bill managed to say, and his voice sounded wheezy. "Those things took Juan. Larry went after him to bring him back."

"Okay," Ray said. "Got it. Now stay quiet and save your strength."

They made it slowly up the stairs, with Bill's breathing growing more labored with each step. Ray heard a slight gurgling sound as Bill breathed, and he started to worry that Bill wasn't going to make it.

"Come on, Bill," he encouraged the sheriff. "Just a few more steps and we're out of here." Bill's face was contorted into a grimace, and Ray could see that the pain must be terrible. They had just reached the porch when Bill's weight seemed to increase. Ray saw Lopez coming over just as Bill muttered one word, "Can't."

He lowered Bill to the porch as gently as he could with Lopez' help. "He's been shot, it looks like," Ray said. "We've got to get him over to Taylor's."

"We can't carry him," Lopez replied, looking around for help that wasn't there, "not if he's been shot."

"Go over there and get something we can use as a stretcher—a cot, or something like that. Anything sturdy enough."

"On my way," she said. "Keep guard here. And keep pressure on that wound. He's not holding it any more."

Ray watched her run across the lawn in the rain, and suddenly he was very glad that she was there. He pulled back Bill's jacket and put the heel of his left palm over the hole he saw there in the shirt, then turned his attention to the doorway behind him.

"Move quickly, Lopez," he muttered.

Lopez was faster than he ever would have thought she could be. In less than three minutes she was coming back across the lawn with Henry and Jackson, who were carrying a box spring between them.

"Let's do this quick," Henry said. "We don't want to give those things time to show up."

"Let's do it, then," Ray said.

"Taylor's getting stuff ready for a pressure dressing," Lopez said.

"And Pauline used to be a nurse," Jackson added. "We'll go get her as soon as we get back." They lay the box spring on the porch floor next to the sheriff. "Deputy, trooper, you each grab an arm. Hank, left leg?"

"Gotcha," Henry said, and in seconds Bill was lying on the box spring. "Don't know how sturdy this thing will be, but it should get us over to Taylor's. Let's slide it to the top of the stairs, and you two can grab it from below."

Two minutes later they set it down in front of Taylor's front door and once more lifted Bill's unconscious form and carried him inside.

"I'm going for the nurse," Lopez said once they had set him down on the floor. "Bring the box spring in and put him back on it. Taylor, can you take me over to her house?"

"You mean go outside?" Taylor asked. "Her house is really easy to find."

"I can take you," Jackson said. "Taylor's still working on dinner for everyone."

"Come on, then," Lopez said. "Ray, could you empty the vehicles and get everything in here? We never got a chance to do that." Ray nodded.

"Hank, can you keep the wound covered?" Jackson asked. "It sounds like the bullet might have nicked his lung. We don't want to let air into it if it did."

Larry walked carefully down the passage that he found on the other side of the rubble. This side was completely different—he was now in what looked to be a natural cavern, not a shaft that had been hewn out of rock. He wondered how and when anyone had ever found this place—it must have been sheer luck that whoever was digging a mine had ended up making contact with a cavern. Or a bitter curse.

The going was fairly good. The floor was somewhat easy to walk on, and someone had smoothed out the surface in several places. Within twenty yards the path started to head rather steeply downhill, and fifty yards down the hill he came to a fork. To the right the path looked wider and smoother, so he decided to go that way. He found three small rocks and put them one on top of another as a cairn, just in case.

Ten minutes later he cursed when he hit a dead end and had to turn back. He probably would have felt even more frustrated, though, if he had known that taking the wrong path had kept him from a direct encounter with the two creatures who were carrying their companion's body.

Emily closed the bathroom door behind her. Immediately she rested her forehead against the door. She hadn't felt this helpless in ages, and she didn't know how much longer she could keep up the control. She took a deep breath and stood up straight, then held her right hand up in front of her face. The shaking was getting stronger. Pretty soon everyone would notice it.

She sat down on the toilet seat cover and sighed. She had sworn off the damned things, hadn't taken one in two months, but she was pretty sure that the current situation would justify a couple of valium. She had always had minor issues with anxiety, issues that grad school had exacerbated to such a point that she had finally sought help to try to keep it in check. The first year had been horrible, but this second year was going so much better so far.

She opened her purse and pulled out her wallet, where she kept a half-dozen tablets wrapped in aluminum foil "in case of emergencies." She unwrapped the pills and simply sat and stared at them. Should she talk herself out of this and face the evening without them? What kind of crazy would she go, though, if her anxiety were to take over? And how would it affect the others? They had enough to be dealing with, without having to deal with her.

"Damn it," she muttered, feeling weak as she pulled one of the tablets from the makeshift container and popped it into her mouth.

"Damn!" she said a bit more loudly as she spit it out into the trash basket.

She wrapped the remaining pills back in the aluminum foil and jammed them back into her wallet. Then she flushed the toilet for the sake of the noise and went back out to join the others.

Twenty-Two
Why

Jackson and Lopez walked quickly down the street and around the corner. Lopez saw the rest of the town for the first time—the street that ran south had two more streets lead off to the left. When they got to the first street and turned east, she saw that it led all the way down to the other north-south street that made the first intersection in town. That made the town a small rectangle with three parallel streets heading east-west and two streets at each end that connected them.

"Not much of a town up here, is it?" Lopez asked, trying not to offend Jackson. "How do you all get by up here? Especially in winter?"

Jackson smiled. "We've spent all of our lives getting by, to tell you the truth. We know how to make it. To tell you the truth, none of us would know what to do if everything were easy. Hell, if anything were easy. We've been dealing with everything that life and Mother Nature dish out for quite a few decades now. It's not that hard when you're used to it."

"But what if there's an emergency during a storm or something? What happens if someone has a heart attack and can't get to the hospital?"

"Well, then, that someone is probably going to die. Dying isn't the worst of all possible outcomes, you know. We're all pretty used to the idea of it being possible for any of us. It's going to happen to every person on this planet eventually."

"Yeah, but—" Lopez started, but she couldn't think of where to go from there.

"What you have to think of, quite simply, is what our alternatives are. You'd have a hell of a time trying to get anyone up here to think they need help in their old age, or that they'd be better off in some sort of retirement home. This is a group of some pretty damned ornery people. And pretty much none of the people who were born and raised here feel comfortable in the bigger towns. Even a town the size of Pine makes me feel that too many people know my business. Too many people think it's too damned important to be telling me what to do. I did my time in that world. Right now, though, I like this one."

He stopped and pointed at a small green house. "Here's Pauline's."

He stood still on the street for several moments. Lopez started forward to knock on the door, but Jackson stopped her with a light touch on the arm.

"She knows we're here," he said simply.

As if on cue, the front door opened and a short woman with thinning red hair and a pair of plastic-rimmed glasses stepped outside.

"What can I do you for, Jackson?" she asked, her eyes on Lopez.

"Bill's been shot, Pauline," he replied. "We need someone to look after him, and you're the best choice for the job."

She shifted her gaze to Jackson. "Bill? Who the hell is Bill?"

"You know. The sheriff."

"We'd really appreciate it if you could help us out, ma'am," Lopez added.

Pauline sighed. "I guess I don't have much choice, now do I?"

"Not much, Pauline," Jackson said.

"I hear tell them Nogglz have come up out of that mine," she said. "Did they shoot Bob?"

"Bill," Jackson said. "And no, it wasn't Naugle's boys that shot him. We don't know how he came to have a bullet in him. Any shots fired in a mine could hit pretty much anyone, though—it could've been his own shot, for all we know."

Pauline didn't reply for a moment, then she finally spoke. "What the hell good is it to have the law up here if they can't even protect themselves? That don't make much sense to me. Let me get my stuff," she said with a sigh. "I'll have to miss my shows for this." She moved back into the house and closed the door.

Lopez kept her eyes on the closed door. "How long do you think she'll be?" she asked.

"Not long, I reckon."

"She's right, you know," Lopez said quietly.

"About her shows? They're probably just trash, like most of the crap on TV that I've ever seen."

"No, about us. We're supposed to be here to help, to protect people. And we're not doing that."

"I wouldn't be too hard on yourself about that," Jackson said. "My guess is that they didn't cover monsters from the depths of the earth in your training. And it's not like you can out-think creatures that don't seem to think at all, and that have all the advantages over you."

"Maybe you're right," Lopez said. "But I feel like I'm not even close to doing my job." She looked back at the house when she heard the door open, and she watched as Pauline stepped outside.

"Well, let's get going," Pauline said.

Ray and Henry were carrying the last armloads of weapons and other equipment back to Taylor's when two more men came around the corner down the street and headed their way. Afternoon was wearing out; the sky had already begun to darken even more, and Ray was starting to feel even more nervous than he had all day. He felt a hint of déjà vu looking at the pair of men who were also very well armed walking towards Sarah's house. It seemed surreal to see the exact same thing happening again that had just occurred an hour earlier.

"What the hell is this?" he muttered, stopping in the middle of the street.

Henry chuckled. "Heckle and Jeckle, at your service."

The two men reached Ray and Henry and stopped. Both of them looked wild-eyed, as if they were on some sort of stimulant. Each carried a sawed-off 12-gauge shotgun in his arms, and each had a pair of pistols in holsters and another sawed-off hanging barrel-down on his back. They stood several moments looking at the deputy. They had to be in their late 30's, and while their weapons looked a bit intimidating, there was nothing frightening about them at all. They seemed to be collecting their thoughts, trying to figure out just what to say.

Henry supplied the introductions. "Hello, Brad," he said quietly. "Hello, Brian. How you doin'?"

The one who had been in the lead and who now stood in front of his brother looked over at Henry and smiled. "Doing pretty good, Henry. We're about gonna go do ourselves some killin', I think. We just got back into town and we heard that somethin's killin' people, and we just watched you all carry a body across the street from Sarah's place, so we figure somethin's in need of dyin' right about now."

Ray looked at Hank. He wanted desperately to tell them that the situation was under control and that they should go home, but he knew that would be a lie.

"So you just got back into town?" he asked. "Where from?"

"Huntin'," was Brian's only answer, and Ray knew better than to ask for any more information—he certainly wouldn't get any more from these two.

"Look," he said, "I know you guys want to do some good, but I wish you'd leave it up to us right now. I don't think you know just what you're going up against." His thoughts betrayed him then, for he found himself thinking, "As if I know myself."

"These things are ruthless," Henry added. "They're going to be a hell of a lot harder to kill than a deer or an elk."

"We done killed a helluva lot worse things things than deer or elk," Brad said with a smile. "You know that, Henry."

Henry sighed. "Yes, I suppose I do know that. But the things that you've killed generally aren't bloodthirsty and ready to kill you."

"Besides," Ray added, "we could really use you guys up here tonight. I've got a feeling those things are going to come after us once it gets dark, and we're going to need all the firepower we can get."

Brad looked back at his brother and smiled; Brian smiled, too, as if what they had just heard was the dumbest statement anyone had ever uttered.

Brian spoke. "Deputy, ain't nothin' gonna come after you if it's dead, now is it?"

Ray smiled in spite of himself. He saw that there would be no argument here that would have any effect at all. He also knew that there was no way that the sheriff would let these two go down in that mine if he were there. Brad and Brian looked far less capable than Larry, Juan and Xavier had looked. But he also knew that there was no way that Bill would have been able to stop them from going.

"They've already killed three people, and they took Juan," Henry said. "Larry's down there now looking for Juan. We have no idea if they're even still alive. We don't need to lose two more people here."

"But I just told you," Brad said, sounding confused, "we're gonna kill them. Ain't gonna happen the other way around. Besides, if these are the Nogglz like I think they are, then we've got a score to settle with them bastards."

"Nogglz?" Henry asked. "What kind of score could you have to settle with them?"

"Family history," Brad said. "When we was growing up, Ma used to tell us about them, how they used to beat people and chase them out of town and what-not. How Naugle sent them down a mine and then blew it up after them. She used to say that if we weren't good, then Naugle's boys—we called 'em Nogglz—would come out and eat us. We just kind of believed her, 'cause there weren't no mine around here that they could have gone down. 'Cept the coal mine up the hill. We didn't know there was a mine in Sarah's basement. Makes sense, though.

"And those sons-a-bitches beat the hell out of mom's Uncle Jeremiah, broke his arm, too, so that he couldn't work in the mine no more. And once he couldn't work the mine, there weren't no reason for him to stay here, so they kicked him out of town. They was real bastards."

"And so you're going to avenge an uncle that you never met?" Henry asked. "How come we never heard this story?"

Brad smiled, and he seemed glad to be the center of attention. "Shee-it, Henry, nothing personal, but you ain't from here. You came later. Most of us here had family in the mines. You know that."

"Besides," Brian added, "you ain't never asked, far as I can remember."

Henry sighed. "You've got me there," he said quietly. He glanced at Ray with a look of resignation.

"These Naugle's boys," Ray asked, "or Nogglz, as you call them. What do you think they want?"

Brad laughed. "They want to kill us, deputy, is my guess. What would you want to do if you'd been trapped in a mine for a whole lotta years? And if you was a mean bastard to start with?"

Ray sighed. "I really don't want you to go down there," he said. "But right at this moment, I can't think of anything I can do short of cuffing you and locking you up somewhere to keep you from going."

Brian's eyes narrowed. "I can guarantee you, deputy, that handcuffing us and locking us up ain't a very good idea at all."

"Calm down, Brian," Brad said, looking at his brother. "He ain't actually gonna do it. He's just saying that's the only way he could keep us from going into the mine to kill these things."

"Oh," Brian said, thinking for a moment. "Good. Sorry, deputy, if I sounded disrespectful or anything."

"Is the mine shaft in her basement, then?" Brad asked. "Is that where we're gonna start?"

"That's where you'd start," Ray replied, "but I still don't think it's such a good idea. We sure could use you up here with us."

"What you could use, deputy, are a few dead Nogglz. Ain't that right?"

Ray shrugged.

Brad nodded to Ray and Henry. "We'll be on our way, then, if you've got nothing else for us."

"Have you got lights?" Ray asked.

"We do," Brian said.

"Well, keep in mind that these things are fast, and they're strong—faster and stronger than you'd expect."

"As long as they ain't faster than a shotgun blast, I think we're good," Brad said. "Thanks for the information, deputy. You all make yourselves nice and comfortable up here. We've got some business to take care of. Let's go, Brian." They stepped past Ray and Henry, who watched them make their way down the street and into Sarah's yard.

"They're going to die," Ray said quietly. "You guys have got yourselves quite a crazy little town up here."

Henry laughed. "Welcome to Canyon Bluff, deputy," he said. "It definitely is a world of its own." He looked back as he heard voices behind them and saw Lopez and Jackson returning. "Here comes Pauline. We're gonna want to get her inside with the sheriff. I sure hope he's hanging on okay."

"Bill's a stubborn one," Ray said. "I just hope to hell that he's stubborn enough to make it through this."

Twenty-three
Up

They soon forgot the man in the water, and they soon forgot even the larger figure who had left them minutes after their return. They had no feelings for their companion who had been unceremoniously dumped over the edge of one of the chasms, and they had no feelings for the one who had kept them fed for so long. They feared him, but they did not feel that he was one of them. They had no memories of who he was or even of who they were, but they did have the urge that he didn't seem to share—the urge to return to the surface and kill. They wanted people to pay for what they had suffered, even if they no longer had any words to express that desire.

Instinct was enough.

So when they went upwards once more, it was no longer to try to find a way out—it was to be out, to go through the hole that they had cleared, to find people that they could kill because they felt the urge to kill. They might not have been evil when they had first been trapped, but they had certainly not been good people who felt the touch of compassion in their hearts. And the long time of isolation and anger before their transformation had become complete, had taken from them any last vestige of humanity, any emotion or feeling at all.

Had they become lost on their own, had no one blown up the mine shaft to trap them, they might have avoided the descent into evil. The rage that they shared and that had engulfed them once they realized what had happened, though, had ensured that their anger would dominate, that their hatred and desire for revenge would be the driving forces behind all their actions. Only that type of deeply internalized anger could have kept them digging for so long, could have allowed them to continue working for so many days when it seemed absolutely hopeless—and for so many years after they had forgotten even why they were digging.

Their companion was gone. He had been the leader of Naugle's boys back in the days when they were still human and they were still living above-ground. After their transformation, though, there was no more leading and following. His loss didn't affect them at all. They simply felt the bloodlust rising in their veins, the vessels that carried so little blood these days because they no longer had any significant amount of flesh on their bodies.

They scurried past Juan's body in the stream with hardly a look his way—they could feel the oncoming night, and they knew that night would be the best time for them to be above.

Unburdened, it took them much less time to get up to the top. They stopped before they approached the hole. The last time they had been up here, light had suddenly come through it. It hadn't hurt them, but their instincts told them to go slowly, at least here. If anyone had been paying close attention to them, that person might have noticed that their ability to reason might have been slowly, very slowly, returning to them.

They looked at each other and they knew what their instincts were telling them. And just as they were about to go through the hole one by one, they heard a voice on the other side of it. Then once more they saw a light shine through it.

Twenty-four
Down

The deputy sure was a wuss, Brad thought. He was pretty sure that he and his brother could have taken care of whatever was down in the mine, and he knew that he wouldn't have lost three people if he had been the sheriff. The things would be dead and nobody else would be. Both he and Brian stopped for a moment when they first entered Sarah's house, but Fogel's body and Sarah's body parts didn't stop them. They'd seen plenty of animals torn up like that, and to them there wasn't a whole lot of difference between an animal's corpse and that of a person—a dead thing was a dead thing, and that was pretty much it.

"That's a shame," was all Brad said when he saw Sarah's body, then he started into the house.

"Yeah," Brian agreed. "She was pretty nice." He followed Brad in. Neither of them thought even for a moment of the possibility that what had happened to her, might happen to them.

The door to the basement wasn't hard to find. "Lights," was all Brad said when he found out that the switch didn't turn on any lights. They both pulled their flashlights from their utility belts and turned them on. "Extra batteries?" Brad asked.

"Yep," Brian replied. Brian also had a headlamp that he was already wearing, and he reached up and turned it on.

Without another word, Brad started down the steps, Brian right behind him. Both of them were feeling the adrenaline rush through their bodies, and they felt completely invincible—they knew they were good hunters, and they were well armed. There was no way that anything could get the jump on them, as long as they were vigilant and quick with their guns.

"Lots of blood," Brian said quietly, looking down at the steps as they descended.

"Looks like these things are pretty nasty critters," Brad said. "Let's stay quiet now, bro. Can't let them hear us comin'."

Brian didn't answer. He simply followed his brother into the basement and over to the mouth of the mine shaft. "Wish I had a headlamp," Brad whispered. "Don't like the idea of not having a gun in both hands."

They played their flashlights on the entrance, then Brad took the plunge and headed in, Brian right behind him. The mine was dead quiet, except for their footsteps and their breathing. They proceeded slowly, listening carefully, shining their lights everywhere they could before taking the next few steps. Neither one of them felt any fear yet—they knew that they would be much more able to deal with the Nogglz than the sheriff and the others had been. Brad stopped at the first beams, recognizing a possible hiding place, and he reached his arm out and played the light in the spaces behind them until he was sure that nothing was there. From there they saw Xavier's body where it still lay, the head cocked at an unnatural angle, the eyes staring at the wall of the mine next to it.

"We'll have to check his place when we get out of here," Brad said quietly. "He's got a really good stereo that he won't need no more. And I don't think he'll have any use for this headlamp, either." He reached down and pulled it from Xavier's head. He turned back up the tunnel and started towards the wall of debris that they could just make out. There was a hole in the upper-right portion of the debris, and they both could see how easy it would be to get trapped in there if something was waiting for them on the other side.

Brad stopped some twenty feet short of the hole, and Brian knew that he was listening. He stopped, too. They both stood completely still for about thirty seconds before Brad turned to Brian. "You hear anything?" he whispered.

"Nothin'," Brian replied. "But it sure stinks to high hell down here."

"I'll go first, then," Brad said. "You cover me, and I'll shine the light back through the hole when I'm clear." Almost as an afterthought, he added, "Stink don't matter. Stay focused."

"Right," Brian replied, and he followed for about ten feet when Brad started for the hole. Then he stayed put, shotgun ready, and he quickly checked the pistols at his waist to make sure they came out smoothly. He watched as his brother slowly neared the hole, his head cocked slightly to the side to put his right ear closer to the hole so that he could listen better. The hole was about chest high, and Brad slowly approached it, shining his light through it. He wanted whatever might be on the other side to know he was coming, because he knew that there was no sneaking up on them now that he was in their world. If anything was going to happen, he wanted it to happen head-on and eyes open.

Twenty-five
My House, My Home

"What do you mean, you're going to stay put?" Lopez asked, disbelief strong in her voice. "Do you understand what I'm telling you? What they've done to three people already?"

"I'm not stupid, miss. I understand exactly what you said. And we're not going anywhere." Arnie Planinsek spoke calmly, but Lopez was sure that he was out of his mind.

"I just don't think you understand the danger that you're facing here," she tried again. "These things are incredibly vicious, and they'd just as soon tear you to pieces as look at you."

Arnie wasn't a young man—already in his late sixties, it looked to Lopez, as was his wife—but he had a sparkle in his eye that made her think of a very young person. He looked at her almost in amusement at her frustration, as if she just didn't get something that should have been very easy to understand. He stood a good six feet tall and didn't seem to be carrying much fat. His face was lean and rugged from the mountain living, but also friendly and caring. It was a nice mixture, Lopez thought in spite of herself. His wife was about her height, and her dark hair was graying. She was Mexican and he had a strong Eastern European accent, which would make sense up in an old mining community. Many of the people willing to work the mines and be treated harshly had been immigrants who didn't have any other real options yet. Even Lopez' own father told her often of his grandfather's years in the mines over in Conejo. Arnie's wife's name was Bernice, and she looked to be kind and patient.

"Look, Miss Lopez," Bernice said now, "I know that you don't understand our decision, but we'll be fine. Really, we will."

Lopez looked helplessly from one to the other, weighing her options and quickly realizing that she didn't have any. Now the sheriff's decision to let those men go into the mine made more sense to her—it wasn't really any decision at all. It was something he couldn't prevent, even though she knew he had wanted to.

"We really can take care of ourselves," Arnie added. "In fact, we prefer it that way. Why the hell else would we be living up here in the first place?"

"Do you need anything?" Lopez asked hopelessly. "Food? Weapons?"

Arnie chuckled. "We've got food enough for quite a while, thank you. Have to up here. And I think we'll be fine in taking care of ourselves."

"All right, then. I've got to get going—you two take care." Lopez turned and walked back out to the street, and she could feel their eyes on her as she went.

"By the way, trooper," Arnie called out, and she turned back to face him. "Has anyone else taken you up on your. . . offer?"

Lopez paused before answering, then decided that he really was curious, and not mocking her. "Just one," she said.

Arnie chuckled. "That would have been Ochko, no?"

"His name is Maurice. I don't know his last name."

"Maurice Ochko. That makes sense. He's pretty much the only one around here who can't take care of himself any more, what with the oxygen tanks and all. Give him our best, will you?"

"Sure," she replied, then turned and walked away. Her street was done—she had knocked on twelve doors and had people answer at four of them, with three refusals and only one man who decided to come to Taylor's for the night. She wondered how Ray was doing on the next street over. It was almost four-thirty and darkness was coming on them quickly, so she started to walk quickly to Taylor's.

As she passed a hedge on her left, she saw a pair of does on the lawn, eating peacefully. They looked up at her and watched her carefully. She slowed down so she could watch them as she walked past. She always loved seeing wildlife, and even their current situation couldn't take that away from her.

The does were completely oblivious to what was going on, she knew, and for just a moment she felt the incredible tension that the day had brought upon her subside. She was suddenly reminded that the world was going on, no matter what was happening in Canyon Bluff, no matter how much danger the people there were facing. Her mind jumped to her son, who would have no idea at all what she was dealing with here. The lack of ability to communicate with the outside world was the thing that frustrated her most. They hadn't been able to let anyone know just how dire their situation really was.

She was sure the state police would send in someone by chopper in the morning if they didn't hear back from them, but the terrain was far too rough to send anyone out in the afternoon who would risk being caught in the dark. And given the fact that the road was out and the phone lines were down, they would probably just be assuming that she and Fogel were incommunicado as opposed to dead and in danger of being dead.

Suddenly she was overwhelmed with the feeling that she might never see her son again. What was going to happen tonight? Maybe nothing, if they were lucky. If there was some sort of attack, where would it be? Whom would they go after first? What would it be like for her son to grow up without either parent?

She gazed at the deer until she had walked completely past them, then she turned her head towards Taylor's and started walking faster again. "I love you, *mi hijo*," she said quietly aloud to her son, hoping that he would know how much his mother loved him if anything were to happen.

Ray was coming down the next side street when she reached it, and he, too, was alone.

"No one?" he asked.

"Just one," she said with a slight smile. "And he's already there, I think."

"My God," Ray said. "These people have no idea what they're up against."

"It's that fierce independence that we're taught from the day we're born. We don't need anyone else—we can do just fine on our own."

Ray shook his head. "Until we need someone else. And then we're too damned stubborn to ask for or take any help. And multiply their stubbornness by twenty in a place like this." He looked back where he had just come from, and Lopez could see the frustration in his face, in the way he walked. "Damn it!" he yelled fiercely, but uselessly.

"So it looks like it's gonna be the ten of us here," Taylor said. "I think we can fit fine."

"And Taylor has enough food ready for a small army," Jackson said with a smile. "You've never seen a big meal until you've seen a woman from a mining town cook."

Taylor smiled. "Back in the day," she told Emily, "that's how we learned to cook. We never knew who was going to be sitting at our table that night, so we always had to cook a lot."

"You should have seen my mother," Jackson added, laughing. "Hell, if the table wasn't completely covered with plates and pots and pans full of food, she thought she'd committed a sin. We had leftover dinners that were bigger than most people's regular dinners."

"Well, who knows?" Taylor asked, a tone of seriousness coming into her voice. "This could be our last supper. It might as well be a good one."

"Can't argue with that," Ray said, then the group was silent for a few moments. He looked over at Pauline, who was sitting on a pillow she had put on the floor next to Bill. "How's he doing?" he asked.

"Pretty much the same as he was five minutes ago, last time you asked," Pauline replied. "Those pain pills are gonna keep him knocked out for a few hours. The bleeding has stopped, but we have no idea what's going on inside."

Lopez stood up from her seat on the couch. "I'm going to check the doors and windows again," she said. "Then we've got to figure out some sort of course of action. I'm going to lose my mind just sitting here waiting for something to happen."

"You and me both," Ray said. Then he addressed Henry. "Anything else in that journal there?"

Henry picked up the book and flipped through the pages. "Not much of anything that's going to help, I'm sorry to say. It's interesting in its own way, but it's pretty much all supposition as far as what happened to the party that Naugle trapped in the mine. What I'm still interested in is what could have carried the one guy off—if that indeed happened. Could be that he wandered off, or that he got into a fight with the others and they killed him, and they didn't want to admit that they'd taken out one of their own. If there really was something down there, though, it's pretty sure that they would have met up with it after they were trapped, one way or another."

"Had you heard any of the stories about 'Naugle's boys' still being around?" Ray asked, taking a seat at the table. "I mean really being there, not just the wives' tales."

"Now, deputy, you can't live in Canyon Bluff without hearing stories about the Nogglz," Jackson put in. "They were our boogeymen, our monsters under the bed or in the closet. When my kids were young, the Nogglz were our mythology, our way of using our past to threaten our children. I used to tell my boys that if they didn't knock it off, the Nogglz would come at night and carry them off."

"You have sons?" Lopez asked from the bedroom. "I have a son. He's six." She appeared in the doorway.

"Had," Jackson said. "Lost 'em both in 'Nam."

"I'm so sorry," Lopez said.

"Thank you, but don't be. That was more than twenty years ago. I've gotten used to it. The wife never did, but she passed a good ten years ago. Without the boys, there's nothing to pull me out of this town. Which is why I get the pleasure of experiencing our current situation."

"Speaking of that," Henry said, "Lopez, you mentioned a course of action. That would be a damned good thing to consider right about now."

"What do you mean?" Ray asked.

"What happens if the shit hits the fan here in the next hour or two?" Henry asked. "Have you thought about how you're going to respond?"

Ray shook his head. "I guess I just figured we'd be dealing with things as they happen. If we hear something, we go take care of it."

"In the dark? Leaving everyone here?"

"What else can we do?" Lopez asked.

"Well, you're talking reaction rather than action. That's giving these things the upper hand, isn't it? That's why I say we should start thinking about it now. When and if they come up here and start attacking people, it'll be a hell of a lot better if you have some sort of plan."

"We'll just give Jackson a gun and send him out into the dark," Taylor said, smiling.

"And thank you very much for that vote of confidence," Jackson said with a laugh. "We could send you out there with a few plates of spaghetti and a bottle of wine. You could calm them down with a good dinner."

"How can you joke at a time like this?" Lopez asked, exasperated. "I don't get it."

"Dear," Taylor said, "things are what they are, and nothing that we say or do at this moment is going to change that. I'm scared as hell, personally, but I'd much rather be able to smile when I'm afraid. That way my fear doesn't own me. A couple of hours ago it was owning me. I didn't like that."

There was a pause in the conversation as they all considered Taylor's words and their own thoughts.

"So what do we do then?" Lopez finally asked. "I've never been in a situation anywhere close to this one, so I'm open to suggestions. Do we go after those bastards, or do we let them come to us?"

"Problem is," Henry said, "with everyone spread out as much as we are, if they do come, there's no reason to think that they'll come to us here. And with blankets over the windows like this, there won't be any light to see from outside to draw them here."

Lopez shot a glance at Ray—she hadn't thought to suggest to the people she had talked to that they cover their windows or turn lights off. She could tell by the way he looked back that he hadn't thought of doing so either.

"So what do we do if something happens somewhere else?" she asked.

Henry shook his head. "The worst part of it all is that if we hear anything going on, it won't be a good idea to go out and try to help out. I've been thinking this through. If we're all in here tonight and we hear shots or screams or something like that, I honestly don't have any idea what we're going to do."

"You stay put," Taylor said. "Every single one of those people has been warned, and every single one has decided to face this on their own. I'd say by the time you hear screams or shots, it's going to be too late anyway. And if you leave here, what happens to the people you leave behind?"

Ray shook his head. "It's easy enough to talk about it when it isn't happening yet," he said. "But once something starts, the decision becomes much, much harder."

"Actually," Jackson said quietly, "it may be much easier to come to a decision now, and make sure that you commit to following it later. Right now we can discuss the situation rationally and consider different plans of action. If things get bad, there isn't going to be a whole lot of rational thinking going on. That's what it was like in the Army, and it made life easier. Orders were orders, no matter what was going on. Now think about it: you hear shots, and that means those things are already there. As fast and as vicious as they seem to be, do you really think that you're going to make it from this house to another house—and you won't even know which one—in time to make any difference? All you'll be doing is making yourself pretty easy targets out there for something that can see much, much better in the dark than you can."

"I don't want to sound like a coward," Lopez said, "but I don't see any way that going out there can help anyone. Like you said, Jackson, once we hear anything it's going to be too late to do anything about it. If we could actually accomplish something, I know it's my job to do anything I can to help people, and I wouldn't hesitate to do so. But it seems to me like it would just be suicide, and us killing ourselves isn't going to be much of a help to anyone."

Ray sighed, a heavy, helpless sigh. "That's what I'm thinking, too. And it goes against everything I believe in as a deputy, everything I feel inside, to hear someone who needs help and not do anything at all to help them."

"Which is why, deputy, it helps sometimes to have these kinds of discussions when logic and reason can prevail," Jackson reiterated. "Once we hear a shot, we aren't going to have any time at all to think things through or have any discussions about what we should do."

Maurice Ochko came out of the bedroom just then. He was one of the older men in a town that was almost all old people, with at least eighty years behind him but still active, still able to take care of himself in this town where the dominant social norm was that everyone takes care of themselves.

"Couldn't help overhearing," he said. "The only thing that hasn't been said is that you'd be damned idiots to go out there. Those things will kill you, I can guarantee you that. I used to hear the stories about what mean bastards they were when they were people, but they ain't people no more, so chances are they're meaner than ever. Unless you want to die tonight, the only thing you can do is stay put. Period. Taylor, you got any cards? I want to play some solitaire."

"So you knew the stories about these guys?" Ray asked.

"Did I know 'em?" Maurice asked with a laugh. "Hell, I made some of 'em up myself to scare my little brother. But they were all based on what we knew—Naugle sent them down to die, and none of us thought for a second that they were actually dead. Mean sons of bitches like that don't die easy and they don't die quiet. We all thought it was a matter of time before they came back, especially since Naugle himself seemed to think so. Why do you think they had that steel door built in the cellar to close up that mine shaft?"

"You knew about the door?" Ray asked. "I was under the impression that it was a secret. That Sarah was some kind of guardian, the only one who knew about the mine in the first place."

"Now come on, deputy, you can keep some secrets in some places, but in a town this size, you can't keep many secrets at all. Those of us who have been here forever know a hell of a lot more than you'll ever get out of us. This ain't the kind of town where people do a whole lot of talkin'."

"I hadn't noticed," Lopez said drily, looking over at Ray.

"Of course you noticed," Maurice said, ignoring the irony in her statement. "We've been told since we were real little that the Nogglz would be back—and that's spelled N-O-G-G-L-Z, by the way. Some little kid drew a picture of them years ago after her pa threatened that they'd come get her if she misbehaved, and she spelled it that way. Her mama showed the picture around, and the name and the spelling stuck. I think it was Jacky's daughter, if memory serves me right. Anyway, we've heard the stories our whole lives long, and most of us just kind of believed them. It ain't like some sort of evil witch or enchanted forest—this was something from our own back yard, people that our parents actually met and talked to and probably hated with a passion."

They suddenly heard a knock on the door. Lopez and Ray drew their pistols and moved quickly towards the door, not sure what to do. Henry and Jackson exchanged an amused look.

"Open the damned door," Maurice said, sounding exasperated. "I can guarantee you that those sons of bitches ain't gonna be knockin' when they get here."

Ray looked a bit sheepish as he reached out and unlocked the deadbolt while Lopez took a step backward to cover the doorway. Ray pulled the door open and they saw an elderly couple standing there as if they were out for a casual evening stroll.

"Come on in," Taylor said. "Just find a spot to get comfortable, and we'll get everyone arranged for sleeping a little later, after we eat. The food's almost ready. Deputy, trooper, this is Jerry Richardson and his wife, Eileen."

Ray nodded.

"It's nice to meet you," Lopez said as she holstered her pistol. "Sorry for the armed welcome."

"Not a problem, young lady," Jerry said. "Under the circumstances, I wouldn't have been surprised if you hadn't even opened the door." He turned to Taylor. "Food is good, Taylor. Especially if you made it. You haven't had us over for dinner in ages."

"Well, there haven't been a bunch of maniacal creatures trying to kill us all for ages," Taylor said.

Jackson laughed. "Now we know what it takes to get a dinner invitation out of Taylor," he said.

Lopez took a careful step out of the door and looked around. Dusk was fading into complete darkness, leaving the town on the verge of night. The rain had turned to an icy mix with a few snowflakes mixed in, but nothing was sticking yet. It wouldn't be long until it did, she could see.

A night in Canyon Bluff hadn't been in her plans that morning. As things stood, she was in a comfortable house filled with the aroma of good food and the sound of pleasant conversation among nice people, up in the mountains where things were supposed to be peaceful and quiet. She smiled as she considered the contrast between the idyllic setting and the horrific reality, but there was no humor in her smile at all. Ray came and stood beside her.

"We got everyone who was willing to come, I think," Ray said.

"I think that we've done all that we can do here so far," she said quietly. "And Ray?"

"Yeah?"

"If anything happens tonight, if we hear shots or screams or whatever the hell there may be, we stay put. Right?" She glanced at Ray to see his response.

Ray seemed torn, and he thought for several moments.

"We can't do anybody any good out there," Lopez said quietly, "and we probably would end up getting ourselves killed doing something foolish."

"I hate to say it," Ray said, just as quietly, "but I think you're right."

"We've made the decision now," Lopez said. "So when we're sorely tempted to rush outside to try to save someone, we don't have to think about it. We stay put."

"Got it," Ray said.

It was a decision that neither of them felt entirely confident they were going to follow later.

Twenty-six
Let 'em in

They stopped when they heard the quiet voices coming from the other side of the hole. The last time they had heard something there, one of their own had been outside, and they had lost him. And light had come through the hole, and they had taken that person. But what were they going to do now? With just a glance at each other, they agreed to hide and to wait and see what these new voices meant.

Instinctively, they were less defensive now. They were starting to feel their strength and their power, starting to feel the strength of the beast that does the stalking. There was no need to fear these voices, they felt, for these voices were in their home, and they somehow knew that they had an advantage.

So when Brad's head came through the hole, he wasn't immediately killed. The flashlight came first, and very soon afterwards they saw his face as he tried to peer through and see what was on the other side. It didn't seem to help much, though, so he put his head and shoulders through. With one arm ahead of him holding his flashlight and his shoulders stuck in the hole and his other arm—the one with the shotgun—stuck behind him, he was as vulnerable as he was ever going to be for several long moments. Any one of the four could have moved in on him quickly and killed him and pulled his body from the hole, but inexplicably they waited.

Perhaps they waited because they were starting to feel the lure of the sport of killing, and killing a helpless person brought little gratification. Perhaps they waited because their reasoning was starting to return to them and they understood that there probably was another person out there. Or maybe they waited simply because they knew there was no hurry—this would be an easy kill, no matter when or how they did it.

No matter what the reason, Brad was luckier than he ever would know. Four pairs of eyes that were adapted to the dark watched him closely in the darkness, just out of the range of his light. They waited quietly and patiently as Brad climbed to the bottom of the rubble and shined his light all around, his gun ready in his right hand. Then a second light appeared in the hole, and then moments later a second head. Soon a pair of people stood in the cavern, shining their lights down the pathway that they would be taking, having no clue that they were being watched by four creatures who were no more than thirty feet from them, hiding in the crevices in the walls and the ceilings.

Without any sort of group consensus or conversation, they decided to allow these two into the caverns. They felt the lure of the outside, of the houses and the lights that they had gotten glimpses of just hours ago. They moved quietly and quickly, almost as one, hiding themselves down an offshoot of the main passage. They knew somehow that these two would stay on the main path down into the earth, because that's what they would have done so many years ago, when they were just like these.

And soon the pair was past them. They moved again, this time out to the hole, and then out to the door that they had destroyed the night before. There were no longer any lights in this room—the other, the one that was gone—had seen to that. And there were no people here to see or to feel or to smell.

They were four creatures who used to be human, but who now moved more quickly than most humans could even imagine. With all the flesh gone from them, they had less weight to slow them down, though the lack of muscle tissue should have made movement impossible.

But move they did, up the stairs and through the house, past the trooper's body and the mess they had made the night before, out onto the porch. It was still dusk, so there was some light. They stayed low, behind the porch railing, breathing the air of the outdoors for only the second time in sixty years. It felt good, and in their own way they could understand why the other had wanted to come out so badly that he had risked coming out in daylight.

Tonight was going to be a fulfilling night, a night during which they could express their anger and hatred in the only way left to them.

Twenty-seven
Bait

Brad felt a shiver run through his entire body, and he would have sworn then and there that he and his brother were being watched. He slowed down and shined his light carefully in every direction, but he saw nothing but the walls of a cavern. They were no longer in a mine. A new thought entered his mind: what if they didn't find anything down here? He and Brian had been assuming that they would meet those damned Nogglz and either take them out or be taken out, but what if nothing happened? Heading back up top without having at least taken a shot or two at something would be almost worse than being killed down here.

Within minutes of walking, he felt the tension ease. He no longer felt watched, no longer felt the presence of anything else other than his brother. The smell, too, was growing weaker. Even though he didn't want to talk down there, he needed to talk over their situation. He stopped.

"What do you think, Brian?" he whispered as his brother came to a stop next to him.

"About what?"

"Are we going to find those things? I thought they were around a few minutes ago, but I don't get that feeling anymore."

"Me, too," Brian replied. "I felt 'em back there a ways, just after we came through that hole. Kept expectin' 'em to attack us."

"If they were there, I wonder why they didn't?" Brad mused. "Were they leading us into a trap or something?"

Brian chuckled. "They didn't need to lead us into no trap, bro. We walked right into the biggest trap in the world, didn't we?"

"That's true. But then why did they just let us walk on by? It don't make no sense."

"Don't make no sense to me, neither. But if they did, they did. We just gotta figure out what we're going to do now."

"Well, we can't go back just 'cause of some feeling, now can we? How would that look? 'Well, we went down there, but we didn't feel like they was down there, so we came back up.' That would sure make us look like idiots, wouldn't it?"

"Pretty much," Brian agreed. "Maybe we can look for Juan if those things aren't down here."

"Juan is dead, bro. But that's a good idea—we can look for the body, anyway. Find out what they did to him. And we'll be down here in case they come back. Hell, as far as we know, they're still down here, just following us until they get the urge to take us out."

Brian didn't reply immediately. "Now why the hell did you go and say that for?" he asked, sounding peeved. "I don't need to be thinkin' that shit down here. 'Specially as you're on point. If they're behind us, I'm first in line."

"And if they're in front of us, then I'm first. Calm down—we don't have any idea where those damned things are." He chuckled suddenly.

"What's so funny?"

"Think about it," Brad replied. "All those times ma told us the stories about the Nogglz, and we never believed her. And now we're down in a freakin' mine huntin' the damned things."

"More like being hunted by 'em," Brian muttered.

Brad chuckled again. "You're probably right there, bro. But if those things are hunting us, let's at least make things as difficult as we can for 'em. We gotta make sure they don't take us out without us taking out at least one or two of 'em. Let's move."

"Let's go," Brian agreed, and they started down the tunnel once more, slowly and carefully.

Twenty-eight
Lyle

Lyle Kapushion sat resolutely in his easy chair, reading for the eighth or ninth time the last book his wife had given to him before she passed on, a large volume that offered a comprehensive history of the Korean War. He'd been around many years, and though he was pretty sure his wife would have wanted him to go with that deputy, he just didn't feel like it. There wasn't any way that anything could get into his house without him being ready for it. His shotgun lay across his lap, a handy tool upon which he rested the binding of the book.

Before him the fire crackled peacefully in the fireplace, with the occasional loud pop that fires will make. His living room was small, as were most of the rooms in the old miners' houses, but small suited him fine. He didn't need a whole lot of room for the few things that he had. Besides, smaller was cozier. That's why he had just the easy chair in there in front of the fire, and the old red loveseat that Margie used to sit in when she was still around. There were two pictures on the wall of ducks taking off out of the water, but other than the lamp by which he was reading there weren't any other decorations.

Lyle's dad—Lyle senior to everyone in CB—had been one of the first miners on site when the coal got started. He'd put in ten years with the company, until the price of coal went down so much that there was no longer any reason to be pulling it from the mountains. Then, when most everyone else packed it up and moved away, Lyle senior got hold of a piece of land, tore down the company house and built himself a nice little cabin, where he and his wife could spend the rest of their years, which they did. It wasn't any bigger than the company house had been, given the limits of the property, but it was a hell of a lot nicer. Lyle junior had grown up here, leaving only for two years of college and two years in the Marines. He saw enough in Korea to make him want to head back to Canyon Bluff where he wouldn't see any more of that kind of thing, where life was much more manageable than it happened to be in any city that he could imagine.

Life was quiet since Margie had passed on two years earlier, so he spent most of his time now reading the books that reminded him of his past. He had hated Korea, but he had an extensive collection of books about every aspect of the war there—he could find out what units fought where and when, what kinds of weapons they used, what kinds of battles they won or lost. It was kind of a therapy for him, he figured, getting to know everything he could about a war that had taken away two years of his life.

His dad had told him all about the mines, all about working for Naugle and being threatened by Naugle's boys. Lyle thought it must have been pretty rough being a miner back then, especially since it wasn't all that uncommon to lose a friend or two in the mines every year or so. It was kind of like the war—you never knew who was going to be the next to die.

Arnie had come over earlier to tell him about Sarah and the trooper who went and got killed and the sheriff and everything that was going on. He told him all about the theory that these were Naugle's boys coming back for revenge after so many years, but Lyle didn't buy it for a second. If he was anything, he was a logical person who didn't believe in shit like a bunch of guys still being alive in a mine after sixty years. That didn't make any sense. Something else had to be killing people, and in his experience, anything that can kill can also be killed. And he was good enough with the shotgun not to miss when he took a shot.

That's why he didn't jump when he heard the thump on the roof. His eyes raised slowly from the book, looking up at the ceiling. No more sounds came immediately. He was surprised—even with the possibility of something terrible coming to try to kill him, a thump on the roof was the last thing he would have expected had he even bothered to think about it. He slowly closed his book and put it on the end table next to him, then lifted his shotgun from where it was lying across his lap, holding it ready as he stood up slowly and quietly and carefully.

He backed himself slowly into a corner, giving himself the maximum coverage of the room with minimal movement of his weapon. In the corner, nothing could come up behind him, and nothing could approach him from the front without him seeing it. He stood, somewhat surprised at how unafraid he actually felt—was he feeling that way because he actually thought he had a chance against them, or because he really didn't care if he had a chance or not? Perhaps death would be the release that some people talked about, the chance to move on, maybe even see his wife and daughter on the other side. There certainly wasn't a lot for him here in CB, and he was damn sure there wasn't anything for him anywhere else.

The silence was punctuated by the hissing of the logs in the fire and the crackle of the wood as the flames burned it away. Suddenly he heard a scraping sound on the roof, and he instinctively raised the barrel of the shotgun to point it above him. There was, of course, nothing to fire at, and the sound didn't repeat itself immediately.

He lowered his weapon and surveyed the room. The drapes were closed tightly on both windows, so there was no way that anything outside could see his position. The lone light on the end table next to his chair did a decent job of lighting the room, though he suddenly wished that the ceiling light also was on—moving over to the entrance to the room, though, would get him out of position and make him more vulnerable. If he did move over there, though, he would also be able to close the door, something that he was also wishing he had already done. It was a tiny room, and just six steps or so separated him from the door and the light switch, so he decided to quickly take care of those things and get right back to his corner before anything really happened.

As his right foot hit the floor for his third step, he suddenly heard his bedroom window break, and a heavy thump as something hit the floor in there. He reached out quickly with the barrel of the shotgun and pushed the door closed, thankful that the door opened inward, and just as the door slammed shut, he heard a series of gunshots from somewhere out in the night. That has to be coming from Arnie's, he thought reflexively as he took two more steps and reached out for the light switch. At that same instant the door he had just closed burst inward and a figure came flying through it.

"Damned cheap door!" he thought, and that was his last thought on this side. His right hand was on the light switch, not on the trigger, and the form that had burst through the cheaply made interior door slammed into him at waist level with a force that broke his hip immediately and caused him to drop the shotgun without ever getting a shot off. As he fell he saw another figure follow the first through the hole in the door, and he never did see the first one get up quickly and turn back to him. Thankfully for him, the creatures were interested more in killing than anything else, and the second one delivered a furious blow to the throat, claws extended, ripping out everything there and showering the room with blood.

All of this happened before Lyle even hit the floor. He landed next to the shotgun, now silent and completely useless without a live person around to make use of it. The power it had given Lyle to defend himself was gone with Lyle.

The two creatures in the room continued to tear at the body, though they didn't do nearly the damage to it that they had done to Sarah's body. There was too much else going on tonight, too many other people to find, too many other opportunities to mete out the vengeance—the justice—that they had waited so long to deliver. Not that they understood a concept like "justice" anymore. They just followed their urge to kill, and the urge this night was strong.

Twenty-nine
Forever Together

Arnie and Bernice had decided that if anything came of the day's silliness, they would make their stand in the den in the basement. After all, there was only one small window down there and one door leading into the room. As far as defensible positions were concerned, this room was by far the best, with the possible exception of the bathroom. But that was far too small.

Bernice was starting to doubt their decision to stay on their own this night—and she'd started doubting it almost immediately. It was a doubt, though, that she would never share with Arnie. She didn't feel that doing so would accomplish anything except get them upset at each other, which was the last thing they needed. But now that darkness had fallen and they were all alone in the quiet in the den, she was wishing that she were over at Taylor's house with the others.

Arnie had a nine millimeter pistol on the table next to his recliner, where he sat trying to read. He also had a shotgun propped up next to the chair, and three more pistols on the coffee table in front of him. Bernice held a shotgun herself on her lap, one that she had used only a couple of times, so she didn't feel completely confident with it. It was better than nothing, though.

Arnie got up once more to check each of the pistols. Clip full, bullet chambered, safety off. It was at least the seventh time that he had checked them, but each time he did he felt reassured for only a few minutes before the doubts started creeping into his mind. Did I get the safety on that one? he would start to think. I might have forgotten to chamber a bullet in that one. He would let the thoughts whirl around in his mind for ten or twenty minutes before he would finally get up again and check each pistol one more time.

"I wonder how Lyle's doing?" Bernice said. She was also trying to read, but rather unsuccessfully. She had no concentration just then, and the printed words meant pretty much nothing to her when she was in that state.

"I'm sure he's fine," Arnie said, trying to sound like he was at ease, like it was just another evening in the house where they had passed so many evenings together. He never would have admitted that he, too, was having his doubts about staying on their own, and that the words "safety in numbers" were leaping into his mind, unbidden, from time to time. His thoughts were on what would happen if those things that killed Sarah came after him and Bernice—he kept thinking about just what he would do, just how he would fire, just what strategy would be best when all hell broke loose, if it even did.

Bernice, for her part, had her mind on her children, Stella and Eddie, both of whom now lived in Denver, many miles away. She wished that she could call them, to let them know how she felt about them, to reassure them of her love. She knew that they knew that she loved them with everything she was, but it would have been nice to once more have the chance to hear their voices, to see and hear all three of her grandchildren. There was a certain finality in the air, a certain dread that she wouldn't have been able to put into words even if she tried. She kept thinking back through the years, seeing Eddie at his high school graduation, Stella at her First Communion, Eddie on the Little League team when there were still enough kids here to put together one team that would travel down to Pine to play the four teams there.

She had tried to write them a letter, starting it four times but never getting beyond a pair of sentences. How do you say good-bye to your children in a letter? Especially when you hate writing? And especially when you probably aren't even going to die?

She felt like she wanted to cry, but no tears would come. And when she thought about it, the tears would be more like tears of joy for the life she had been able to lead than tears of fear or terror or grief. It was odd because as she sat there in the dead quiet of that awful evening, her mind focused more on the blessings she had been able to experience than the possibilities of what might or might not happen to them.

"It's been a good life for me," she told herself.

And just as she had that thought, she and Arnie both jumped as they heard the sound of breaking glass upstairs.

"Living room window," Arnie said quietly as they both stood up. He reached for a pistol, then looked at the shotgun. He was more confident of his aim with the pistol, though, so he held onto it and moved the shotgun to a position in front of him, leaning against the coffee table.

"Arnie," Bernice said quietly. "I love you. Thank you for everything."

Arnie looked over at her. "Now Bernice," he said, starting out in a slightly scolding tone, until his eyes met hers. "I love you, too, sweetheart. We're going to get through this, though. You'll see." His words, though, felt suddenly empty and weak. He looked up as they heard swift footsteps crossing the main floor, scurrying lightly and quickly just above their heads. In moments, they heard the footsteps on the stairs leading down to the basement, and then all sound stopped. They stood motionless in the silence, waiting. Both of them wanted to be closer to the other, yet neither of them wanted to move. Arnie could hear his own breathing, and he could feel it become harder to breathe as the tension grew into an almost palpable force.

When the scratching sound on the door started, he glanced over at Bernice, and he was proud of how strongly she stood there. She was saying something quietly, and he heard the barest whisper of the Lord's Prayer. That's probably what I should be doing, he told himself. The scratching was a long, slow, steady sound as if someone was dragging their fingernails from the very top of the door to the very bottom.

"What the hell," Arnie said quietly, and lifted the pistol. He fired at the door, and a bullet hole appeared about eighteen inches above and a foot to the left of the doorknob. They heard a snarl and a scream, as if from two different animals. He quickly shot twice more, spreading the bullets apart, but there was no response from the other side. He and Bernice stood stock-still, waiting, eyes not daring to leave the door.

Arnie started to think that even if he hadn't killed something, he might have scared them away.

When the door burst open five seconds later, it did so with a violence that neither one of them could have imagined—the door simply blew in, taking part of the frame with it, and both Arnie and Bernice responded by opening fire in that direction. The speed of the creatures that came through the door, though, was too much for their reaction times. There were two creatures in the room with them instantaneously, and none of the bullets hit their marks. One of the Nogglz seemed to bounce off the wall behind them and pounced on Bernice, slamming her to the floor. The other jumped and grabbed the ceiling fan, using his momentum to catapult himself straight onto Arnie, grabbing him by the chin and the back of his head and pulling hard, breaking his neck easily and instantly. It felt the life leave the body and then turned to its companion as if to see whether it needed any help with the killing. But Bernice was already gone, her body dropping to the floor, a pool of blood starting to form immediately from the gaping wound where her throat had been.

Neither Arnie nor Bernice had had the chance to see the shoulder wound that one of the creatures had, though the wound had done nothing to slow it down or keep it from killing them.

* * * * *

The creatures looked at each other, and this time they weren't nearly as bothered by the light as they had been before—though it was a bit uncomfortable, their instincts didn't scream out for them to destroy the lights as they had had to do before. They were standing more upright now, too, now that they had more space and were no longer navigating underground caverns and passages. They both felt it—something was coming back to them, and they had no idea what it might be.

They looked down at the bodies and they felt sheer exhilaration, as they were doing something that they had waited for decades to be able to do. They had no idea who these people were, and it truly didn't matter. The killing felt good, and the killing was necessary. They didn't know why, but they needed to do more.

Thirty
The Elderly

"So, what do you think the average age in this house is, deputy?" Taylor asked with a smile.

Ray looked surprised at the question. There were other things on his mind.

"Excuse me?" he asked, not quite sure that he had heard correctly.

"The average age. Of all us people here. I'd say it's somewhere in the low 50's, wouldn't you? And that's because you four out-of-towners lower the average significantly."

Ray didn't answer immediately. He looked to Lopez, who looked just as confused as he felt.

"You're probably right," he finally said. "But I don't get your point. Why is that important?"

"Important? I don't know that it's important at all. It's just the way things are. I think it shows just what kind of a community we have here. You're sitting there worrying about the people who aren't here, but that's mostly because you aren't familiar with who we are. Look, we all live up in the mountains far away from everything, in a town that doesn't even have a store, and that's our choice."

Ray was still perplexed. "And?"

"So you're sitting there stressing yourself out about people who are willing and able to make a choice like that. People who are independent, who are interested in living life on their own terms. We're a dying breed, deputy, the kind of people you don't see too much of any more. Some of us are here because our grandparents were among the founders of this town. They worked the coal mine day after day, year after year, and they provided for their families doing thankless work far under the ground. After years of that, it's damned hard to go back to 'civilization,' as some people call it.

"People here are used to doing things their way, and they don't like or appreciate interference. That's just the way things are. You two in the uniforms and Emily here are the only ones here who are surprised that more people didn't come over and stay in this house tonight."

Jackson chuckled. "I'm actually surprised you got this many. I didn't think you'd get any more than one. Maybe two. I'm only here for Taylor's food."

"What I'm saying, deputy, is stop beating yourself up over this. It's not a failure on your part, and it's not a statement about you by any means. It's just a bunch of people reacting to a situation in the way that comes most naturally to them."

Ray thought for several moments. "Thanks for saying that, Taylor," he finally said. "That does help. The hard part is just not being able to do anything. I'm not used to sitting quietly while something goes after people to kill them and mutilate them. It goes against everything I feel is right."

"And what's happening here right now goes against everything that we know is even possible," Jackson said. "Tell me, can you give me a profile of these 'criminals' based on your previous experience? Can you tell me what their M.O. is, how they're going to go about doing what they do? Can you tell me their motivation or what they hope to accomplish here?"

Ray shook his head. "I have absolutely no idea about any of that. Hell, I don't even know how many of them there are."

"And I'll bet you they can function perfectly well at night, too. We can't. And one of them took out an armed trooper in broad daylight, so the advantage is definitely on their side."

"As much as I want to do something," Lopez added, "I can't think of a single thing that would be productive that wouldn't get me killed. And I've been trying to think of something for the last hour. I'm with you, Ray—sitting here just feels wrong. Completely wrong. But if there's nothing else that can be done, then sitting here can't be wrong. Besides, we have these people here to watch out for—if we go out there and get killed, what happens to them?"

Ray sighed. "I guess we just have to keep revisiting the decision to do nothing. I don't know what I'm going to do when we start hearing things."

As if on cue, a gunshot rang out in the night. It was muffled and not very clear, definitely from inside someone's house, Ray thought. Everyone in the room looked up, their nerves on edge. The single shot was followed quickly by two more, then there was silence.

"Three shots," Ray said. "We have to hope that at least one of them hit home."

"And this is the part where I just can't stand sitting here," Lopez said quietly.

Suddenly a series of shots rang out, lasting only two or three seconds. Then there was silence.

No one spoke.

"Do you want to go?" Ray finally asked Lopez. "I'll go if you do. I don't think we'll do any good, but I'll go if you do."

Lopez exhaled the breath that she had been holding, and slumped back in her chair. "Go where? We'd be stumbling around in the dark with no idea where to go. We're where we need to be right now," she said quietly. "What we've got to be doing, I guess, is figuring out just how we're going to defend this place if it comes to it. Who do we need where? Who sleeps when? It's only six o'clock right now—" she looked at her watch again. "It's only six o'clock? That doesn't seem possible. I would have said it was at least ten or eleven."

"It's been a long day," Henry said. "Hell, you haven't even eaten dinner yet."

"And you should eat something," Taylor chided him. "This isn't exactly a normal social situation, but there are still some social norms that apply. Such as 'my house is your house.' If someone goes hungry in my house, that's your fault, not mine. We may be stuck here together against our will, but that doesn't mean that you're not still a guest."

"Thanks much—I appreciate that. Right now, though, I really don't have much of an appetite. Let's just figure out what to if things get bad."

"I thought we already made that decision a while ago," Jackson said. "If you go out there, that will be nothing but foolhardiness."

"You'd be idiots," Maurice interjected.

"But if we stay in here and do nothing, that will be torture," Ray sighed. He got up and walked to the picture window, which they had covered completely with blankets when it became too dark to see Sarah's house any more. "I haven't heard anything else," he said, his head bent as he tried to focus on listening. "There's no way of knowing where those shots came from, but there sure haven't been any more."

"I suppose we'll find out in the morning," Lopez said, not sounding too sure of herself.

"I suppose," Ray agreed. "But we've got a long night ahead of us before the morning ever gets here." He looked over at Bill, who was still unconscious on the box spring. Pauline still sat next to him, watching over him. He wished that Bill weren't out of it, that he could provide some guidance.

Thirty-one
The Bastard II

Deep in the mine shaft, the creature that had kept them alive, the one who had been down there for many years before they were trapped with it, felt something disturbing, felt a loss. They were far from him for the first time since they had arrived, and his connection to them was suddenly weak. The fact that they were no longer in the caverns themselves had changed something. He suddenly felt nervous, anxious. The glowing food on the walls had managed to sustain them for all this time and they had forged a connection throughout the years, but that connection was now threatened.

He and his partner had found the caves many years before, long, long before the mine shaft had been created, long before those people had come down there to explore, to look for whatever it was they searched for. The pair had been mountain men, tough and resilient and daring, but when he had broken his leg, his partner had left him there to die. But he hadn't died. He had come across the glowing moss and worms on the walls by accident as he tried to drag himself out. The food had kept him alive, but it had also extracted a high price: his almost immediate addiction to it had kept him from leaving, had kept him from ever wanting to leave. His leg had healed leaving him with a limp, but his flesh wasted away from his body; that had left him with a greatly diminished frame, but somehow much more strength and agility.

He had been there when the first miners had broken through into the caverns from their mine shaft some ten years later. He had had to kill only one of them to scare off the others, though the respite had lasted only a pair of decades before the groups of men had started to explore. He had taken one of them and killed him, but that hadn't scared the others away—they had come back quickly, all of them at once, and they hadn't been there long before a massive explosion had sounded all through the caverns.

He had taken them one by one and he had helped them to stay alive. The company was good for him when he desired it. He had been able to dominate them easily because of the strength he had gained from the food and his ability to move in the dark. There had been six of them, but when the first one had challenged him the first time, he had killed him quickly and viciously, and then turned to the others to see who else wanted to challenge him.

None did.

He watched as the five slowly lost their bodies and their minds and their ability to think. He felt kinship with them, though he never had felt that he was a part of their group. He saw that his intellect had not diminished nearly as much as theirs, for he was still able to think and to plan and to react with intelligence rather than instinct. Speech had left him completely; thought had not totally gone. Over the years they became more subservient to him, yet they continued to go up to the top of the caverns to move stone from the part of the shaft that had collapsed in the explosion. They were obsessed with doing this, even though he didn't see what good it could do. He didn't try to stop them because it didn't make sense to do so—he knew that they could never leave the caverns for good, that they would have to be back to eat of the food upon which they had been subsisting on for so long. They couldn't stay alive without it, he was sure. Besides, they took frequent breaks from their work. He often took advantage of that fact to go up and replace much of the rubble that they had removed, or to collapse the roof of the narrow tunnel they were trying to clear.

But now one of them was dead and the others were out of the cave. He no longer felt them close. He didn't know what to do about this—to try to keep them there when they came back to feed, to just let them do whatever they were doing, to go out and find out what they were doing. . . but the outside frightened him more than anything else. There was nothing for him out there, he knew already. He had left once before from the far, far hole—the hole the others might have discovered if they had not been so obsessed with moving the rocks—and his one encounter with a person had shown him that he had no business up there. The terror in the hunter's eyes when he saw Matthew—yes, that was his name, Matthew—had made it very clear that there would be nothing for him but pain if he were to stay up top. Besides, the further he had gotten from the food, the weaker he had felt, the stronger the draw to come back had been, and he did not want to risk not being able to do so another time. The man up top had taken a shot at him as he had run away, and he didn't want to face any more rifles for any reason.

But then, he did not have the rage that these others had, the thirst for vengeance that drove them constantly to dig through tons of debris for decade after decade. He didn't share the maniacal bloodlust that coursed through what was left of their veins. He couldn't understand them, but that was partly because they had lost so much of their minds, and all that seemed to be left was the need for revenge.

He didn't know what to do. There was another man in the water, and there were also new intruders in the caverns that he hadn't yet seen or heard—but he could feel their presence. And he didn't like it. His world was his world, and there was no room in that world for intruders. He had allowed the five to live long, long ago, and he was no longer sure that was the right thing to have done.

He needed time to think, but he didn't feel that he was going to have too much time at all. Things were moving very quickly. They would be back soon, he knew they would. They would weaken quickly being away, and they would have to come back to feed.

Thirty-two
Jupiter Rising

They didn't spend nearly as much time with their victims' corpses this night as they had the night before with what was left of Sarah's body. Not ten minutes after their attacks, they all were outside once more and they grouped back up, the four of them, on the roof of Lyle's house. They were elated, they felt powerful, and they felt that there was much more to do with the night. They had no plans, they had no schedule, they had no specific ideas of what they were doing; they just felt compelled by their bloodlust to find new victims, and their instinct told them that the houses all around them were full of victims. Wherever there were lights, they felt, there would be someone to kill. Perhaps their long-buried memories were surfacing, or perhaps they were learning anew something they had long before forgotten.

They hardly felt the cold, though the temperature was a good thirty degrees below what it always was underground. They sat on the roof, naked and quiet, anxious to keep going but also feeling the need to rest. Their lives underground had consisted of nothing but moving rocks for so many years—moving rocks and exploring a bit and eating and sleeping. Their exploring, though, was always cut short by their desire to move the rocks and get back out into the world. And it was cut short by their need to eat the glowing food and drink the water of the stream, the two things that kept them alive, that kept them able to continue on their quest for release and revenge.

Sometimes the Bastard went with them in their exploring. They felt a bond with him, but they didn't understand the bond. They knew that he was more powerful than they were, and they knew that he could kill them with almost no effort at all. At first, when their minds were still functioning, they feared him and they feared what he could do to them, especially after he made an example of Cody—a brutal, terrifying example that they definitely didn't want to experience themselves. But it was an example, a way of killing that they were now emulating in their own victims.

But the addictive and the degenerative qualities of their only food source worked quickly, and their minds didn't last long. They now had no memory of the early days—they lived now almost exclusively for the moment, following their drives instead of their ideas, their instincts rather than their reason and logic.

And there was a house right next door that they hadn't been in yet, and there was a light in that house that drew them instead of repulsed them, as lights had done just a very short time before. When they moved they did so quickly, jumping from the edge of the roof to the ground, then quickly jumping the fence between the houses. Even though they moved with speed, they were also wary, their eyes always on the windows to make sure that no threat faced them from inside. The light was on in a room at the back of the house, and when one of them climbed a short way up into a tree, he saw no one in the room—the others knew this without him having to say anything at all to them. One of them leaped through the closed window, the broken glass having no real effect on what could only be called his skin except for a few superficial scratches. The others followed him quickly into the empty room.

They quickly went through an open door into the hallway from that room. From the hallway they found the living room and the kitchen, and they found three closed doors. One by one they smashed in the doors, none of which had been locked—the knowledge of the function of doorknobs was obviously something that had escaped from their minds. One door led to a small closet, one to the bathroom, and one to a bedroom, all of which were empty. In the bedroom one of them was mesmerized by glowing objects on the ceiling—they weren't exactly the same color as the glowing food in the caves, but he wasn't able to distinguish between nuances such as shade any more.

It had no idea that Eileen Richardson had left her son's room exactly as it was when pneumonia had taken him when he was just twelve years old. The creature couldn't know that every couple of years she replaced the glow-in-the-dark stars and planets because she often felt the urge to visit the room late in the evening before bed to think of her son and how much she missed him.

It had no way of knowing any more what it was looking at, even if such a thing had been invented before he had been lost to the mine. Right now he knew that he was hungry, so he jumped quickly to the top of the dresser and reached up and ripped off of the ceiling the biggest chunk that he saw. It didn't feel like the moss, and it was harder than the glowing worms that lived on the walls of the cavern, but he didn't take the time to allow such things to register in his mind—he thrust Jupiter into his mouth and tried to chew it, without any luck. It wasn't squishy like the worms, or smooth like the moss, and what was left of his teeth weren't able to chew anything at all. Just as he was about to spit it out, a reflex action forced him to swallow, and the object lodged in his throat, which had grown much narrower over the years.

Suddenly, he was no longer able to breathe, but he had no idea what the problem was. He felt the object lodged in his throat, but even stronger was the sudden desire to draw in air, the sudden panic that came with not being able to do so. He was unable to understand the connection between the plastic Jupiter in his throat and the pain in his chest, the overwhelming urge of his body to draw in more air. His hands reflexively came up to his throat, and his dark and empty eyes widened in sudden ignorant and impotent fear. He looked to the other three, who had entered the room behind him and who now stood watching his desperation. They had no idea what was going on, no idea what he was doing.

He began to flail about wildly, knocking the lamp on the dresser to the floor, punching through the sheetrock in the wall nearest to him. His desperate movements didn't last long—as his body had withered, his lungs also had grown smaller, with far less capacity than they had had before. They didn't know that their breathing was even more important to them now, that they now breathed at least forty times a minute because each breath accomplished so little for the body as a whole. In a matter of one minute, his body gave out and he fell to the ground, lifeless.

The other three looked at each other. They felt nothing, for this had nothing to do with their revenge. The gratification of killing was the only real feeling that they had now. One of them moved over to the body that lay on the floor and lifted the head to see if there was any response, then dropped it back to the floor, which it hit with a loud, dull thud. He looked back to the others, and saw one of them on the dresser, reaching for the ceiling, where the glowing stars and planets were. He pulled down a glowing star and put it into his mouth. He was lucky—the star was very small, and there was no taste to it at all. He spit it out, looked up, and ran out of the bedroom.

There was no one to kill in this house. They had to go to another house. They were now three, but that was of no concern to them. Nothing was really of any concern to them except the urges that came to them, and they were only a concern until the next urge came.

Thirty-three
Bennie and the Steel Door

Bennie Marasco sat calmly in his basement, not at all worried about what might pay him a visit tonight. In fact, he was thinking about moving from the recliner to the cot so that he could get himself some shut-eye—he wasn't going to be like those others, who were sitting around waiting for some kind of disaster to hit. His father had built this basement many years before as a refuge, some sort of end-of-the-world place, and he had built it strong and almost impenetrable. Bennie had been a kid when his dad had done all the work, talking all the time about the "Red invasion," or something like that. He had learned later in school that he had been talking about the Soviet Union, but that fact never impressed him much. It was still just a basement to Bennie.

All that notwithstanding, Bennie was glad for his father's effort now. As he sat there reading, he started to think that he really should have asked some of the others to come down into the basement with him. He just hadn't thought about it at the time. Besides, there was room for only five or six people down here, so just whom would he ask and whom would he leave out? None of his neighbors knew about it anyway, so far as he knew, so it really wasn't any big deal. Add to that the fact that he had to use a gallon jug as a urinal as long as he was down there and it might not have been too comfortable for everyone. His father hadn't thought everything through.

He knew the walls were made of cinder block, not drywall, so there wasn't any way that anything was getting through them. The door was solid steel—something his dad had found when they had torn down the old armory over in Grand Junction and sold everything they could. Of course, Bennie didn't know about the door in Sarah's basement. If he had known, he wouldn't be feeling quite as safe. But he still would have been fine with staying there.

Bennie kept a journal, a rather detailed one about his years on this planet. He had hardly ever left Canyon Bluff, from the time that he was born until this very day. He never really had any need to do so—everything he needed was here except his groceries, and he got those every other week on his run to Pine. This was where his roots were, where his family had lived. Even though he didn't have any blood family left, he knew that everyone in town was a brother or sister to him when all was said and done. They had all been through everything together, from the early days when their dads still worked in the mine all the way through the last several decades as family after family, person after person had left the town for more opportunity, for schools for the kids—CB's school had been closed some fifteen years ago, with a final graduating class of two—for jobs and shopping and movies and sports.

He didn't blame them at all. No one did. He understood that the younger people didn't have the ties to the town and the people that he and his generation had. He understood that when you have kids, the important thing was to find opportunities for the children, and if there weren't any where you lived, then you just had to move, now didn't you?

When he heard a window break upstairs, he closed his journal slowly and carefully, set it down on the table beside him and listened. He heard footsteps scurry quickly across the floor above him, several sets, as far as he could tell. From what he heard, they were checking out the whole house, looking for someone or something. He really had no idea what these things could be, for he hadn't seen them at all and the deputy's description had been rather vague. Until the window broke and he heard the footsteps, he had been skeptical of the things even existing. "Come on," he had told the deputy. "Are you trying to tell me that these are the men that were trapped in the mine sixty years ago? And that they're still alive?"

The deputy had been unsure of himself, but he had stuck by his story. And he had been very disappointed when Bennie had refused his suggestion of staying with the others tonight—Bennie knew that he'd be fine, but he could tell that the deputy thought Bennie was signing his own death warrant.

He heard light, quick footsteps on the basement stairs then, and Bennie suddenly was paying closer attention. The other half of his basement was filled with odds and ends that he and his wife had accumulated over the years, so he knew that whoever was out there would have to make their way around all the crap to get to the door. The basement floor was concrete, so he heard no further footsteps. The silence was beginning to become overwhelming when he heard the slightest touch on the other side of the door. As secure as he told himself he felt, Bennie found himself reaching for his rifle. He cursed under his breath at the thought of having given his pistols and his sawed-off to his son, who he thought would probably need them more in the city when he had moved. A rifle in a small room would be bulky and difficult to aim quickly, he knew, and he tried to reassure himself that things wouldn't come to that.

His eyes widened quickly when he noticed that he had neglected to lock the deadbolt. That meant that the only thing between him and whatever was out there was an unlocked door. "Shit!" he muttered aloud in spite of himself, then stepped over quickly to the door. He had no way of knowing that the Nogglz had no idea how to use a doorknob, so he reached out quickly and turned the knob that set the deadbolt with a loud thud.

He also had no idea that the Nogglz had been at the point of turning around and leaving when they heard the noise that told them that someone was behind the door.

Almost instantly, before Bennie was able to take even one step back, something slammed into the door from the outside. Bennie's eyes were on the lock that he had just set, and he was surprised to see just how much the door actually moved in the frame from the impact. He didn't even want to think about what would have happened if he hadn't been able to close the deadbolt. As it was, a second loud thud caused the door to move again, and Bennie's mind went from the confidence he felt in the strength of the door to the doubts he suddenly had about the frame that his father had built so many years ago. What kind of wood was it? he wondered. How many of these blasts could it endure? He realized that the only true barrier between himself and whatever was out there was the wood of a door frame that had been put in place decades ago, and he had no idea how thick the wood was or how strong it was.

The third blast came almost immediately after the second, and the thought that they must have been taking turns out there leapt into his mind. How many of them were there? he asked himself frantically. How much strength did they have? How long could they keep throwing themselves at the door?

He backed away, his rifle now held ready before him, pointing straight at the door. Bennie was now terrified as the blows on the door seemed to be never-ending and the strain on the doorjamb seemed to be taking its toll—with each impact, the door seemed to move in just the tiniest bit more.

This might be it, he told himself in disbelief. I should be over there with the others. You arrogant old man! You idiot! He suddenly spied his journal on the table, and he quickly reached over and grabbed it, putting it into the bottom drawer of the small dresser that served as a pantry. He closed the drawer quickly just as the doorjamb gave way and the door collapsed inward. One of Naugle's boys burst into the room with unimaginable speed and rushed over to where Bennie stood, turning back toward the door far too late to accomplish anything, far too late even to get off a useless shot from his now-useless rifle. As he tried to lift it and point it, the creature reached out swiftly and smashed it from his hands, his claws leaving deep gashes in Bennie's arms as they swept across the flesh.

Bennie looked his death straight in the eyes, and his fear grew in his last moment of life as he saw deep, dark pools of nothingness staring straight back at him from a face that had skin stretched tautly over the skull, pulling the mouth back in a horrible grimace and creating eye sockets that were far too deep to be human, far too deep not to be terrifying. The eyes were dark and horribly empty. And Bennie's last thought before the next blow ripped the skin from the left side of his face and sent him into shock was one that would have surprised even him: My God—these poor men. The third blow, one that came from the second creature to reach him, mercifully sent him into unconsciousness; then the third creature also was upon him.

Thirty-four
Contact

"I think we made a big fuckin' mistake," Brad hissed, shining the dimming light from his flashlight in every direction, but still finding no clue as to which direction they should take. "This cave is huge, and we're about as lost as lost can be."

Brian didn't reply, for he saw no need to do so. They were completely lost. They had been for quite a long while. Since neither of them wore a watch, they had absolutely no idea how long it had been since they came down into the caverns. He was hungry, but he was even more thirsty. They had both thought things would be over with pretty quick—one way or another—and they hadn't planned on spending so much time below ground or traveling so far.

"We're pretty much screwed," Brad said in a low voice, still leery of the idea of having the Nogglz hear him and be able to sneak up on him in the dark. He didn't mind the thought of dying, but he at least wanted the chance to blow away one of them and take it with him.

"Well, we've still got my flashlight and the headlamp," Brian offered. "Should we just start going back the way we came?"

"Do you even know what way we came, bro?" Brad asked sarcastically. "'Cause I ain't got any idea which way is which, much less which way we've been coming."

"I think I do," Brian said. "Gimme the light. I know which way we came." He reached out and took the light from his brother's hand and turned around and started down the passage they had just come down. He really didn't know which way to go but he did have a pretty good hunch, and Brian knew that his hunches were usually pretty good.

In one minute, they reached a fork that they hadn't noticed before when they were walking in the other direction. Brian took the left passage without hesitation and they started climbing; just three or four minutes later he stopped. Brad, who had been following closely because they were using only the one flashlight, bumped into him from behind.

"What the hell, Brian?" he whispered. "Tell me if you're gonna stop like that!"

"I put up my left hand," Brian replied, but before Brad could protest that it was too damned dark to see anyone's hand go up, he added, "Looka there. Up ahead."

Brad looked closely in front of them, and as his eyes adjusted he was able to make out a greenish glow that seemed to be coming from around the next bend in the passageway.

"What the hell is that?" he asked. "Did someone bring a freakin' lava lamp down here?"

"I dunno," Brian said matter-of-factly. "But I sure didn't expect to see no light down here."

"Well, let's find out what the hell it is. And since we didn't see this before, I'm guessing that you ain't got the slightest idea where we are or how to get back up top."

Brian moved forward slowly without answering, Brad right behind him. "Don't shine that light too far ahead," Brad warned in a whisper. "We don't want to give ourselves away if there's something up there." Brian responded by lowering the light to the ground right before his feet and slowing down. Soon they reached a wall that blocked their view of whatever was glowing, and Brian turned the light off and stopped behind the wall. They both were baffled by the idea of seeing any light at all down so deep underground.

Brad moved ahead of Brian, kneeled down and peered around the wall. "Holy shit," he muttered, almost to himself. "The whole damned place is glowing!"

Brian stuck his head around the corner, too. His eyes widened as he saw the glowing growth all through the chamber, but he didn't say anything. In addition to whatever was all over the walls, there were hundreds of points of light, too, something that was glowing slightly brighter than the other stuff. On the far side of the chamber, there was an indentation at the bottom of the wall, and he was shocked to see someone lying there, illuminated by the glowing material that was all around him.

"Look!" he whispered, pointing directly ahead. This time Brad saw his hand as a silhouette in the glowing light, and he saw the body lying on the other side of the chamber.

"Who the hell is that?" Brad asked. Whoever it was, was lying at a level slightly lower than the floor of the chamber, so they weren't able to get a full view of him.

"Don't know. Looks kinda like Juan, but they made it sound like he was dead."

"Well, there's only one way to find out, isn't there?" Brad said, taking the flashlight from Brian, turning it on, and starting across the chamber. As he neared the body, he saw that it was Juan, and that he was lying in a stream of water that was only a few inches deep.

"Shit, that must be cold," Brian said quietly.

"You ain't kiddin'," Brad replied. He kneeled down and grabbed Juan's wrist, feeling for a pulse but putting his fingers in the wrong spot. "I don't feel no pulse," he whispered.

"That must mean he's dead," Brian replied. "What should we do?"

"Ain't nothing we can do," Brad said. "We can't carry him with us or anything. But we know where he is at least. 'Cept we ain't got the slightest idea where we are."

"Listen!" Brian said in warning, and they both heard rocks falling somewhere in the caverns.

"Shit!" Brad hissed, and he scurried back to the spot behind the wall where they had just come from. Brian was right with him, and they both tried to quiet their breathing.

In a matter of moments, they heard a low growling sound from the chamber. Brad leaned down as far as he could towards the floor and slowly stuck his head out around the wall and held his breath as soon as he saw the three creatures that now stood near Juan's body, their attention focused on the wall in front of them. He could see only their silhouettes against the glowing green, and he watched as they reached out their hands and took small chunks of the glowing matter between their fingers and then ate them, slowly and carefully. They also reached out and pulled down the brighter objects, putting those, too, into their mouths and chewing.

Brad wanted nothing more than to start shooting, but his position made that impossible. He watched a few more seconds then moved back, leaning back against the wall next to Brian. The darkness here was barely touched by the glowing, so they couldn't see each other at all. He desperately wanted to tell Brian that there were three of them, to get his shotgun ready so that they could blast them to hell, but it was too dark for hand signals and too dangerous to talk—the Nogglz were only some thirty feet away. He knew that they would hear him as soon as he said something, as soon as he made any sort of noise at all.

He was frustrated—to have come all this way for no reason. To have the things right there, not just in range but at almost point-blank range, and to be sitting here too damned scared even to take a shot. Screw it, he told himself. Gotta do what we gotta do.

He pulled his pistol from its holster, felt to make sure that it was cocked, then leaned towards where he knew Brian was sitting next to him and whispered, "Lock and load, bro. I'm going for it."

He stood quickly and stepped to the left, starting to bring the pistol up to get a couple of shots off at the creatures. But in the dark there were many things that were completely unseen, such as the rock overhang that extended into the end of the passageway where it met up with the chamber. He had no idea that it was there until his head smashed into it, immediately stunning him and causing him to drop his pistol and fall to the floor. Brian, who had been following his lead, ran into his body and fell with him, dropping his weapon, too.

"Oh, shit," Brian said quietly, and not because he was falling. He glanced to his right to see the figures already moving quickly towards him—one was already upon him just as he hit the floor, and he never saw coming the back-handed blow to his temple that knocked him unconscious. Brad lay still under Brian's body, too stunned to be able to move or to know what had happened.

Thirty-five
Out

"This silence is starting to get to me," Lopez said, standing up once more and walking into the kitchen. She came back moments later with another small portion of spaghetti, surprised at how hungry she suddenly was. She hadn't thought about it at all, but she hadn't had any lunch—nor had Ray or Bill for that matter. The entire day had flown by faster than any day she could recall in her life, but she still couldn't believe that it was only eight o'clock at night. They had been working on dinner for the last couple of hours, but not everyone was able to eat depending on how jittery they were.

She was thinking mostly about her son, about the fact that she still wasn't able to get him any message at all letting him know where she was, what she was doing. In a small way, she felt it was a good thing that she wasn't able to do so—she didn't have any desire at all to tell her parents what had happened in Canyon Bluff that day and what was still happening. She could only imagine what kind of worrying that would cause. But the idea of being killed here in CB without ever having the opportunity to say good-bye, on a day that had promised to be nothing but routine when she had woken up fifteen hours earlier was not an idea that he found to be particularly pleasing.

And as she thought about him, she wanted less and less to go outside and risk being killed. But as the evening dragged on, even still in its early hours, she also wanted less and less to be sitting in a dining room of a stranger's house—no matter how nice and welcoming that stranger was. She was especially disturbed by the fact that her job was to protect and serve, but instead she was sitting in a comfortable if crowded home, with no clue at all what was going on in other houses.

On the other hand, she told herself, she was protecting and serving the people in the house with them, and everyone had been given the chance to be there.

But that wasn't enough for her. She couldn't feel right, no matter how much she wanted to get back home and see her son, no matter how unsure she was of what might be going on. She had to get out and see if there was anything she could do, anything that was needed.

"I'm going out," she said abruptly to Ray, then she looked at Jackson and Henry. "No one is at all obligated to come with me, but if anyone's up for it, one of you is more than welcome to come. Someone needs to stay here, though."

"I'll go," Jackson said quickly, surprising her.

"Count me in," Henry added.

"I'm willing to go, too," Ray said.

Lopez lifted her eyebrows in surprise. "So now everyone wants to go. What happened to our decision?"

"That was then," Henry said. "This is now. Gotta be able to change our minds."

Lopez sighed. "This is extremely risky. Ray, you and I can't go together. How about if we each pair up with Jackson and Henry and alternate patrols?"

"Sounds good to me," Ray said. "As long as I'm not sitting around here with nothing to do."

Lopez was torn. While both Jackson and Henry had volunteered to go with her, she didn't want either of them going. But she couldn't take Ray and it would be sheer stupidity to go out there alone.

"All right," she said finally. "Henry, you'll come with me now. Jackson, you'll go out with Ray on the next patrol."

"Sounds good," Henry said, standing up and walking over to the coat rack. Lopez watched him as he went, looking for any sign that he might not be able to move as quickly as they might need to move. She had her doubts, but she didn't have her choice. He looked like he'd be okay, just not particularly fast.

"Don't worry," Henry said as if reading her mind. "I still do a lot of hunting in the woods. I can move when I need to move. I won't slow you down."

"How many lights do we have?" Lopez asked, moving over to the bookcase where they had stockpiled the supplies that they might need. "Do we have two headlamps?"

"We actually have three," Ray said, picking two of them out of the pile and turning them on to test the lights. "And we have plenty of batteries, thanks to Taylor. Both of these take three batteries, so you can carry extras with you."

"I'd rather carry an extra headlamp, too," Lopez said, fitting the one that Ray handed her on her head. "But I'm not going to leave you guys without. We'll each take a flashlight, too."

"What are you planning on?" Ray asked.

"What do you mean?"

"Are you going inside houses? Are you trying to find those things? Track them down?"

"I don't think we're ready for that. Let's just call this recon. Once we get an idea of what's going on out there, we'll be able to come up with some sort of plan. Maybe." She was already questioning her decision to go out, but she wasn't about to share that fact with anyone. "Are you about ready, Henry?"

"About as ready as I'll ever be."

"You sound surprisingly cheerful," Lopez remarked. "Is there some sort of secret death wish I need to know about?"

Henry smiled. "I've been penned up with Jackson and Taylor for going on ten hours now," he said. "Even going outside and getting torn to shreds will be a welcome break."

"My thoughts exactly," Jackson said, laughing. "You'd better be careful that you don't jinx yourself with your shitty jokes. Or jinx someone else and end up killing them. Karma can be a real bitch, you know."

Henry looked at Lopez. "Don't you fret now, trooper. It just feels good to be doing something. I'm not about to go and get you killed."

"All right. There are what—three long east-west streets and two cross streets here?" She looked at Emily. "Can I borrow a piece of paper?" She took the sheet and picked up a pen from the table. She quickly drew a small diagram of the streets. "We're here right now. More or less. We'll head west, to this corner, then go south to the third street. What's it called?"

Jackson smiled. "Third street," he said with a chuckle.

"Okay. Then east on Third, north on this cross street, then west on Second Street."

"Actually," Jackson said, "That one's called Oak. We're on Main. We have Main, Oak, and Third."

Lopez looked at him carefully to see if he was messing with her. Jackson shrugged. "You learn to leave rhyme and reason behind when you come to CB."

"Tell me about it. So Ray, you know where we're going in case it starts taking too long. We shouldn't be more than twenty, twenty-five minutes."

"Yep. Are you going in any houses?"

"We'll have to make that call out there. If there seems to be a need to, then we will. But probably not."

"May I say," Taylor interjected politely, "just how incredibly dumb this seems to be?"

"Of course you may," Henry replied.

"I'm with Taylor," Maurice said from across the room. "Why the hell are you going out there again?"

Lopez smiled. "Because we've got to. Someone's got to."

"Got to, hell." His tone was conversational, not confrontational, and he shrugged his shoulders. "Seems to me it makes much more sense to stay put."

"It must be something about these badges," Lopez said. "Sometimes I think they make us stupid or something."

"Henry ain't wearing no badge."

"But Henry's been doing stupid things his whole life long," Henry said. "Are we ready?" he asked Lopez. She was already at the door, reaching for the knob.

"Let's go," she said, pulling the door open and letting in a burst of cold air. They both slipped outside quickly and closed the door behind them. They heard the sound of it being locked.

Lopez was surprised to see a thin layer of fog lying over the ground. It was snowing very lightly, and a thin covering had fallen since they had locked themselves inside. In any other situation, she thought, it would look pretty. Right now, though, it was just the way things were and they didn't have any time to stop and admire the beauty. Their minds were on other things.

They walked straight out the walkway to the street, where they positioned themselves in the center and turned left. They stuck to their plan, walking at a slow but steady pace—they both knew that the more quickly they walked, the more likely they would be to be careless, to make some sort of mistake that could cost them dearly. The town was spooky at best—completely quiet and almost completely dark. They caught an occasional glimpse of lights that were on, but for the most part everyone had turned them off.

"I'd like to know where those shots came from," Henry said in a very low voice, almost a whisper. Lopez didn't answer—they both knew that there was no way of knowing for now, and no way of finding out unless they were to search every house in the town.

Their lights reflected off the fog, barely penetrating it, so the snow beneath their feet was almost invisible to their eyes. Lopez tried to keep the light trained on the houses that they were passing, with only an occasional glance downward—if anything was going to come after them, the chances were that it would come from one of the houses. Both she and Henry turned around completely from time to time in order to make sure there was nothing behind them, but there seemed to be nobody and nothing around. Lopez was glad to see that Henry seemed to know what he was doing.

"Army?" she asked.

"Yep. Korea."

It took them about two minutes of slow going to reach the end of the street, and they followed their plan and turned left. So far, neither of them had seen anything at all that seemed even slightly suspicious or unusual.

Lopez suddenly stopped. "Henry," she said quietly, "we have a broken window over here."

He stopped too and looked. In the light they both shined over there with their headlamps, the broken window looked ominous.

"Damn," Henry said. "Now's when I would want to go into the house and find out what's happened in there. If anything. This is Lyle's place."

"This could be the house from which we heard the gunshots," Lopez offered.

"It definitely could be that."

"Let's keep track of the houses that seem to have been compromised so that we can make a plan to canvass the town in the morning," Lopez suggested. "We're going to have to start finding out what's been happening sooner or later, but not right now. Not in this dark, not when we're the most vulnerable."

"Right. That's Lyle's place, like I said. Broken window."

"We can mark them on the map when we get back." She pulled a pen from her pocket and pushed up the sleeve of her coat, then wrote "Lyle" on the inside of her forearm.

She was surprised by the lack of sound—the night was completely and eerily silent. It was something that she wasn't used to experiencing. She wasn't sure what she had expected, whether she had thought that the darkness would be full of the sounds of people being killed by creatures or what, but the quiet was disconcerting. It scared her more than any sounds of violence ever would have.

"It's too quiet," she whispered, and Henry nodded his head in agreement, the light from his headlamp jumping in the fog.

"Kind of hope it stays that way," he whispered back, then added nothing more. Lopez took that as partially a statement and partially a hint, so she said no more.

They walked quietly to the end of the street, then turned again. Henry suddenly whispered "Wait!" and held up a hand, and they both stopped. Lopez looked over at him, then down to where he was looking. She saw what looked like a mess in the snow—a bunch of footprints that didn't seem to have any sort of pattern or sense of direction to them. It was impossible to tell if they were of one person or of ten. They were all over on Henry's side of the street, coming out only a foot or two into the street, mostly staying inside the yard of the house they were passing. It looked like a bunch of kids had been playing tag in the snow, she thought, trying to distinguish some sort of rhyme or reason in the randomness of the impressions.

"Is that blood?" she asked suddenly, noticing traces of color mixed in the white and the dark.

"Think so," Henry replied. The beam from his headlamp raised slightly as he looked at the yard, then moved slowly back and forth as he surveyed the area. The yard was full of the footprints.

Lopez slowly looked over the street ahead of them, trying to keep the light from moving too quickly, and she saw just at the limits of the light similar footprints crossing the street ahead of them. "There's where they crossed," she whispered to Henry.

He followed her gaze, then looked back at the yard and the house behind it.

"No sign of anything happening here," he said quietly. "Other than the footprints. No broken windows, no door open, nothing like that."

"Maybe they went in through the back," Lopez replied. She had started to feel almost safe as they walked, but that feeling was now history. Now she felt tense, as if those things could be anywhere around them at this very moment. Her adrenaline had kicked in with a vicious rush as soon as she had seen the footprints. "It's weird, though," she added. "This house is pretty much the farthest house of all from Sarah's place, from the mine shaft."

"That is strange. This is Arnie and Bernice's house. They've probably locked themselves away in their basement."

"I didn't think the mining companies went to the trouble of putting basements in these houses. That sounds like a lot of work."

"Just a few, for storage, mostly. This house used to be the company store. Bennie's house used to be the saloon. He's got a basement, too."

"I still want to know how or why these things got this far out."

"I wouldn't expect them to be following any pattern, but who knows? Maybe they just worked their way this way from house to house. Maybe following lights. Beats the hell out of me."

"So what do we do?" she asked.

"Keep walking, I guess," Henry replied. "This is recon right now, like you said. No engagement if we can help it."

Lopez didn't reply, though she hoped to hell that Henry's last statement would prove to be accurate. She felt the limitations of their current situation, the power of the immense darkness around them, the extreme vulnerability of their position, weapons or no. She didn't know how they would fare against something that was stronger than them and much faster than they were. Without being able to see fully and clearly, she didn't really feel like finding out. She wrote Arnie's name on her arm.

When they had slowly walked past the house, she looked back and saw that one of the windows on the far side of the house was broken. "It looks like they have a preferred method of entry," she told Henry. He looked in the direction her light was shining.

"Maybe they just don't get doors," he said. "But windows sure are the easiest, especially if you don't care if anyone hears you or not."

Lopez stared at the broken window for several long seconds, wondering what they would find in the house if they went in now.

"Let's go," Henry said. "It looks like they're out, and I for one do not want to run into them out here."

They moved on, now with a stronger fear and a building sense of dread.

Thirty-six
Visitors

By the time they had finished with their fifth "visit," they were feeling something that they hadn't felt before. They weren't sure why they didn't feel as strong as they had before, why their strength seemed to be failing them. The last door hadn't been nearly as easy to smash, and they didn't feel nearly as fast as they normally felt. They forgot about Mattie and Janie Aguiar's bodies, which lay at their feet. They looked at each other, knowing somehow that they all felt the same thing. Though they didn't know what was going on, they knew that they needed to go back to the caverns, to go back to their home.

They looked around themselves and felt the gratification of having done what they had come to do, having addressed their lust for vengeance, though the gratification would be fading very soon. It was a very important feeling to them, though, one that would continue to drive them.

They stood in the Aguiars' bedroom, where Mattie and Janie had simply gone to bed, choosing not to believe the trooper's warning when she had come to warn them of the danger. But now the "ridiculous paranoid fantasies" that they had accused Lopez and the sheriff of concocting were standing over their bodies, standing in the puddles of blood that had just recently been pumping through the veins and the arteries and the hearts of the old couple.

But they didn't stand there long. Almost simultaneously, they turned and left the bedroom, leaving the tell-tale bloody footprints that on any other day would be something extraordinary. Tomorrow, though, the prints would be just another indication of where the Nogglz had been and what they had done.

The three leaped out the window through which they had come in, and they started running together back towards Sarah's house, leaping over the Hellers' hedges and Jackson's fence, paying no attention to the snow that now covered the ground or to the few lights that they saw in windows. They came out into the main street just east of Rita's at the same place where they had crossed the street before, ensuring that Henry and Lopez wouldn't see their tracks immediately when they turned west more by chance than anything else.

The porch of Sarah's home was now almost like home to them—they started to feel a certain level of comfort and belonging when they reached it. One of them stopped to look back across the street at Taylor's house, drawn by the light that sneaked past the edges of the blankets in the windows that faced the street. While it felt that it wanted to attack, it also felt it wasn't possible now, that something else must happen first.

If it had stayed there just thirty seconds more, it would have seen the door open and two people step outside—easy targets for them, even in their weakened state. Instead, though, it turned and followed its companions through the house, past the bodies, into the basement and down into the mine shaft.

It never took them long to get from the blocked section of the mine shaft to their feeding ground, and as they came closer to it, they started to feel the anticipation of pleasure. It was something that they couldn't associate with eating, of course, but which nonetheless came to them as they neared their source of nutrition. For decades they had eaten only of the glowing moss and the glowing worms on the cavern walls, never being able to consider just how such a nutritionally poor diet could maintain their bodies, their strength, and their speed. Never had they been able to consider just how quickly the moss and the worms regenerated on the walls upon which they hung. They had four feeding grounds, but this one that was closest to the mine entrance was by far the richest and the most accessible.

They slowed as they approached the chamber, for they all smelled the same thing—something different that they now recognized as human. There was a person down there, and they suddenly became tense, sensing some sort of confrontation.

When the first one turned the last corner that led to the chamber, he saw Juan's body lying in the stream where they had put it hours earlier. He began to growl softly, as did the others behind him—they didn't remember Juan, and they didn't remember putting him there. To them, now, he was an intruder, though a completely inert one—why was this human not moving?

A calming thought came to their minds, and they knew that the Bastard was there, the one who had taught them of the feeding, the one who had shown them the caverns. The one who had allowed them to live even though he easily could have killed them. He wasn't in sight at the moment, but he was near, and he was letting them know that it was okay that the body was there, that there was a human present. Their soft growls died down, and they turned to the wall and began to feed, almost immediately feeling their strength grow.

Suddenly, a sound came from behind them, to their right, from the other path that led out of the chamber. They quickly turned to look, to see another person already starting to fall, and then another come from behind the wall and tangle up with him, and then they were both falling. Almost instantly they were over there, the first one there hitting the top human in the head hard enough to knock him out. He was about to strike the one below him, but it looked like that one already was almost unconscious.

They all three stood and looked down at the two men on the floor of the cavern. Had they had the ability to think, they would have been surprised at their lack of anger at these two, at their lack of a desire to kill them and rip their bodies apart. Somehow, the fact that these two were down here in the caverns—just as Juan had been in the mine shaft—made them less of a threat, and took away the association that they had made between revenge and the town. This wasn't the town, so these weren't people that they needed or wanted to kill.

The Bastard came slowly out of the passage, looking curiously at the bodies and at the three remaining Naugle's boys. He felt no threat, though something told him that he needed to get rid of the objects that were lying on the floor near the bodies. He picked up the pistol and the shotgun, then found another shotgun around the corner in the dark. He took them across the chamber to the same spot where he had thrown the dead Noggl hours earlier, and he tossed the weapons into the depths of the darkness.

The others were back, as he had known they would be. After all, they needed the life-giving sustenance that grew so abundantly on the wall. They needed the place, and he liked to think they needed him—for he most certainly needed them. His years before they had come had been lonely and desperate. Though he knew he was not a part of the group of them, he did know that he was the strongest and the fastest, and therefore they must obey him. He had no desire to return to the outside world, for he had completely forgotten about it in the many years that he had been down there. He also had no hatred to drive him to find the outside world, no desire for revenge, no bloodlust that needed to be fulfilled.

There was no longer anything interesting about the two on the ground any more, so the Nogglz went back to the wall and continued to eat for several minutes. After they had eaten their fill, they all drank from the stream in which Juan lay and they lay down on the floor to sleep. To them, sleep was very necessary, though they rarely slept for more than an hour at a time. There was much more killing to do, but it would have to wait until they awoke from their naps.

In the meantime, the Bastard grabbed Brian by the collar of his coat and dragged him further into the room. When he came back, Brad was coming to, shaking his head groggily until the creature hit him in the face and knocked him out once more. Then he dragged Brad's body over by Brian's and left them there while he moved out of the chamber and deeper into the caverns. He already had slept, and he was simply gratified that the others had returned. He felt a loss, somehow, but he wasn't sure what it was—somehow, the others had been more when they had left than they were when they returned.

Thirty-seven
Hair

Ramsey Stefanic made her way slowly over the snowy street, cursing her arthritis constantly, cursing the pain in her knees especially, the pain that made walking such a slow and painful task for her. She wasn't too fond of the darkness, either, and she cursed her own neglect for having forgotten to buy new batteries for the only flashlight she owned. It still put out a bit of light, but not nearly enough to make her feel at all comfortable or safe.

She had been sitting around all evening wondering if she had made a mistake in not going to Taylor's with the others. Her house was cold and lonely at night, but she normally didn't notice that fact because she went to bed about eight. Tonight, though, she had been unable to sleep. For the first time in a very long while she was reminded of just how cold and lonely—and long—night could be. She had heard the gunshots earlier, and she wasn't sure but she thought that she heard someone scream later. It didn't matter whether she actually heard the screams or not because every sound that she heard fed her imagination, told her that those things were just outside her house, ready to break in and rip her to pieces.

She had grown up hearing about the Nogglz. Grandpa had enjoyed teasing her when she was very young, telling her about "Naugle's boys" and the things that they would do to people when they finally came back up out of the mine. She had only believed it until a certain age, of course. She grew old enough to believe the other kids when they told her that no one could live down in the mines that damned long, that they would have died from starvation in a couple of weeks. But they were still a good story to scare the kids with, and she had told the story herself to her two sons when they were much, much younger. She remembered that her boyfriend in high school had even suggested that they make the Nogglz the high school mascot—"Ladies and gentlemen, here are your Canyon Bluff Nogglz!"—in the days when they had a school. It wasn't an idea that anyone took seriously, though everyone could see the irony and humor in the thought.

By the time ten o'clock came around, she was jumping out of her skin. She figured it was time to get over to Taylor's—or at least try to do so. I get killed out on the street or I sit here and wait for them to come and kill me, she told herself, and she knew that of the two choices, the former was by far the most appealing as far as death was concerned. Hell, at least she'd be *doing* something.

So she had gotten dressed and put on one of her wigs—the black one—and put on her heavy coat and stepped outside, thinking immediately that she was making a huge mistake. A quarter mile, she told herself, that's all I have to go. Maybe those things are busy with someone else right now, and they aren't going to see me. Maybe I'll even make it to Taylor's.

If her husband were there, she knew they would have been with the others all evening. He would have made her go. And he would have made sure there were fresh batteries for the flashlight, too—he was good at that sort of thing, and she most certainly wasn't. But he hadn't been around for fifteen years, and she did pretty good for herself, thank you very much. Besides, who ever would've thought that she'd be out in the middle of the night because Naugle's boys had come back from the dead?

She reached Main Street and took a left—just a hundred yards more. In the dim light of the flashlight, through the veil of mist that often made it impossible to see the ground, she suddenly saw many, many footprints in the snow. They were small footprints that didn't look like they came from any kind of shoes that she was familiar with. They looked almost barefoot, but they were really too scuffed to be able to see them clearly. She shifted the flashlight to her left hand and made the sign of the cross with her right, reflexively starting to say a Hail Mary as she walked. She tried to pick up her speed, but her legs weren't willing to do what her brain told them to. Her heart started racing even faster, and for a moment she thought how easy a heart attack would make things.

But no heart attack was coming, and she made her slow and steady way down the street. She reached Taylor's walkway just as the Nogglz came out of Sarah's house, well rested and ready for more havoc. A new sensation had worked its way back into their minds, that of enjoyment of what they were about to do. Catching sight of Ramsey making her way along Taylor's walk jumpstarted their killing instinct—she was halfway to the door already, and they had a good hundred yards to cover to reach her. They could get her.

Ramsey, though, made one of the best decisions of her life right then, and it probably couldn't even be called a decision. Fear got the best of her, and she yelled out Taylor's name as loud as she could when she was still ten yards away from the door. The hell with the doorbell—if they heard her, the door would already be open by the time she got there. "Open the door, Taylor," she yelled a second time, and at her last word the door flew open, and the deputy stood there looking wide-eyed out at her.

"Holy shit!" he exclaimed, taking a step outside, planning to help her inside. He took her arm as she reached the screen door, then he caught a flash of motion just inches from his face. His gaze had been focused on the old woman, and he had thought that he'd have plenty of time to make sure everything was clear once she was inside. He hadn't thought at all that there might be something right behind her.

The creature also had been completely focused on the woman—what was left of his memory told him how gratifying it would feel to grab her head and break her neck. His last few steps he was moving fast, looking only at her head, which he would be in range of quickly. He only noticed the other person out of his peripheral vision, which was severely deteriorated because of all the years he had hardly used his eyes at all. As his arm was reaching, he realized that he could kill both of them very quickly—the others would be behind him because they always were, and he could kill quickly.

The claws that used to be fingers closed on her head, but something that he hadn't expected happened—they didn't grab a head. Instead, he found himself holding something and he had no idea what it was, and his confusion made him stop cold for a full second.

Which was just enough time for Ray to hurry Ramsey through the door while at the same time lashing out as a reflex action at the beast that was suddenly standing next to him. The blow wasn't a strong one but it was direct, landing squarely on the creature's nose. Ray didn't waste any time at all finding out the effect of the punch—he followed Ramsey into the house and Lopez slammed the door shut just as the creature let out a loud, long, blood-freezing scream.

"I didn't hit him that hard," Ray said to the room in general as he caught his breath. "The thing must be more pissed that he didn't get to kill someone."

Ramsey looked around herself at the other people in the room, and then suddenly her eyes widened as she seemed to realize just how close the call had been for her. "Oh, my," she said, and Lopez reached out and caught her as she fainted.

Thirty-eight
Pondering

Lopez felt shivers run up and down her spine at the howling that was coming from outside. Either those things were becoming bolder, she thought, or the creatures hadn't had any idea that there might be someone else behind the door. In the first case, the people in the house might be facing a pretty rough time of it; in the latter case, they might benefit from the stupidity of the Nogglz. They all had heard the scream of the first one, and everyone's imagination had supplied a different reason for the scream—frustration, anger, pain. But when the other two had caught up with the first one, they had added howls of their own. They seemed to be like dogs who picked up on other dogs' howling, just because.

They didn't stay in one place and howl, though. Almost immediately, there had been footsteps on the roof, and it sounded like the other two had each run to separate sides of the house. Suddenly, the howling stopped. There was nothing but silence.

"Everyone just stay calm," Lopez said firmly. She felt pretty confident in their plans and their preparations—since she and Henry had returned from their "patrol," they had been productive. They had found out that any attack was likely to come through the windows, so they had done everything they could to minimize the chances of that. Two of Taylor's rooms were completely shut off, and they had made a quick trip out to her garage in back to bring in some of the spare lumber that her husband had accumulated over the years. Taylor was a good sport about letting them drive nails into the door and window frames ("Nail holes in the frames or being torn limb to limb—hard choice," she had said philosophically), and they had been able to reinforce all of the windows in the rooms they were occupying.

Lopez looked around the room. Jackson held a shotgun and Henry had a pistol. She herself was carrying the shotgun from her cruiser and her sidearm. Ray also had a shotgun and a pistol. Lopez had gone out of her way to remind everyone not to start shooting indiscriminately at the first sign of trouble. What they didn't need was for a bunch of elderly men to try to recapture their glory days or earn bragging rights by bagging a monster. She didn't get the feeling that Jackson or Henry were that type of elderly men, but one never knew.

What she didn't like was the fact that their position was purely defensive, but there was truly nothing they could do about that. She looked at her watch: 10:30. Still a lot of night left, still a lot of dark. And the dark was incredibly unforgiving of mistakes, especially when your enemy seemed to have built-in night vision.

She was glad of one thing: Ray and Jackson had just been getting ready to go out on another patrol when they had heard the woman's calls, and she couldn't help but think that they wouldn't have come back.

But where had the Nogglz been?

As if reading his mind, Ray caught her eye from across the room. "So where do you think these things were all that time?"

"I don't know," she replied. "Inside someone's house somewhere, maybe."

"I don't think so, trooper," Jackson said, still listening intently while he spoke. "Hey, can I call you something other than 'trooper'? That's been kind of bothering me all evening."

"You can call me Alex if you'd like. It's short for Alejandra."

"Good. Alex it is. Well, Alex, my guess is they get tired. If they've been doing a lot of attacking and killing the last twenty-four hours after sixty years of being stuck in a mine, they're going to tire out. And probably get hungry, too. Have they been eating their victims?"

Lopez glanced at Jackson with distaste, but then realized that the question probably was an important one. "We couldn't tell, really," she said. "At least with Sarah, things were all over the place—it was impossible to tell. The one that got Fogel didn't have time for anything like that. And we don't know what happened to Juan. Or Larry."

"Or Brad and Brian," Ray added.

"Or those two," Lopez said. "They're probably still down there in the mine, dead or alive. Maybe they're feeding off them."

"Alex," Taylor said with repulsion. "I know we've all been thinking that, but let's not say it, okay?"

Lopez shrugged. "Will do."

"No matter what," Jackson said, "there's got to be some sort of food source down there that's kept them alive all these years. Food and water. Maybe they had to go back down to feed. Maybe their mothers forgot to pack a lunch for them to take along."

Lopez was silent for a few moments. "If that's the case," she said quietly, "I'm starting to get the feeling that we should be across the street, guarding the entrance to that mine. If they have to go back and forth, they'd have to go by us both ways."

"Nope," Ray said. "You're forgetting the one that got your partner. He came from the back yard somewhere."

She sighed. "You're right. So it wouldn't have been that easy."

"Not at all."

She raised her eyes to the ceiling, realizing that they hadn't heard a sound for several minutes. "Where do you think they've gotten to?" she asked no one in particular.

Ray shook his head slowly, looking around at the walls and the ceiling as he tried to hear something from outside.

"I've got no idea," Jackson said quietly. "To someone else's house, maybe? Or maybe they're outside this house, strategizing, figuring out the best way to attack."

Taylor chuckled. "From the sounds of it, those boys weren't bright enough to strategize when they were human. And it doesn't sound like they've actually grown smarter over the last sixty years."

"Maybe not smarter," Ray said, "but they certainly are meaner. And there's nothing more difficult to fight than something that's just pure mean, that doesn't have any sort of conscience or compassion. Especially when they're stronger and faster than you."

They all were startled by a loud noise that came from the floor next to the couch. Both Ray and Lopez pointed their weapons immediately in that direction, but Jackson just laughed softly.

"Don't worry yourselves," he said. "That's just Maurice. The man can sleep anywhere, anytime, believe me."

"That was a snore?" Ray asked, lowering his pistol. "Hell, I wouldn't be able to sleep right now if you gave me the most comfortable bed in the world and a pair of silk pajamas."

Lopez looked at him quizzically. "Silk pajamas?" she asked.

Ray laughed sheepishly. "They're amazing. The most comfortable things in the world. You ought to try 'em sometime."

Taylor laughed. "Forgive me if I find it hard to picture you in silk pajamas, deputy. That's just not a picture that wants to stay in my brain, if you know what I mean."

"Look at us here," Jackson said calmly. "People are dying, there's things out there that could kill us in a heartbeat, and we're talking about the deputy in silk jammies."

Taylor looked puzzled. "What else are we going to talk about, Jackson?"

"Maybe about how quiet those things are being," Jackson replied. "We haven't heard a sound for a few minutes now."

"It's kind of creepy," Lopez said. "Disconcerting. I don't know what to make of it."

"Do we still go out on patrol?" Ray asked.

"Let's hold off on that for a while," Lopez said. "Let's let things calm down a bit. It sounded like the one that you hit was pretty pissed off."

"That works for me," Ray said, a bit relieved.

"Now that it's a bit quieter," Taylor said, "let's get Ramsey settled in, shall we?" Ramsey was lying on the couch, where they had put her when she fainted, and she was just coming around. She looked around at everyone, obviously unsure of where she was for several moments. When her location sank in, she looked over at Ray, who was standing in the doorway between the rooms.

"Thank you, deputy," she said. "I don't think I would have made it in here without your help."

"You're welcome," Ray said. "I don't think either of us would have made it in here if that thing hadn't gotten your wig like it did. Confused the hell out of it just long enough for us to get in that door."

"We got lucky," Ramsey said, running a hand over the thin gray hair that covered her head. "I don't know what made me put that thing on."

"I don't know either," Ray said. "But let's hope that luck holds."

Thirty-nine
Bear

For many, many years, Naugle's boys hadn't had any stimulation of their minds at all. Living in the darkness, addicted to their only source of food, existing from day to day with nothing to do but explore caverns and more rocks, they had stopped using their minds completely. Some of their degeneration had to happen because of their diet, but they knew nothing about chemicals and vitamins and other things that had strong effects on their bodies' systems. Their memories had faded, their ability to choose between two options had died, the gift of being able to plan their next moves had completely faded. When they had come out into Sarah's basement twenty-four hours earlier, they had been completely mindless creatures that had as their goal the one passion that had remained entrenched in whatever was left of their psyches: vengeance. Their only driving force was the need to kill, and their first kill had not satisfied that lust.

This new night, though, had started a process that they didn't notice themselves. Even had they noticed it, they would not be able to understand it. Being up above again, seeing the houses in the town—most of which had actually existed while they were alive and walking the streets themselves—had started to stir memories from deep inside of them. They weren't conscious memories, but feelings of familiarity, feelings even of belonging. They were far too far gone to be able to consider the possibility that they had something in common with the people of the town, but they noticed that the feelings they had this third time up and out in the open were slightly different—the first time running through town and smashing into houses had happened in a place they knew nothing about. This time, though, they felt that they knew the town just as they knew the depths of the caverns, the routes that led deeper and deeper underground, the places where their food grew, the places where they could find ample water.

The frustration with the wig had made the one who missed the kill more infuriated than he had been before. While his first temptation had been to hurl himself through the window of the house and start killing, something had stopped him from doing so. He stood, howling and staring, for many long seconds, then with a prodigious leap he caught hold of the edge of the roof and swung himself up onto it, looking for any way into the house he could find. There was none, just the pipes that were smaller than he was, and he quickly jumped from the roof and ran from the yard, the others quickly on his heels.

The houses were no longer strange objects to them—they recognized them as places where they could find people. Whereas before they looked only for light, now they looked even at the houses that had no lights shining as possible targets for attack. They weren't actually regaining their ability to think, but they were becoming able to recognize on a very basic level just what things might be.

They scurried through the yard behind Taylor's and across the second street, and all three noticed at the same time the lights that were on in a house to their left. In the complete darkness of a town without streetlights far from any other town, even the dimmest light was easy to see. They veered left almost as one, slowing down a slight bit as they approached the house. One thing that they were beginning to feel was that there was no need to hurry, though the experience they had just had with the woman who had escaped them seemed to contradict that feeling.

There was just one window with light in it that they could see, in the back corner of the house. It was a tiny home, a rectangle that couldn't have been more than 40 feet long and 20 wide. It was also very old, and there had been a day when they would have recognized it as a typical miner's house, built by the company and designed for bare subsistence living—no extras and no luxuries, just four rooms to do with as you please, plus a small bathroom that had been added on when the town had added running water. At one time, entire streets had been filled with identical houses all the way down—quick and easy and cheap to build, made for a populace that wasn't at all discriminating, people who were glad to have a roof over their heads.

The frustrated one approached the door, something in his mind reminding him that this was how the old woman he had almost killed had gone into the house. It wasn't a window and it didn't need to be broken, but it looked just like the rest of the wall to him, just different. He reached out and touched the knob, and he pushed and then he pulled with no result at all. Seeing a door open told him nothing about knobs and twisting, so even had the door been unlocked, the knob would have done him no good.

He looked over to the others, who were squatting down, watching him, unsure of what he was doing. They were starting to get a bit impatient, because they felt that the light meant that someone was in the house. They were anxious to get back to their sole purpose in being there. With a snarl, he took a few steps back and then launched himself into the window that looked out onto the street, his arms before him to shield him from the glass. The window shattered and even cut him in a few places, but he felt no pain—he hadn't felt any pain for many years. He landed on all fours in the middle of what looked to be a living room, and he heard the thuds as his companions landed on the floor near him.

He didn't feel the way that he had felt before—he now felt compelled to look around himself, to see the things that surrounded him. There was no thought involved with the looking, but the compulsion was there. This was something to which he was connected, like the chamber with the moss on the walls and the hole in the rubble through which they had first left the caverns after decades. There was nothing but a small couch, an end table with a lamp, a coffee table, and a small TV on a table in the room, plus some sort of picture on the wall behind the couch, but these things he needed to look at, to actually see now instead of just rushing by and searching for their next prey.

There was no way for him to know that sixty years earlier, this had been his house, his home that he had shared with his wife and daughter. They were long gone and over the years many different people had lived here, but that fact didn't change his ties with the place.

So he looked, and he saw. And then he knocked the television set from the table, noticing that the sound of the breaking tube was a good sound, one that gave him just a touch of pleasure. He knocked over the coffee table, but that sound did nothing for him. The lamp breaking made him feel good also, but ripping the cushions of the couch had no effect.

Though he had no idea what was happening, he was once more learning, once more starting to feel and to experience. The decades in the dark had taken away almost everything he knew and thought he knew, but it wasn't all gone. Some of it was coming back.

In the meantime, his companions had searched the house and found an older man in his bed in the bedroom. Chuck Ramirez had been napping when Ray had come by his house earlier, and when he slept, there was no waking him. He slept often in the day, preferring to be up at night when there were better TV shows on. Chuck was almost eighty, and television was almost the total extent of his life any more. There wasn't much that he enjoyed doing, and there weren't too many people in town that he gave a damn about. At least, not enough of a damn to hang around talking about all sorts of bullshit with them. His TV was company enough, and since he didn't have any family left anywhere, he basically had no reason at all to leave CB and go somewhere else.

So they found him in his bed, where he had been trying to sleep because his satellite dish was getting no signal and there was nothing to watch. He hadn't been doing a very good job of sleeping because he had slept so much during the day, and he had sat up in fear when he heard his front window crash in. What the hell could that be? he wondered, instantly recalling stories of random deer leaping through people's plate glass windows before, but not daring to get up and go look. His fear had grown even more when he heard the footsteps in the other room, and he held the bedcovers close to his chin, wanting to hide beneath them as a little child would, but wanting to see what was in his home.

He screamed once when the other two found him. They leaped to the attack immediately, one jumping up on the bed and grabbing his head, breaking his neck quickly, while the other grabbed one of his arms and dragged him out of the bed, then ripped open his ample stomach with one vicious pass of his claws. The spilling of the blood and the entrails awakened the bloodlust in them even more strongly, and they went on a rampage after their first kill since coming back up, ripping the body into bits much as they had done to Sarah's body the night before.

The other, however, did not take part in the mutilation, even after he came to the door and watched the other two rip apart Chuck's body. Instead, he turned to the other room behind him and slowly walked into it. He found there Chuck's homage to his wife and his daughter, the room where he kept their belongings from so many years ago, from the days before Elisa had taken Sammy for a drive down to Pine, a trip that was supposed to take only a couple of hours, but that had become never-ending when her car had slid off the road and fallen into the river fifty feet below. Neither of them had had a chance, and he had kept the room as a monument to their memory. Now, so many years later, the colors of the pictures and the dolls and the stuffed animals and the clothing were all faded away, but he kept everything clean and in place anyway. They'll throw it away when I die, he always said. Until then, it's fine as it is.

The creature's attention was caught by a large object that sat on the bed—a teddy bear, something that he didn't recognize or comprehend, but that he felt, smiling at him. Another feeling came to him suddenly, and if he were able to understand it, he would have known that the first glimmer of a true memory, that of his own daughter who had owned just such a teddy bear herself, was welling up in him. He almost tried to retrieve the memory, but it was a futile effort. The memory had no chance to be realized as a memory, though it did affect his feelings very deeply. And instead of being focused only on revenge, all of a sudden he was overcome by a feeling of loss, too, a feeling that he couldn't figure out, but which held him in its grip nonetheless.

Suddenly his feeling of a need for vengeance grew stronger, grew huge inside of him, and he let out a savage growl and sped into the other room where the other two were finished with their cruelty. He looked at them both and then turned and ran back to the living room, jumping out the window and heading straight for the house next door.

Forty
Sniping

Frank was tired of sitting around and waiting. He had never been very good at either, and this night was driving him crazy. Thirty years in the Army hadn't prepared him well for retirement. Instead of being relieved to have a more relaxed lifestyle, Frank was one of those people who missed the activity, the always having something to do that usually came in the form of orders from someone else. Of course, once he made First Sergeant he was able to give many of those orders himself, but he hadn't liked the amount of time the job kept him behind his desk.

Right now he was wishing he had a night scope for his rifle, something that would allow him to see outside and pick off whatever the hell it was that was running around town. He wasn't sure if they were killing or not, like the deputy had told him they would be, but he knew they were there. He had heard the shots earlier in the night, and he had heard screams a couple of times. He sat quietly in the dark in his tiny attic, looking out the window that had been built in, probably to make it look like a two-story house years back when someone was trying to make money here, trying to sell houses and property but not finding enough suckers to buy in.

Frank had bought in later, but he wasn't a sucker about it. He had grown up in another mountain mining town, but that place had become a ski resort and summer playground for people with tons of money. That wasn't a crowd that he wanted to have anything to do with. When he was a kid, his mother used to tell him about Canyon Bluff, where she had grown up, and how much more isolated it was than Gunstock, which had started growing even when he had been young. He had been here a few times and decided to make it his home when he finally retired from the Army. His wife had passed on some five years earlier, so it was an easy decision to make to go someplace where he could be alone when he wanted to and get out in the woods when he wanted to.

He was one of the younger residents of CB, not quite sixty yet. He was living in a dying town, he knew, but that was fine with him as long as it lasted long enough for him to die there. He made his monthly trip down to Pine for his groceries, but that was pretty much the extent of his contact with the so-called civilized world anymore.

At the moment, his attention was focused down the street, where he thought he had seen movement in one of the windows of Chuck's house, the only window with lights on. This was the most frustrating part—there wasn't enough light anywhere else for him to see whether anyone—or anything—actually left the house once there was no more movement to be seen. The falling snow didn't help matters, no matter how light it was. And he had just seen a silhouette on the blinds as someone walked in front of the lamp—that could have been Chuck, for all he knew. He had been tempted to try to squeeze off a round anyway, but he knew that the shadows gave no clear indication of where the actual body was on the other side of the screen.

He wished more people kept lights on and blinds open at the same time. Then he might have been able to accomplish something. As it was, he was stuck there just watching, and that made him feel helpless—but at least he wasn't cowering over in Taylor's house just so that he wouldn't have to be alone. That would have been pretty pathetic, though he had to admit that he understood why the people who were there had decided to go. It was just a fact of life: not everyone was able to take care of themselves, and some people needed to be around others to feel safe. From the looks of things, the safety was more of an illusion than a reality.

Suddenly, he thought he saw another dark flash of movement on the lawn across the street, two houses down, next to Chuck's. He couldn't be sure, though, as the darkness was complete—there was no moonlight or starlight, and certainly there were no streetlights in CB. That was the yard of one of the abandoned houses, so those things wouldn't be finding much in there. It was possible, though, that they were coming towards the light in the house across the street, where Jackie and Hoss lived.

He knew that Hoss would be pretty well armed, but he also knew that Hoss couldn't see a damned thing even with his glasses on. And the only person more stubborn than his wife, Jackie, was old Hoss himself, so Frank wasn't surprised at all that the two of them had decided not to join up with the others and to ride the night out at home. He leaned forward and raised the window another twelve inches, to make more room for him to aim and shoot if he needed to. Then he raised his rifle from his lap to a ready position—the light in the living room was on, and the curtains were drawn—maybe he could watch their backs for them from here. He put his cheek against the stock, but didn't look down the sights yet—he needed to have as broad a view as he could.

As hard as he looked, though, he still couldn't see anything going on. He kept his eyes trained on the area around Hoss' window, half-expecting at any minute to see some form silhouetted against the light as it looked into the house. He didn't expect to have much time to squeeze off a shot, so he had to be ready to fire as soon as he had a target.

Time seemed to stand still, and his breathing was becoming difficult, as he was alternately holding his breath for the possible shot and then breathing deeply to recover. The silence was intense. It seemed as if there was nothing alive and moving in the town at all; even with the window open, he could hear none of the tell-tale signs of life that one normally hears in areas where people are living. He could hear his own breathing only, and he would have sworn that he could hear his own heartbeat as a pulse in his ears.

"Okay, you assholes," he said quietly, more to simply break the silence than to express any real thought, "it's time for you to show yourselves and let me get a shot off."

But Frank's logic was flawed when he thought that the lights were the most important target for the creatures. He had made a serious mistake when he raised the window before knowing just where his enemy was—all three were indeed on the lawn across the street, and they had been about to burst through the lighted window. But then they were suddenly more attracted to the sound of the window opening and the feeling that where there was sound, there was someone. When one looked up at the window from which the sound had emanated, it was able to see the rifle barrel pointing out of the window. It didn't know what it was, but it felt that it meant danger and it wanted to face that danger head-on.

So Frank sat for three more minutes after telling the Nogglz to show themselves, three minutes of tension and the beginning of worry as the thought that something was going wrong with his plan started to nag at him. Where were they? He knew that if they had been going for the light, they would have been there already. Just when he decided to close the window and move downstairs, he heard the slightest of creaks from the roof above him. He only had time to look up in the direction of the sound when the window before him filled with a form that came from above and landed on the roof in front of the dormer, grabbing the barrel of his rifle and causing him to fire off a round as his finger slipped from the trigger guard to the trigger. The shot flew harmlessly across the street and buried itself in Hoss' lawn, a fact that did Frank no good at all. The rifle was ripped from his hands and tossed down to his lawn just as a second form jumped down and immediately crashed through the window and onto Frank before he had a chance to move from his chair. Frank didn't last long as his throat was ripped out savagely, then his neck broken as the creature twisted his head viciously as if it were trying to pull it off.

* * * *

Almost immediately, the first creature was inside as well, tearing at Frank's body with inconceivable fury, but the rage didn't last long at all—once they realized that there was no life in the corpse any more, they stopped what they were doing. They turned slowly to look at the third one, who still stood on the roof before the window, looking in at the gruesome havoc that his companions had perpetrated.

Something was trying to make its way into his mind, something about having come up quietly on his prey, something about having an advantage in the darkness, something about strength versus weakness. But it wouldn't stick with him, so eventually he simply turned his head back to the light toward which they had been moving originally. With a mighty leap he jumped to the ground, followed closely by the other two. They weren't moving in a hurry. The urgency behind their revenge was fading, so it didn't seem to be wasting time when one of them stopped to pick up the rifle that had been flung to the lawn minutes earlier.

It was a curious thing—it was cold and hard and strong, and it was familiar. He ran his claws over the wooden stock, feeling the smoothness of the wood, and then put what once had been a finger on the trigger. It was unfortunate that one of his companions chose that moment to grab the barrel and pull it closer to his eye in order to be able to look into the hole more closely. When he pulled, the other's finger pulled on the trigger and the resulting blast from the semiautomatic rifle ripped through his companion's eye and blew a large piece out of the back of his head. The body flew backwards several feet and landed hard on the thin layer of snow.

The one holding the weapon jumped at the sound of the blast, the strength of the recoil, and the sight of the flame that leapt from the barrel of the weapon. He held on to the weapon, though, and sniffed at the smell of spent gunpowder, then dropped it on the ground. It was still dangerous. He went over to his companion who lay on the ground and kicked him, but there was no response at all. He looked to the other one, who was looking at the light in the window of the house on the other side of the street, and the two of them started quickly across the street.

Their dead companion was already gone from their minds.

They were already beginning to feel tired and weak, and they were beginning to feel the call of the cave.

Forty-one
Sins of the Fathers

Taylor jumped a bit at the sound of the gunshot. She glanced at the clock on the wall—it was only twelve-thirty, and there was still plenty of night left before them. Her eyes met Jackson's, and she saw in his eyes the same questions that she had herself.

"I never can tell if a shot is a good thing or a bad thing," she said aloud.

"Well, we can hope," Jackson said, "but given that we know there are at least five of those things and we've heard just single shots, I'm not so sure that they're a good sign at all. Now when we start hearing someone going at 'em on full auto, then there might be a good chance that they're out there making a difference."

"Good thing this is amnesty night, Jackson," Ray said. "We don't want to be hearing about people walking around with fully automatic weapons."

Jackson smiled. "Come on, deputy," he said lightly. "That's just a figure of speech. You know that."

"Of course I know that," Ray replied.

Taylor was starting to feel the weight of the many hours that she had been without sleep. "I wish there was something we could do about those damned things. They were hateful when they were Naugle's boys, and they're even worse now as creatures from the depths of the earth," she said, sounding exasperated. "I wish we could just go out there and blow those things away."

Ray shook his head. "I wish we could, too, Taylor, but it's not going to happen without a whole lot more resources. We'd need light, plenty of it. Given the fact that we've got very little of it, we're pretty limited in what we can do. And guns or no, if we can't see out there, they'd be able to pick us off at will in the dark. Hell, even with the headlamps and the flashlights, you can only see in one direction at a time, which does you no good if something comes sneaking up on you from behind or from the side."

"Actually, that brings up a pretty interesting question," Henry said. "I've always been under the impression that if we were deprived of light for long periods of time, we'd actually lose our sight, not have it get better."

Nobody replied immediately. Finally, Taylor broke the silence.

"And?" she asked.

Henry shrugged. "Just thinking out loud, mostly. I'm wondering if there's some sort of light source in that mine."

"You mean like in their rec room where they play pool all evening?" Jackson asked.

"Or the lamps in their living room. Who knows? It's just a thought," Henry replied. "I'm just wondering what kind of creatures we're actually dealing with here."

"I don't know," Taylor shook her head sadly. "I just know that I've lived here sixty years without anything really happening. Everything that's changed here has changed slowly—people leaving, the school closing, all of us getting older. I've walked these streets almost every day for six decades, and now just like that it's all different. There's almost nobody here younger than fifty, and none of these people deserve to be dying the way that they must be dying."

"The sins of our fathers," Jackson said quietly. "The people who are here today are paying for something that happened when we were too damned young to have anything to do with it, if we were even born at all. Hell, Sarah was just a little girl when those boys were trapped down there, and she was the first one to get killed."

"It isn't fair at all, if you ask me," Lopez said. "Not that fair has anything to do with this kind of thing."

"'Fair' is a relative term, that's for sure," Jackson replied. "There are plenty of people who were more than happy to see those bastards trapped down there, and most of 'em knew what had happened to them even if they said they didn't."

"Whether anyone knew about it or not," Rita said, "doesn't mean that there was anything that anyone could actually do about it. What could they do—go down and clear out the mine shaft of the rubble? Not with Naugle still on the job. And by the time he was gone, there wasn't a soul here who would've thought that those men were still alive down there. Would you have thought that they could have survived even six months in that mine?"

Jackson shook his head. "Not for a second. But whether it's fair or not, it's happening, isn't it? And just like there wasn't anything anyone could do back then, it looks like there isn't a thing for us to do about it now, either."

"Not 'til first light, anyway," Lopez said. "We definitely can't go on any sort of offensive until we have some light." She looked over at Ray. "You gonna make it, deputy?" she asked.

Ray looked up quickly, surprised that she had addressed him. His eyes had been closing of their own volition in spite of his determination to stay awake. He grinned sheepishly. "Sorry about that. They're closing on their own. Just came over me all of a sudden."

"If you want," Lopez said. "Get a bit of sleep. We're good for now, until our next patrol."

Ray looked groggy, but he stood up and started to stretch. "No, I'm fine. Just too much sitting and not enough doing."

"It's funny how when we were young like you we thought we could go forever without sleeping," Rita said, "but it isn't until we get much older that we actually are able to go for a long time without it. Would you like some more coffee, Alex?" she asked Lopez, who shook her head.

"No, thank you," she said. She pushed her cup away from her. "I've already done my bladder a huge disservice by drinking as much as I have. It does taste good, though—just like campfire coffee used to taste. I haven't tasted it perked over a flame for years."

"It is good, isn't it?" Jackson agreed. "Every time I taste it like this, I wonder why we settle for that drip stuff all the time. Just 'cause it's easier doesn't mean it's better."

"It's like most things in life, Jackson," Taylor said. "We find quicker ways to do things and then we just do them because everyone else does. I guess we think that we're going to find something better to do with all that time we save. But we don't, do we?"

"What's that? Find something better to do?"

"Exactly. Because there really aren't too many things that are better to do. Just different. Hell, most of the people I've ever known save their five minutes here and ten minutes there just so that they can watch an hour more TV every day."

Jackson nodded. "Yeah, I do miss the old days in a lot of ways. I used to help my mom in the kitchen—it'd take her two hours to make dinner sometimes. And she was fine with that. It was something she really liked doing. Most of the time. And she was really good at it."

Lopez got up and stretched. "Yeah, but then all the food was eaten and all her work was for nothing. Now she can do the same work in a quarter of the time."

"And what, though?" Taylor asked. "My mother was the same way. It didn't matter what happened to the food she made—she loved the process, she loved the artistry. And she took a lot of pride in the food she made. Maybe that was the most important thing, that she had something that she could be proud of because nobody else in the whole world could make what she made in just the same way."

"You got that right," Jackson added. "Pride is pretty much dead these days. Not too many people take pride in the jobs they do. They take pride in how quickly they get them done, no matter how shoddy the work is. I had a plumber up a couple of years ago, and he replaced some pipes in my basement. The son of a bitch was pretty pleased with himself that he did the job so quick, but he was back up here six weeks later fixing the crap that he'd screwed up on."

Lopez laughed. "You guys crack me up," she said. "You've got these crazed beasts outside killing your neighbors and you're sitting here completely helpless, and you take the opportunity to philosophize about life and living. I find it downright amazing that you're able to take this all so calmly."

"But what's one to do, Alex?" Taylor asked. "There truly is nothing that we can do about the situation that we haven't done already. If this were a normal night, we'd all be sleeping right about now, wouldn't we? There really isn't much of anything else that we can do while we play this damned waiting game, is there?"

"Of course not, Taylor. Like I said, I think it's great. You could sit here worrying and whining and feeling sorry for yourselves and being scared, but instead you're finding other things to talk about."

Jackson stood. "Well, Alex, when you get to be our age, you get to realize that worrying and being afraid are almost always wastes of time. Now if you'll excuse me, I'm going to go get rid of some of this coffee."

"And could you check on the candle in there, Jackson?" Taylor asked. "I've got another one if it's burned down too far."

"Will do," Jackson said, and he turned and left. Lopez admired the way that the man still carried himself with pride and dignity at his age.

Lopez turned to Taylor. "So what do you think is going to become of this town now, Taylor?" she asked.

Taylor sighed. "That's a very good question. I'm afraid I don't have an answer. Most of the folk here have stayed because of their ties to the past—this is where they grew up, this is where they have the wonderful memories of their childhood, even if those memories are a bit rosy-colored. Or they own their houses and there's no way that they'll ever be able to sell them, so they're stuck here. Most of us thought that when they closed the school down in the eighties that that was going to be the death knell. For the most part, it was. That was when all the people with children pretty much had to leave if they wanted their kids to be able to go to school. That left the older folk, and the town's been dying ever since. It's been more than ten years."

"Do you think you'll be able to stay here after all this?"

Taylor laughed without much humor. "I've got enough work to do just dealing with the here and now," she said. "I haven't thought one bit about tomorrow or the next day. I guess we'll see what those days bring, and then deal with them on their terms."

"I have to say," Lopez said, "You all are pretty hardy people. Most folks would've given up long ago, but you're pretty tenacious."

Taylor smiled. "Tenacious, Alex? Or afraid? I think the line between those two is a pretty dim one, at best."

"I don't get what you mean. You guys are taking this all in stride today—you aren't freaking out or anything. Nobody seems to be particularly afraid of what's going on."

"That's a different kind of fear. The threat here is the threat of being attacked, of maybe being killed. That's much different than the fear of change, the fear of making new beginnings in new places at our age. Personally, I'd much rather face a dozen Nogglz than move into a retirement home somewhere that I'm unfamiliar with. A new start scares the hell out of me; dying doesn't scare me all that much."

"I'll second that," Jackson said, returning to the room. "Your candle's fine in there, Taylor—at least another hour. But Taylor's right, Alex. Change is much more frightening to most people than anything else. How else can you explain a bunch of old people like us living out here in the middle of nowhere, miles from the nearest services? I've been lucky enough to live a pretty long life, and I want to end it right here in the place I've lived most of it. That's just the way it is. I don't want to go anywhere else and start all over again. Not at my age. Makes no sense."

Lopez nodded, thinking. "But I still admire you all," she said after a moment. "Not everyone could do what you guys do."

"Most people wouldn't want to," Taylor said with a laugh. "Hey," she added, "anyone up for a game of poker?"

* * * *

Emily sat in the corner now, curled up with a notebook on one of Taylor's recliners. She felt as if she hadn't said a word in hours, and that was probably true. But she had never listened so much in all her life, and she had never written down as many notes as she had this night. Every now and then Jackson or Taylor or Henry would look over at her to see how she was doing. They seemed to know what she was up to, and they were content to let her be, to let her write. After all, they were the ones whose words and ideas she was recording for posterity.

Emily was amazed at the power of listening. When she wasn't a part of the conversation, she heard so much more. When she gave up thinking what she wanted to say, she heard more of the nuances of the voices, more of the inflections on certain words that gave them different meanings.

She only hoped that somehow she would be able to do justice to what she was hearing on this long, cold, dreary night.

Forty-two
Awakening

Brian woke up with the worst headache he had ever had, even worse than the one he had after falling out of the tree when he was out hunting with Brad. He hurt, but he didn't dare move in case whatever it was that had hit him was still around. After a few moments, he recognized that the pain was coming from one particular place where he had been hit. When he tried to open his eyes he found out that only his left eye would open. In the dim green glow of whatever was on the walls, he tried to see all that he could about his surroundings.

Unfortunately, he had been knocked to the floor facing the wall, so all that he could see was a rock wall and the glowing stuff that looked like moss to him. His dad had told them about stuff like that that he had seen in caves before, glow-in-the-dark moss that lit up whole rooms. They had believed him completely when they were little, but as they had grown up they had become a bit less trusting of their father's stories. I'll be damned, Brian said to himself. You were right, dad.

He wished that he knew whether Brad was conscious, too, as that would make things much more simple for him. He had pretty much always followed Brad's lead since they were kids, even though Brad was younger by a year. In a way he had been lucky that he had gotten a brother who was a born leader, for it made Brian's life easier all the way around. Brian simply didn't like being the decision-maker, the person who came up with ideas and who decided what to do and when to go where. He was definitely the best shot, though. Right now he found himself almost paralyzed with indecision—should he move so that he could see around himself, possibly alerting his attacker to the fact that he was conscious, or should he lay there still and silent until Brad was conscious, too?

But what if Brad needed his help? What if he was hurt badly and couldn't move?

But what could he do even if that were the case?

Brian decided first of all to take stock of what he still had with him. He had no idea where his flashlight had ended up, but since there was no light to be seen it must have been broken. But both he and Brad had brought small penlights with them, stuck in their pockets as a back-up. He moved his right arm so slowly that it seemed to take five minutes to get his right hand from the floor of the cave to his right cargo pocket, and he felt the reassuring shape of the penlight through the fabric. He felt encouraged that his movement hadn't brought any unwanted attention his way, so he weighed the option of rolling over or propping himself up a bit so that he could turn his head the other way. He decided on the latter, as it seemed to require the least movement. Besides, he had no idea what he might roll into behind himself if he did roll over.

Since his hand was already there, he decided to pull the penlight from the pocket, a feat that took a good two minutes. He was sure Brad would compliment him on his stealth, for he was moving his hand and arm so agonizingly slowly that the motion almost couldn't be detected unless someone were looking very closely. He thought of Brad as he did so, and the times he had seen his brother move so very slowly when an animal was in range. It was almost as if Brad were staying still, but the gun that was being held at his side somehow made it up to his shoulder, pointing confidently at the animal that Brad wanted to kill.

Once the light was in his hand, he pulled his arm closer to his body, moving his hand until it was right under his head, where he would have to push down in order to prop himself up. This maneuver, too, took several minutes to execute. Once his hand was in place he pushed down upon the ground, lifting his head several inches above it so that he had enough space to turn it easily and look in the other direction. He was moving slightly faster now, spurred on by the confidence that was rising in him due to the lack of sounds and the lack of response to his movements so far.

As soon as he lifted his shoulders high enough and turned his head, he dropped back to the ground so that he could pretend he was still unconscious if necessary. He could see almost the entire chamber in the dim glow from the moss now, including Brad's inert form just a few feet away from him. Other than Brad, though, he couldn't make out any other forms—he remembered that there was someone in the stream, but his vision of that area was blocked by Brad's body. The lack of any living forms gave him confidence, and he decided to find out if Brad was awake.

"Brad!" he hissed, and even his whisper sounded loud in the chamber, so loud that he was sure that Brad would have heard him if he were conscious. He waited several long moments for some sort of response, but when there was none he repeated his effort. "Brad!" he whispered a slight bit louder, "Are you awake?"

Brad was either still unconscious or faking it, so Brian knew that he would have to decide what to do on his own. He figured Brad must still be out, otherwise he would have told him to shut up. Or he might not have told him to shut up if he was afraid that something would hear him. . . Brian wasn't sure what to think.

He lifted his head the slightest bit so that he could get a good look around the chamber. It was eerie and kind of cool, he thought, the way that the moss was glowing everywhere. And there were these little spots of glowing light in the moss itself, brighter than the moss, that he couldn't figure out. Even in the glow it was extremely dark, though his eyes had adjusted to the darkness by then. He could see as well as he was ever going to be able to see down there.

But he saw nothing other than Brad. No other bodies, no dark forms, nothing moving at all. He listened as carefully as he could, but he heard nothing, either. No footsteps, no creepy sounds, no sounds of something slithering in the darkness. He had a feeling that they were alone, that there was no one and nothing else with them in the chamber, so he slowly rose up to one knee and kind of scooted over to Brad.

"Hey, bro," he said quietly, shaking Brad by the shoulder. He didn't dare use the light yet—he wanted to save the battery until they really needed it. Brad didn't respond at all, and Brian grabbed his brother's wrist and checked for a pulse. He did have a heartbeat, which was obviously a good sign, but a heartbeat wouldn't do him any good unless he could wake up.

Brian looked around again, taking in the entire chamber now that his head wasn't on ground level anymore. He saw the body over by the wall, lying in the water that he could just make out in the glow of the moss. Now that he saw it, he also noticed the very slight trickling sound that the water made as it flowed along the wall of the chamber.

He scooted over to the body, using the penlight for just a second to find out who it was.

"Bravo, Juan!" he muttered. "You got here first. You must be one cold son of a bitch, though." He stuck his fingers into the water to confirm his suspicion—the water was frigid, and it wouldn't have surprised him a bit if Juan had already frozen to death. And if he hadn't frozen, whatever had caused that wound on the side of his face definitely could have killed him, too. He grabbed Juan's wrist, and for several seconds he wasn't able to make out any sort of pulse. That didn't surprise him, though—his dad had taught them all about how the heart slows down when bodies are cold. It was something they needed to know because of all the winter hunting they did—if someone got hurt, you sure wouldn't want to leave them out in the woods just because you thought they were dead because you didn't feel a pulse first thing.

Brian stuck with it, and several seconds later he was rewarded with just the slightest sign of a heartbeat. Then he felt it steadily, weakly, and he knew that Juan was alive. He grabbed the pants leg that was nearest and pulled the leg out of the water, then pulled the other leg out, then grabbed hold of Juan's belt and pulled his hips out of the water. Finally, he grabbed the collar of his coat and Juan's hair to hold his head up, and pulled the rest of the body out of the water. "Good thing you're small, man," he muttered. "If you was Jake, I would've left you in there."

"Brian, is that you?" Brad said quietly from behind him. "What the hell happened?"

"Got cold-cocked, bro," Brian said, turning quickly and scurrying to his brother's side. "You okay, man?"

"Feel like my head got bashed in," Brad said. "And I must've landed on my arm bad, 'cause it hurts like hell, too. What the hell hit us?" He forced himself to sit up, but he wasn't able to use his left arm to help himself.

"Don't know," Brian whispered, "but we better keep it down. I don't know where those things got off to. They must live down here. Could be back any minute."

"Well, I don't aim to wait for 'em," Brad said. "We gotta get our asses out of here."

"I hear you there, but what should we do about Juan? That's him over there, and I don't think he's going to be waking up for a while."

Brad looked at the dark form on the floor for several long moments. "We gotta leave him, then, and come back for him once we get out of here."

"We can't just leave him!" Brian protested.

"You gonna carry him all the way out of here?" Brad demanded weakly. "Hell, we don't even know how to get out of here, when it comes right down to it, do we now? How we gonna find the way if we're dragging around Juan all unconscious-like?"

Brian thought for several long moments. "You're right. It just don't seem right, though, to leave him here."

"It seems right if it's the only choice we have, don't it?" Brad forced himself to his feet, and reached into his right cargo pocket, where he found a penlight identical to Brian's. "Now we ain't got a lot of light this way, so first thing we gotta do is see if our flashlights and guns are still around anywhere. I think we were back this way when we got attacked."

"Brad, do you remember those things eating? Were those the Nogglz? Those guys that were trapped down here like a hundred years ago?"

"I don't know what else they could be, man. Somehow that moss crap must keep them alive. It sure don't look like it fills 'em up good, though. I sure as hell wouldn't eat that shit."

"But how can they be so strong, if they're so damned skinny?"

"I got no idea, bro." He was now on the other side of the chamber, shining his light over the floor. "But I can tell you that our flashlights and our guns are gone as hell. All I've got is the one in my ankle holster, and I don't know if it can kill these things. So I'd say let's just get the hell out of here and come back with some big guns. Some fuckin' bazookas if we can get our hands on 'em."

"I'm all for that first part, gettin' out of here, but you can come back on your own, as far as I'm concerned." Brad didn't answer. "You know which way we're going?" Brian added.

"Up," was all Brad said, and he started walking, his left arm hanging limply at his side. Brian followed him closely so that they could both see from the one penlight—there was no use using both of them if they didn't need to.

Forty-three
Diminishing Returners

Immediately after leaving Frank's yard, the remaining pair killed Hoss and his wife. The couple had been asleep in bed and hadn't fully realized what was happening, so they were easy to kill, far too easy, and there was no gratification in killing them. If they could have thought, they might have considered the idea that they had spent their revenge and that they were now killing for the sake of killing simply because they didn't know of anything else to do up here. Or they might have attributed their lack of enthusiasm in their last kill to the exhaustion that they were feeling, the need that they had for their nutrients, the withdrawal symptoms that they were feeling from not having eaten enough of their food in the last twelve hours. Or perhaps they were just getting tired of killing, or their lack of passion might have had something to do with the fact that three of their companions were now dead, leaving only the two of them.

But all they could do was follow the impulse that drew them back to the mine, the need to eat, the need to rest.

They didn't bother going through Sarah's house this time, instead choosing to take the vent the other had shown them that led down into the mine shaft from the cliff behind her yard. The darkness of the shaft felt comfortable to them, felt known, felt right. As much as they had wanted to be above to take the revenge that they weren't even conscious of, it felt much better being below in the mine. They couldn't have known why, but the fact that they belonged here was important to them. They no longer belonged above with the houses and the streets and the people. They were creatures of the cavern now, and the closer they got to their feeding ground, the more relaxed they felt, the more energetic they became.

They moved more slowly this time. The caverns were familiar to them, but they simply didn't have the strength to speed through the passages as they were used to doing. They kept up their pace as much as they could, though, for they needed to feed, they needed to put more of the drug that kept them going into their systems.

If they had been paying more attention, they would have noticed Brad and Brian, who had heard them coming and had ducked into a recess in the wall near the passageway that led up. But they were focused only on moving forward, only on reaching their feeding ground. Brad and Brian hadn't covered much ground since they had left the feeding chamber some twenty minutes earlier, as they had taken several wrong turns and ended up moving in circles. They were lucky that they heard the Nogglz coming toward them, lucky that one of them had made a low growling sound as it was walking. They were heartened by two things: only two Nogglz walked by them in the dark, as far as they could tell, and the fact that the creatures were using this passage meant that they were finally on the right path.

When the Nogglz reached the feeding chamber, they stopped momentarily. Something was different, but they weren't sure what it was. There was a body on the ground, out of the water. Hadn't there been something else? Hadn't things been different when they had left the last time? But they couldn't remember things as they had been, so after a moment or two of confusion, they began to scrape the moss from the walls and to pull down the glowing worms that hung on the walls and put them into their mouths. They didn't need much, so they were done feeding rather soon. They felt their energy returning to them, and some of their enthusiasm for getting back up top and continuing their task.

Just as they finished eating, though, the Bastard returned to the chamber and found them there. He was immediately taken aback, for he did have a memory of how many of the others there had been. While he couldn't have assigned a name to the number five, he knew that the fact that only two of his companions were here meant that they were fewer, meant that he was in danger of losing all of the companionship that he had down in the cavern. He remembered the years of being alone in a vague, simplistic fashion, and he didn't want that solitude, that loneliness to return. And as he looked about the chamber, he noticed that something else was missing—there had been other bodies on the floor, but now there was only one. And it had moved.

He felt a sudden surge of loss, of desperation. And he didn't know what to do about it.

He walked into the chamber, and the other two bowed as he came closer. The two Nogglz knew that they had nothing near the strength of the Bastard. They hadn't even been the strongest of Naugle's Boys to begin with.

The Bastard looked first at the spots where the other two bodies had lain. He didn't have the capability to remember details about them, but he did feel the loss, and he did know that something had been there.

Then he went to the Nogglz and stood before them, looking them over as they cowered before him. None of them had voices to speak with or words to use if they could have spoken, but when the Bastard reached out and grabbed the second Nogglz by the arm and pulled him to stand next to the first, then moved to the empty space next to him and pointed to the ground, they understood what he wanted. They had no way to explain anything to him, though. And the memories of the others were very quickly becoming almost non-existent. They were only able to point upwards, to point to the surface where they had lost the other two.

There was no decision made, no thought processes involved—the Bastard simply turned away and left the chamber, heading out the way that the other two had come in, and they followed behind him. They moved silently and swiftly this time, and even though they had wanted to sleep, they knew that they were bound to follow him who was larger and stronger than they.

In just five minutes, they came up behind Brian and Brad, who didn't hear them coming at all. With two wicked backhand blows, the Bastard knocked them both unconscious, almost killing Brian and certainly causing a severe concussion, without even slowing or interrupting his stride. They would be there later, just as the other companions had been there so many decades before.

He didn't want to end up alone again, and he would not do so. If there was a threat on the surface that was killing his companions, then he would simply have to take care of that threat before it could take the other two.

When they reached the hole that the Nogglz had dug out of the rubble, the Bastard stopped suddenly and examined it. He had been up here many times before to sabotage their progress, but he had never passed through the opening. He looked at it with what could only be called distaste and he seemed to be pondering just what it meant; the truth was that a very basic idea had just began forming in his mind, an idea that would keep these other two with him when they got back.

Forty-four
Jackson

Ray and Jackson were in their coats and ready to head out into the darkest time of the night, the two-in-the-morning darkness that would let them see nothing at all if it weren't for their headlamps and flashlights. Each carried a shotgun, and each had a pistol in holstered on his belt. They had all decided that this was the appropriate way to be armed for the patrols.

They stood with Lopez looking down at the hand-drawn map on the coffee table in the living room.

"So one more time," Ray said, pointing at the map, "we're going to check the windows on all the occupied houses on this side of this street, and on this side of the next street over. I think it's still too risky to take the walkie-talkies. We don't want them hearing us if we can help it. We'll start from here and head east, then come back west on Oak, then back east on Main. You guys took twenty-five minutes. We shouldn't be any longer than that."

"Good luck out there," Lopez said. "It's too bad we can't wait four more hours until it get light."

Ray pulled back the blanket over the window and looked outside at the cold darkness, then shook his head. "We've got to do something here," he said. "There may be people out there who could use our help."

"All right then," Jackson said. "I'll follow you."

"And you have the extra batteries, deputy?" Taylor asked from the table where she still sat.

"I've got them, Taylor—thanks." He nodded at Lopez, then left; Jackson followed him and Lopez shut and locked the door behind them.

"They're out of their minds," Pauline said quietly, sounding weary. "That's the problem with being young—you've always got the idea that you've got to be doing something, even if being patient and waiting until daylight is the best possible thing you can do. Waiting is still doing something. Besides, Jackson isn't all that young."

"But waiting is just letting those things attack other people," Lopez protested. "We've got to do *something.*"

"Waiting can help them to stay alive so that they're still in a good condition to actually do something later when they have some daylight to work in. They aren't going to be able to do anything helpful at all if they're dead, now, are they?"

Lopez didn't answer for several moments, mostly because Pauline had said exactly what was on her mind, even if she didn't want to be thinking that way. "They're going to come back just fine," she finally said.

"This one's still intact," Ray said quietly, after he and Jackson had passed the house. "One down."

They moved through the yard to the house next door, since there was no fence there. This was Lyle's house, a small white structure that could only be called a fixer-upper. It looked white in the flashlight's beam, but it was hard to tell if that was truly its color. When they reached the side of the house Ray played the light over the windows, and they both saw at the same time that one of them was broken.

"Shit," Ray muttered, not sure what to do. Their plan had been to check which houses showed signs of being broken into, but he was now feeling the need to check inside the home to see if anyone was still alive inside.

Jackson was thinking the same way, for he said, "This is Lyle's place. Alex told us the window was broken when they were out here. Do we check inside, or do we stick to the plan?"

Ray hesitated, then he thought of Sarah's remains, the body parts that he had seen less than eighteen hours before, the death that had started this whole mess. If that's how Sarah ended up, he thought, then there isn't really much chance that anyone in here can be in better shape. But what if?

"Let's stick to the plan," he said quietly. He didn't share it with Jackson, but a sense of dread was creeping up on him, a sense that something was about to go terribly wrong. He chalked the feeling up to the fact that he had been awake and on edge for nearly twenty-four hours, and to the fact that he was cold and engulfed in the most intense darkness he had ever experienced. He felt that the beam of the headlamps were completely inadequate for the task at hand. They were especially ineffective through the falling snow. There could be a very real threat anywhere around them and the lights wouldn't allow them to see it until it was too late. But they were all that they had. He was beginning to doubt the wisdom of being outdoors, but here they were, and they needed to get going.

They headed for the house directly behind Lyle's house. This one looked completely quiet, and they found no broken windows as they checked it quickly.

Jackson, too, was feeling a sense of urgency. He felt as if he were being watched, as if something were very close to them, biding its time. He, too, attributed the feeling to his imagination, because he knew there was no rational explanation for any such feeling. They hadn't heard any noises, and they hadn't seen any sort of movement at all. Anything that he felt had to be due to his imagination.

"I don't think I've ever seen a night this dark," Ray muttered, half to himself. Whenever he turned his head and tried to see anything that wasn't in the beam of the headlamp, he saw nothing but the nearest snowflakes and the snowflakes behind them that grew progressively dimmer as the light weakened with distance.

"Welcome to what the night used to look like," Jackson said quietly. "Before we decided that we had to light up every square inch of everything, this is what things looked like."

"It sure puts us at a disadvantage," Ray said. "I can understand why people wanted to light the world up. It's scary this way."

Jackson chuckled. "Scarier when you've got a bunch of homicidal beasts roaming around town."

The next house was also clear. The next, though, had a broken front picture window.

"I'm not sure just what we're accomplishing here," Ray said suddenly. "Some sort of inventory, maybe, but I'm not sure what good—" He stopped suddenly, and Jackson understood that he had heard something. They both stood perfectly still, perfectly quiet. Ray turned his light off, and Jackson followed suit. They both heard footsteps on the lawn to the side of the house in front of them, slow, steady steps.

"Sounds like a deer," Jackson whispered, but Ray didn't reply. They both listened closely as the footsteps continued to move slowly towards the front of the house, and suddenly Ray turned his light back on, looking in the direction of the sound.

They both exhaled suddenly with relief. Jackson had been right—a young buck stood in the yard looking at the light, frozen in place.

"I'm glad you were right on that one," Ray said, relieved.

"Me, too," Jackson said. "I'm not right often, but I'm glad I was now. He's a young one. Look at those antlers. He's got quite a few years ahead of him."

Before they could become too relieved, though, the deer suddenly jumped high in the air and came down running, moving out of the beam of light. Something had spooked it, but neither Ray nor Jackson had heard anything at all.

Ray tried telling himself that they had spooked it, that it had just taken the buck a few moments to be properly afraid.

It didn't work, though—he didn't believe it.

Both of the men had their guns ready, but they weren't sure where to point them, if anywhere. They still hadn't heard or seen anything.

"I think it's about time to get back inside," Ray said. "I've got a really bad feeling about being out here."

"That's fine with me," Jackson replied, and they turned and started walking towards Taylor's house. Neither of them wanted to spend another moment outdoors.

They both stopped suddenly as the light from Ray's headlamp revealed what looked to be a pair of legs, but legs that were inconceivably thin, as if the skin covered not a bit of muscle. Both of them took in the basic details of the legs in the second or so that the light was still directed at them; Ray looked quickly at the face of a creature that neither of them ever could have conceived of, a monster that stood staring at them as if it were unsure what it should do.

The Bastard stood before them, taller than they were and somehow horrifying with its lack of essence, with its wiry form that made it look as if it must be dead, not somehow alive and walking around in the middle of the night. His eyes were the worst part, though—deep, dark and disturbing pools of nothingness, of inconceivable and incomprehensible pain. Its hands came up to shield its eyes from the light and they saw that they were more like claws than hands, small and strong with sharp thick nails at the ends.

"Oh, God," Jackson said. "Was that a man?"

They didn't know that this was the first time it had been out of the caverns in almost nine decades, that it wasn't quite sure what it should do—it would have been fine backing off and letting the people be, going back into the cavern and continuing to live down there. It had come up because it was afraid of losing its companions, but it was pretty sure now that rather than attack these humans, it should go about closing the hole that the others were using to get out.

In fact, it had just started to turn around so that it could go back underground when both Ray and Jackson shot at it simultaneously.

Because it had just started to turn, Ray's bullet hit it in the upper left arm, smashing the bone. Jackson's bullet missed the mark. The sound of the shots had made it jump with unbelievable speed, so that their second shots both passed through empty air, crossed the street and another yard and went through Taylor's yard before hitting her house. Ray's bullet lodged in the dirt in the window box on the side window, while Jackson's bullet crashed through the window and hit Eileen in the temple, instantly killing her as it lodged in her brain as she lay sleeping in Taylor's other recliner in her bedroom.

Their third and fourth shots passed harmlessly through the air as they tried unsuccessfully to follow the creature's jump. Ray fired a fifth and sixth shot, hitting nothing, but Jackson decided to save his bullets when he saw that firing was a waste of effort and ammunition.

Their ears were filled with the enraged howl of a creature in pain, a creature who moments before had wanted to do nothing but go back home, but that now needed to defend itself, to make sure that these people would not be able to hurt it anymore.

"Run!" Ray cried out, reaching out and grabbing Jackson's right arm and starting out towards Taylor's house. Jackson started with Ray's pull on his arm, but he had been closer to the creature when it landed. He almost instantly took the brunt of a blow to his left shoulder, a blow that crushed the bones in there immediately. He cried out in agony, falling to the ground, his mind and body suddenly plunged into shock.

Ray stopped when Jackson screamed, and he turned around quickly. He had heard Jackson land just after he screamed, and his headlamp illuminated Jackson's face, which was gruesomely contorted with pain. His right arm crossed his chest and his hand was at the shoulder, but he wasn't able to hold it. At the edge of the light, Ray saw movement. Even before he was able to look that way, he saw a claw appear in the circle of light and reach for Jackson's throat. He instinctively turned his head and fired, but he shot at empty space. He looked quickly back at Jackson and saw the claw then rip back, tearing open Jackson's throat as it went. Ray fired again. And again. And then he was out of bullets, and he knew that Jackson was dead. He turned and ran.

He was quickly across the street and through the first yard. As he came closer to the side of Taylor's house, he yelled out, "Open the door!" He came around the corner of the house and a sliver of light appeared as the door opened the slightest bit. He reached the walkway and turned around quickly and ran backwards to the door, making sure that nothing was behind him.

"Clear!" he yelled. "It's only me!" The door opened all the way and he stumbled inside.

Forty-five
And Then There Were. . . .

Lopez paced back and forth, waiting for Ray and Jackson to return. She didn't feel right being away from any action, any danger. She knew in her mind that she was right where she needed to be, but her heart told her a different story. She stopped and regarded the fire—its smoke outside was probably a beacon to the creatures and it should be put out, but it was also the only heat in the house. Several times she had considered dousing it, but she knew that putting out the fire would be akin to giving up, and she wasn't about to do that, no matter how hopeless things seemed.

She rechecked her pistol for the hundredth time, then picked up the shotgun from the table and made sure a shell was chambered. She looked at Taylor and Henry and Emily, who had been there to help since this whole thing had begun—had it really been less than 24 hours ago?—and she wanted desperately to reassure them that things would be okay. She couldn't do it, though, and she knew that all three of them would see through any attempt of hers to give hope in a situation that was completely hopeless.

Suddenly they all heard shots outside, then heard the blood-chilling shrieks of the creature and the breaking of a window somewhere in the house. Then came Jackson's scream of pain. Then shots. Then nothing. Lopez was beside herself, agitated beyond belief, wanting to be outside helping them where she was supposed to be.

The short silence that followed the bursts of sound hung heavily over the group, and no one seemed to want to break it. They all knew what they were waiting for—either voices outside and then someone pounding on the door if the shots had hit home, or the sounds of some sort of attack by creatures that tended not to make much noise at all. They looked at each other, their eyes betraying their fear and their sudden lack of hope. It seemed to everyone in that instant that it was over for them.

Then a shout came from outside. "Open the door!" she heard Ray yell, and she moved quickly there. She positioned her foot about four inches from the door, then unlocked it and pulled it open until it hit her boot. She knew that a strong force would be able to force the door open even with her foot there, but she had to at least do something.

She peered through the narrow opening and saw a headlamp appear around the corner, then it turned and faced the other way as Ray turned around.

"Clear!" he yelled, then, "It's only me!" She waited until he was five feet from the door to throw it open; as soon as he was inside she slammed it shut, her foot once again blocking it until the locks were engaged. The news she had just heard made her heart drop.

"It got Jackson," Ray said, trying to catch his breath. "It was so damned fast. I think we hit it, but it still got Jackson after it was shot." He stood bent over with his hands on his knees, staring at the floor.

Nobody replied. Partly because the loss of Jackson seemed so impossible, partly because there was nothing to say.

"Damn," Taylor finally said. "I'm going to miss him."

Henry shook his head ruefully. "That's assuming we make it through this and are actually around to miss anyone."

As if on cue, they heard a thud on the roof. There were some soft, slow footsteps directly over their heads, and then another thump as something else landed a few feet away. Then there were two sets of footsteps moving above them, slowly and quietly. Lopez fought the temptation to start shooting through the ceiling at where she heard the sounds. She knew that only blind luck would be on her side then, and she'd waste precious ammo that they'd more than likely be needing soon.

She looked at Taylor, who was staring at the ceiling, then at Henry, who was leaning back in his chair, his eyes also fixed above where the sounds were coming from. No one spoke until Emily broke the silence several moments later.

"I guess this isn't a good sign," she said, so quietly that Lopez almost didn't hear her.

"Doesn't seem to be," Henry said. He looked across the room at the others who were sitting on the couch or lying on the floor. Everyone but Bill was awake, and everyone was staring at the ceiling. "Any ideas on what to do?"

Lopez smiled wryly. "I was just about to ask you the same thing," she said. "I've got a couple of guns and I know how to use them, but then, so did the others."

"We do have a limited number of entrances they can get in," Ray said, "but we also have a limited amount of firepower; and we really have no idea how many of them there are."

"From the sounds," Lopez replied, "I'd say that there are no more than two on the roof right now. But if they're not on the roof, we can't count them. I say we keep a close eye on the front door and blast anything that tries to get in."

"They're not using the doors," Ray said quietly. "They're coming in through the windows still."

Henry stood up. "They know that we use the front door because that's how Ramsey got in. And that's how you got in just now. I don't imagine them having all that much brain power to work with, but there's a chance they've learned about doors." He paused and looked up at the ceiling. "I truly hate having to go to the bathroom while those things are up there. But I really do have to go. It feels like I'm setting myself up for a very ironic and very embarrassing ending, though." He smiled as he turned toward the tiny hallway.

"Then we'd have a story to tell about you for years to come!" Taylor said with a laugh.

Emily was perplexed. She didn't know how she could laugh at such a time. They didn't seem to be too worried about what was going on, and they didn't seem to be taking it nearly as seriously as she wished they would.

Taylor noticed the way that Emily was looking at her. "Don't worry, dear," she said with a smile. "I am taking this seriously. But if I'm going soon, I'd rather go on my terms, not theirs. Smiling, not crying."

"But these things could kill us. And they're probably going to."

"And there's not a damned thing I can do about it. Oh, I'm scared alright. And I miss Jackson already. I feel like a part of me has been ripped from me. But I know that what's going to happen is going to happen. And if I can't do anything about it, then I can't do anything about it. Sitting here and crying and worrying isn't going to make a bit of difference, except for making my last few hours on this planet a bit pathetic. I don't want to go out being pathetic."

Henry had stopped at the door. He chuckled. "I think most of us have spent enough time being pathetic during our lives. We don't want to make our deaths pathetic, too."

Emily shook her head in wonder. "Well, I have to say that I really do admire your attitude. If I ever make it to your age, I hope I'm able to face things as well as you face them."

"You just stay focused there, Emily, and you'll make it to our age," Henry said.

"I hope so," Emily murmured, just as another loud thud sounded on the roof above. She raised her eyes again in a reflex action, then lowered them almost immediately. "I feel like an animal in a cage, just waiting for someone to come along and destroy me. And there's nothing I can do to change the situation on my own. I don't like it."

"It's called 'being out of control,' honey," Taylor said. "Not like the way you act out of control, but not having any control over an outcome. It's one of the worst things in the world for some people. But you just have to accept it for what it is, let it be, and ride it out—and just wait for the moment when you suddenly gain some control. We're doing all we can, really—it's just that our options are so limited. And the tide will turn. If you learn how to ride out the times when you have no control, you're going to enjoy life a whole lot more. Won't worry as much."

"She's right," Henry added. "Right now we can't do a thing about those buggers up on the roof. We have no chance at all to affect the situation. But once one of them shows their face, we're going to have our chance. We've just got to be patient. Most people try to fix things that are out of their control, and things end up not so well."

"You just have to remember," Taylor said, "that there is a difference between sitting around and doing nothing and sitting around waiting until the situation turns in your favor. Sometimes waiting for that is the best thing we can do, no matter how helpless or hopeless we feel."

Emily sighed. "I see your point. It doesn't make me feel any better, though."

"Right now, I don't know that there's anything that could make any of us feel any better," Taylor said, then she turned slightly to look at Lopez and Ray. "One thing that I will say, though, just in case I don't get a chance to say it later: I thank you three for all that you've done for us today. I'd feel terrible if I didn't take the chance to thank you."

Lopez and Ray looked at each other. They were both thinking the same thing, that their help hadn't amounted to much of anything. They had no idea how many people had died so far, and they didn't have a single shred of evidence that showed that they had helped anyone in this town.

"I guess you're welcome," Lopez said quietly. "We really haven't done anything, though." She looked back up at the ceiling. "And I for one have no idea what we're going to do now."

"Let's not get too squishy here," Henry said. "We still have a chance to make it through this fine, as long as we don't lose our edge. We're still inside and relatively safe, aren't we? And in here, we have the advantage until they do something to take that away. Now really, I do have to go." He turned and left the room.

"He's right," Lopez acknowledged. "And we've got to keep that advantage as long as we can."

"Just so everyone knows," Pauline said suddenly, "it looks like the sheriff may finally be waking up."

They all looked over at Bill, who had been unconscious since Pauline had shown up hours earlier. His eyes were flickering, and suddenly his arms were moving slightly, too. Ray was immediately at Bill's side.

"Hey Bill," he said quietly, "it's good to have you back."

The sheriff's eyes opened, and he looked at Ray. It took him several moments to recognize the deputy, but when he did, he lifted his left hand and put it on Ray's shoulder.

"Grenades," he said softly, struggling to get out the word. "Larry's house, in the bedroom. Trap door." He coughed suddenly, and Ray was alarmed to see a pink tinge to the saliva that escaped his mouth. He looked at Lopez.

"Did you hear that?" he asked her, and she nodded.

"Five-second fuse," Bill added, sounding weaker with each word. "Blow tunnel at midnight. Larry said."

"We can't blow the tunnel with Brad and Brian down there," Lopez said.

"The sheriff doesn't even know that those two morons went down there," Taylor said. "He got shot before they went."

"Nonetheless," Ray said, putting his hand on Bill's, "it might be a good idea to get those grenades and at least provide ourselves with another option."

"Another?" Taylor asked. "I wasn't aware that we had any to start with."

Ray turned back to Bill. The sheriff's face was pale and drawn, and now that he was conscious again, Ray could see that he was in a lot of pain. He looked at Pauline, who seemed to read his mind.

"That's what I was planning," she said. "He'll feel better once we get some more morphine into him." She pulled a small box from her bag and opened it.

"You've got to be kidding me," he said. "How do you get hold of morphine? Is that legal?"

"Up here when something happens, we don't always have time to ask that question, now do we? And sometimes we need to take care of someone's pain before they're able to make the trip down the mountain."

"But you can't just give him morphine without a doctor around," Ray protested, and Pauline stopped as she was shaking pills from a vial into her hand.

"Seems to me, deputy," she said, sounding a bit peeved, "that you're not all that used to life without choices. Some things just have to be done. Now do I help him with his pain or do we argue about what's legal and not and let him lie here in agony?"

"Sorry," Ray said quietly. "Go ahead." Life without choices—the words struck him hard. He looked around at the others in the room, all of whom were looking back in his direction, either at him or Bill or Pauline.

"You know, deputy," Henry said, "sometimes life just deals you a hand of cards that has no chance at all of winning. If you're playing poker, you always have the option of folding. In life you can't always fold. You've got to play those damned cards even if you know you're going to lose your ass in the process."

Ray looked back at Bill, who was looking back at him. He saw the pain in Bill's eyes, and he saw the gratitude there as Pauline gently lifted his head and put two pills into his mouth, then helped him take a drink of water to wash them down.

These people up here, he suddenly realized, were pretty extraordinary.

The door to Taylor's bedroom opened quietly, and Jerry Richardson poked his head out and looked into the room.

"Henry," he said quietly, "do you think you could come in here a moment?"

Henry turned around in his chair and looked. "Absolutely, Jerry. I'll be right there." He turned back to the table as the door closed, and caught Emily's eye. "Jerry's a shy one. Great guy, but quite the shy one." He stood, and added, "You should come, too."

"But he asked just for you," Emily protested.

"Just a hunch," Henry said. Emily paused for a moment, then followed Henry as he went into the bedroom.

They both stopped cold when they saw the scene before them in the dim light of the small lamp on the nightstand. Jerry sat on the edge of the bed, staring quietly at his wife, who was lying in Taylor's recliner.

"She's dead," Jerry said simply and sadly. "I think a bullet came through the window."

"Oh, my God," Henry said quietly, stepping over to look at Eileen's body. He saw the blood on her left temple and turned and noticed a hole in the curtain next to her. He lifted the curtain and felt the cold air coming into the room, and he saw the broken window through the boards that they had put up earlier. There was no more than four inches of space there for the bullet to get through.

"Jerry, I'm so sorry," he said. "This is terrible."

Emily had no idea what to do or what to say.

"Could you give her her last rites?" Jerry asked. "You used to be a priest, didn't you?"

"Jerry, that was years ago. Many, many years ago. I left the order—I'm no longer able to do official things like that."

"I don't care if it's official or not," Jerry said quietly. "Someone needs to give her the last rites. It doesn't matter if some order doesn't recognize you or not, does it? She deserves to get them."

Henry sighed. "You're right," he said. "She does deserve that. And no, it doesn't matter. Given the circumstances, it really is the only right thing to do, isn't it?" He looked over at Emily, who was still standing just inside the closed door, looking helplessly at him.

"Could you sit with Jerry?" Henry asked her, and she moved over and sat next to him on the bed.

"I guess we should start, then. Do you want anyone else in here, Jerry?" Jerry shook his head, his eyes not leaving his wife. "Okay, then." Henry moved to the front of the chair and crossed himself slowly. "In the name of the Father, of the Son, and of the Holy Spirit," he said, softly and firmly.

Emily watched with fascination, and she felt her arm move as she put her hand on Jerry's back between his shoulders. She looked over at him and watched the tears run down his face quietly, and she felt her own tears coming, too. And as she watched Henry give the last rites, she couldn't remember him saying a word during her interview with him about ever having been a part of any kind of religious order.

They were done in a couple of minutes. Henry stepped over to Jerry and put a hand on his shoulder. "Would you like someone to stay in here with you?" he asked.

Jerry shook his head. "No, thank you," he said. "I'd kind of like to be alone, please."

"You've got it," Henry said, and Emily stood, too.

"Let us know if you need anything," she said softly.

"I will," Jerry said without turning to look at them. "Thank you both very much."

"You're very welcome, Jerry," Henry said, and they quietly let themselves out of the room.

Forty-six
Grenadiers

The news of the death in the next room hit everyone hard, but no one harder than Ray.

"That could have been my bullet," he said.

"Or Jackson's," Henry replied. "Don't start thinking too much about this right now. We've still got a lot of night ahead of us."

"That we do," Lopez agreed. "And now that we know about the grenades, we have a job ahead of us. I don't want to sound cold and callous, but we've got to stay focused on what we're doing and grieve later."

Ray looked at her for a moment with a confused look on his face. "You're right," he said finally. "Let's get this done."

"So where did—does Larry live?" Lopez asked.

Henry sat down at the table and pulled his map in front of him.

"He's on the west side street," Henry replied. He made a mark on the map. "You know, it's odd that those two streets never got names. He's just a few doors down from Brad and Brian. Just head down to the end of Main here, take a left, and his is the fifth or sixth house down. On the right."

"So two minutes, tops," Lopez said. "One minute if we're not trying to defend ourselves."

"Pretty much," Henry replied. "There's nowhere you can go in this town that takes a long time to get to."

"You can't really be serious about going out there, can you?" Taylor asked. "After what just happened to Jackson?"

"Completely serious," Ray said quietly. "Because of what happened to Jackson. And Eileen. We've got to stop these things somehow before what happened to them happens to everyone else."

"It may not be such a bad idea, Taylor," Henry said. "We haven't had enough time to notice any definite patterns, but there does seem to be the hint of a pattern so far. At the beginning of the evening we heard gunshots for a while, then they stopped. And it was after they stopped that Alex and I went out there, and we didn't see anything going on at all. Then a while later, things started up again. My guess is that they need to get back down in the mine for some reason. Maybe they need to feed or something."

"That's quite a stretch," Lopez protested. "How can we possibly know if they've gone back down or not?"

"We can't," Henry replied. "That's why I call it a guess. But it's an educated guess. And if you're going for grenades, you're going to go whether they're down there or up here, aren't you? But if you go out and don't see or hear any activity, there's a good chance that they're back down in the mine. And that might be just the right time to use those grenades."

"But what about the people down there?" Lopez asked. "Brad and Brian, and that other guy—"

"Larry," Taylor said.

"Larry. And what about that first guy, Juan, I think his name was? What if he's still alive?"

The entire group was silent for a few moments.

"Have we seen anything at all in the behavior of the Nogglz," Henry asked, "to indicate that those men might still be alive down in that mine? And if they're dead and we don't blow the mine, we've lost what could be our only chance to stop those things. They're too fast for us to shoot, especially in the dark."

"And if they're alive," Taylor argued, "then we're dooming them to exactly what Naugle did to his boys."

"It's not exactly the same thing," Ray put in thoughtfully. "What he did was done with malice aforethought. If we blow the mine, it will be done with no malice at all. And to be completely honest, I can't imagine a scenario with them still alive. We've seen what those things can do up here. How is anyone going to survive down there on their turf?"

"It does seem pretty far-fetched that they could be alive," Lopez agreed. "As much as I hate the idea, this sounds like something we may have to do."

"They have been down there a really long time," Emily added.

Taylor sighed. "There's a part of me that says you're all right, and that we've got to do what we've got to do. But there's another part that says we can't do it because they may still be alive down there."

"Which part is the strongest?" Henry asked.

Taylor looked him in the eyes and thought for a moment. "The first part," she finally said quietly.

* * * *

"I don't like the idea of you two going out there together," Henry said. "If things go bad, that can be pretty disastrous. Besides, you said yourself that you couldn't go out together."

Lopez shrugged. "Those were patrols," she said. "This isn't. Besides, we can't risk having what happened to Jackson happen to you, too. I know you want to go, but it just isn't going to happen. Sorry."

Lopez and Ray both held their pistols up, ready to use them, and they turned on their headlamps as Henry turned the deadbolt knob to unlock the door.

"Are you two ready?" he asked.

Both of them nodded.

"Ray?" Henry asked. "You're good?"

"I'm good," Ray said, nodding his head.

They hadn't heard any sounds on the roof for at least fifteen minutes, but they had absolutely no idea what they were about to face. Henry opened the door and they moved quickly outside, Lopez in the lead. She moved out far enough to be able to look back and see the roof. Though the light of the headlamp wasn't as bright as she wished, she still saw the footprints and scuff marks in the snow that had been accumulating, signs of something that seemed to be no longer there.

"Looks clear," she said quietly. "Let's go."

They moved quickly to the street and went left, slowing themselves down by constantly having to turn around to sweep their lights through the darkness. The snow was falling light but steady and a breeze had picked up, pushing the snow sideways, still making it difficult to see any distance at all in the beams of the lights.

They reached the unnamed cross street and took another left, moving as quickly as they dared, and sixty seconds later they were in front of Larry's house.

"This must be it," Ray said. "Green house with yellow yard-sale curtains. I wonder if the yard sale was up here or down in Pine." He went to the door and tried the knob, which turned easily in his hand. "It's unlocked," he said, pushing the door open and moving inside. Lopez followed immediately, and they closed the door behind them. They didn't dare to turn on any lights.

"In the bedroom," Lopez said. "A trapdoor. Probably under something or in the closet."

"Let's see," Ray said. "Kitchen there, bathroom. . . that leaves this door." He reached out to open it, but the knob wouldn't turn in his hand. "Holy crap—it's locked," he said, sounding confused.

Lopez smiled in spite of the tension she was feeling. "You're welcome to use my living room and kitchen and bathroom if I'm not here," she said, "but don't even think of going through my private stuff. Here, stand back."

It only took her four kicks until the door gave way to the force behind her boot. The bedroom that the open door revealed was furnished simply, with nothing but a twin bed and a dresser and a night stand, with a picture of a woman in a field above the bed.

"Wow," Lopez exclaimed. "That's a Wyeth—I'm impressed."

"A what?" Ray asked.

"The print there. It's by Andrew Wyeth. He's a painter."

"Oh," Ray said, looking quickly over the painting. He turned and started looking over the floor. "I'll check under the bed and dresser. You take the closet."

Lopez moved over to the closet and tried to open it, only to find it locked. "Damn," she said. "Another locked door. And this one swings out."

Ray stepped over and ran his fingers over the top of the door frame. When he brought his hand down, he was holding a key. "Don't need to kick," he said.

Lopez shook her head. "So what's the point of locking the door if you're just going to put the key right there?"

Ray chuckled. "Don't need to have a point. Some people just like to *feel* that something's locked up tight."

When she opened the door and looked inside the closet, her headlamp revealed at least ten rifles leaning up against its walls. "He certainly did like his guns," she said.

"That's quite a collection," Ray said. "I'm impressed. And there's a handle for the trap door." He stepped inside the closet and moved a couple of the rifles, then opened the door.

"I think we're lucky it wasn't booby-trapped," Lopez said.

The space beneath the door was small, and it held four small boxes and several clear plastic bags. Ray reached for one of the bags first. "You want any dope?" he asked. "We've got a few dime bags here."

"Don't think so," Lopez said. "Let's get a look in those boxes."

Ray pulled the boxes from the space and handed them out to Lopez, who put them on the dresser one at a time.

"Let's see what we've got," she said when they had all four boxes. "The biggest and heaviest one is going to be the grenades." Ray opened that box and they saw that she was right. She picked up another box. "I hate to invade his privacy, but if he has anything else here that will help us, we've got to know." She opened the box and looked inside. "Photos," she said. "None of our business."

Ray had picked up another box. "This one's full of medals. Looks like Army." He lifted one out and held it up in front of him. "Holy shit," Lopez exclaimed. "That's a Medal of Honor."

"So he's a Medal of Honor recipient?" Ray asked, sounding duly impressed.

"Well, not necessarily. That could be his father's. Or an uncle's, or another relative's. It's still pretty impressive to find one of those way up here." She picked up the last box, the lightest of the four. "Letters," she said quietly. "Someone named Sandra. Postmarks from 1967. That's almost thirty years ago. He was probably in 'Nam then. The address says APO."

"Damn," Ray said. "I wish he would have come out of that mine." He suddenly felt much less sure about blowing up the tunnel; Larry had suddenly become a human being with an identity and a past; he was no longer just the name of a person Ray didn't know.

Lopez stayed quiet, but she too suddenly felt more torn about what they were planning to do. Was it really necessary? Would it really help?

"Well, we've made it this far," she said. "Let's get back."

Ray picked up the heavy box with the grenades and they started to leave, but Lopez suddenly stopped. She grabbed the other three boxes and put them carefully back into the space under the trap door, replaced the plastic bags, then closed it. Then she shut and locked the closet door, putting the key back atop the door frame.

"Now we can go," she said.

When they reached the street, she stopped once more. "Listen," she whispered, and the two of them stood quietly in the falling snow.

"I don't hear anything but the breeze," Ray whispered back.

"Exactly. What if Henry was right? It seems too quiet for them to be up here. I'm thinking they may be down below right now."

"Which means that now would be a good time to blow the tunnel if we're going to do it."

"That's what I'm thinking."

"But how can we be sure that they're down there?" Ray asked.

"We can't. But the middle street there bisects the town. From there we should be able to hear anything going on, even if they're inside a house.

Especially if they're still going through windows."

"Or get ourselves killed if they're lying in wait."

"That's another possibility. But it looks like now may be do or die time. Of course, we can always head back to Taylor's and take a nap."

"Tempting," Ray replied, smiling. "Very tempting." Then they started walking quickly to their right, towards Oak Street.

Forty-seven
Back Home Again

The trio on the roof sat quietly for a while, not looking at each other, not feeling any compulsion to do anything at all. They were all covered with a thin layer of snow. The bloodlust had left the pair of Naugle's boys, and when it dissipated it took away all reason for them to be where they were, all reason for attacking anyone at all. They were sure that there were people in the house below them, but they didn't care, if caring was within their capacities. All of them felt weak, and the Bastard felt agonizing pain in his arm where he had been shot. Because there was no flesh there, the bullet had shattered the bone and exited the other side. His instinct told him that he needed to get down to the feeding room, to put his arm in the water of the stream that ran through it. His instincts were right, too, for the water had proved in the past that it had healing powers that he never would be able to understand.

They were also starting to feel the cold—it was past three in the morning, and the night cold had come close to reaching its lowest point. Their home in the caverns never had been warm, but their long exposure to the lower temperatures on the surface had started to push them to their limits. While none of them had any sort of conscious wants or needs, all three of them did want to go home.

One of the Nogglz was the first to stand, and he slowly walked to the edge of the roof and leaped to the lawn below. He was quickly followed by the other two, and the three creatures who had been moving at high speeds all day long now slowly made their way back across the street, their skinny corpse-like bodies showing no sign of the energy that they had been showing all day. As thin as they were, it was no surprise that they had limited reserves of strength.

The Nogglz felt no sense of elation, nor did they feel any sense of loss for their three dead comrades. They really didn't feel anything at all. They didn't have any idea that they had lost anything. The Bastard, though, did feel that something was gone, something very important. He knew that they were fewer, and he knew that leaving the caverns had caused them to lose something, had been very negative for all of them. Suddenly, though, he felt lighter. As he was thinking of the loss, he suddenly remembered the gain—there were three more down there now, three new people who would take the place of the others. And they would be as they were before.

All of a sudden, one of the Nogglz stopped and turned, looking back over the town. The other two stopped also, watching him. He stared at the town for ten long seconds, then started running back to it, leaving the other two to watch him go.

But they were weak, and they were hungry, and they felt no calling to follow the other one. They simply turned back around and headed home. The Bastard felt the loss again, but his pain overruled his desire to bring back the one who had fled.

As the remaining Noggl passed through the front door into Sarah's house, he had no interest at all in what was there in the darkness—no interest in the body parts or the remains of the people they had killed. The caverns beckoned him, called him, compelled him to come back and to feed of the glowing moss and to drink of the chill waters of their depths. Into the basement they went, almost obediently, following a call that they did not understand, feeling that their hunger and thirst would soon be satisfied, and that their wounds would soon be healed. The Noggl felt comfortable once they hit the mine shaft, and even more so after they made their way through the hole that he had helped to create, through which they had escaped.

Then, when the mine shaft stopped and the caverns began, he felt his old ways of being coming back to him, the easy existence of eating, sleeping, and moving freely through the caverns in their own world.

Here, they wanted for nothing, and here they belonged. No matter how many people they killed above, they still were not a part of that world, and everyone and everything in it was foreign to them, even if, deep inside, there were memories that they could not access about a time that was different, a time when they were different.

The darkness was comforting. The profound silence, too, helped to calm him, to destroy the agitation that had defined his last twenty-four hours. As they made their way deeper below the surface, the fact that he had satisfied his bloodlust helped him to forget all that they had just been through, helped him to lose the desire for revenge that had driven them to the outside in the first place. That desire was his last link to the top.

About halfway to the feeding room, they stopped as they heard noises ahead of them. They weren't able to see much of each other in the complete darkness—even with their eyes that had adjusted so well over time, no light was no light. They could make out each other's forms, but nothing else; not that there would have been anything to read in their eyes, anyway, had they been able to make eye contact. The Noggl didn't have enough of a memory to remember Juan or Brad or Brian, and noises here in the cave were a threat to him. The Bastard, though, remembered, and he had an idea of who was there. They stopped and waited, and in a matter of minutes, a person in a small pool of light made its way towards them.

Behind the man with the light was another man. They moved very slowly, as quietly as they could, which to the Nogglz wasn't very quiet at all.

The scuffle was brief. In fact it was hardly a scuffle at all—with two quick blows each, the creatures knocked both Brian and Brad out. They stood for a moment and looked at the bodies. Blood was oozing from a new wound on Brian's head. The Bastard reached down and pushed off Brian's headlamp, then grabbed his shirt at the neck and started dragging the body behind him. The Noggl did the same thing with Brad. This would be slower, but it was necessary.

* * * *

The one who had left moved quickly down the street and through a pair of yards to the next street. Something was tugging at his memory, pulling him back to one of the places where they had been earlier. It was an incomplete memory of something he had held in his hand and that he wanted to hold again, but he couldn't match what was happening in his mind to anything there in the town. He had no idea where to go to find it again. He knew where and how to find his food in the caverns, but he was unable to make any such connections up here.

He saw a broken window and ran to it, leaping through it on the run. He scurried through all of the rooms looking for the something, but he didn't find it. The dead body on the floor meant nothing to him. He was becoming frustrated, though he had no idea of just what frustration was.

He left the house through the window, then found the next broken window and entered the next house. This time he was rewarded, for in the second room he entered he found the teddy bear that he had thrown down earlier. He had no idea why he had wanted to see it again, but here he was, and here it was. He picked it up almost tenderly, then slowly sat down, his back against the wall and the teddy bear in his hands.

Forty-eight
Out

Larry was about as lost as he had ever been, which was something that hadn't happened often to him. Added to his disorientation, the hunger and thirst that he was feeling were starting to overwhelm him. The fact that his flashlight was almost dead didn't fill him with confidence. The only thing that gave him any sort of hope was the lack of an explosion. As long as he was within hearing range of grenade blasts, he could figure that there was still a way out of this damned place.

It was already past one o'clock, so the sheriff hadn't done what he had told him to do at midnight. He wondered if it was because the sheriff was still waiting for him to show up or if something had happened to him. Both possibilities made complete sense.

The darkness was deep down here, and it grew more oppressive as his light dimmed. He had found himself in an extremely complex labyrinth that had more passages than he ever would have imagined, and he constantly had to climb up and down, sometimes squeezing through tight spots that grew almost too narrow for him. And all the time he had been listening for any hint of the enemy. He wanted either to take them out or to avoid being taken out himself from behind without a fight. He had even pulled out his earplugs in order to hear better. He knew that promised to make things unpleasant if he were forced to fire his shotgun without getting them back in.

He wasn't sure, but the passage he was in now seemed familiar. At this point, though, it didn't really matter. His light would be out soon, and that would be the end of things for him. He'd keep moving, of course, feeling his way through the caverns, but he knew that the chances of him finding a way out were pretty much zero.

But then he heard something up ahead. It sounded like someone moving, like slow footsteps. He was cautious. He had given up on Juan being alive long ago.

He turned off his light and moved carefully forward, his right arm outstretched and sweeping back and forth to feel for any obstructions. He still heard the sounds growing slightly louder, but he could see nothing at all. All of a sudden, though, he was almost sure that he saw the slightest bit of light up ahead. A person?

He decided to move ahead and verify what he was seeing before he made himself known. He knew from experience that jumping the gun could be disastrous. An extra minute or two wasn't going to hurt, while the possible consequences of making a mistake were too drastic to take the risk.

Suddenly the footsteps stopped. He heard what sounded like someone hitting someone else, then a grunt of pain and a pair of thuds. Then there were growls and hisses, and he moved his shotgun into a ready position, his finger on the trigger.

He didn't want to guess at what had happened. He truly had no idea. If he got his mind fixed on one idea of what had just gone down and it turned out to be wrong, he could end up making a fatal mistake.

The noises changed, and it sounded like something was being dragged off to his left, though he knew that with the echoes in these passages there was no way to be sure of directions. Soon the sounds were gone completely and he relaxed his grip on the shotgun. In the complete silence, he took the risk and turned on his dim flashlight again.

He moved forward as quickly as he dared, and in just fifty feet he came across a larger passage crossing the one he was in. And there was light there. The floor and the walls were smooth here so there were no signs to read, but on the ground ten feet away was exactly what he needed—a headlamp with a strong light. He cautiously approached it and picked it up, his hands immediately becoming sticky. He could see that the band that went around the head was covered in blood. On the ground, too, he now saw a small pool of blood. He flipped the switch and a stronger light filled the corridor.

"I'll be damned," he muttered. What were the odds of this?

He looked down the passage and fought the urge to follow the direction in which he thought they had gone. He had been down here too long without food and water, and he was completely disoriented. He had a strong hunch that going in the opposite direction would finally get him out of the caves.

With a sigh, he turned around and started up the corridor.

Forty-nine
Done

"I had forgotten how much blood there was," Lopez said as they climbed the stairs to Sarah's porch. "Hell, with all that's been going on, I had almost forgotten that Fogel's dead."

"It's strange how that works, isn't it?" Ray asked. "Too much to think of today, that's for sure."

They moved quietly into the house, both of them guided by the light of Lopez's headlamp. They dodged Fogel's body and moved to the basement stairs, where Lopez stopped.

"We have to be completely sure that we want to do this before we go down there," she said. "Otherwise, there's no reason at all to go."

Ray thought for several long moments. "I want there to be another option," he said. "But I can't think of one. And we haven't seen or heard any sign of them up here. We may not get another chance like this."

"I'm pretty sure we won't. But then there's Larry and Brad and Brian and possibly Juan to think of."

"We talked about that. As long as it's been, I think the chances are that they're dead already. And what happens if we don't blow it?"

Lopez sighed. "We do it, then?"

"I say we do it."

"All right." She turned and started down the stairs with Ray right behind her.

Three minutes later they were in the mine shaft where it had collapsed, where the tunnel showed itself, where the Nogglz must have first emerged.

Ray opened the box of grenades. "Five seconds?" he asked.

"Five seconds," Lopez replied. "How do we want to do this? Try to get all of them in there at once, or throw them in one at a time? Or two at a time?"

"There are two of us, so let's go with two to start. We each take one, pull the pin, toss one right after the other. You toss first."

"Okay. And don't forget to cover your ears." She reached out and took a grenade; Ray took another out of the box, then set the box on the ground.

"Ready?" he asked.

Lopez took one last look at the tunnel so she could gauge her throw.

"Wait!" she cried out. "Hold on!" She reached up and turned off the light of her headlamp. "Is that a light on the other side?"

"Damn—it is a light."

"Who's over there?" Lopez asked loudly. There was a long pause with no sound.

"Just me," finally came a voice in reply, though neither of them recognized whose voice it was. Suddenly the light was brighter as they heard the sound of someone crawling into the tunnel from the other side.

In less than a minute they were helping Larry out of the tunnel on their side.

"My God," Lopez said. "We almost trapped you in there." She turned her headlamp back on. Larry looked tired and disoriented, but also a bit peeved.

"You were supposed to do that more than an hour ago," he said. "Where's the sheriff?"

"Shot," Ray said.

Larry grunted, then he reached out and took the grenades from them.

"You two get out of here," he said. "These things could bring the whole place down on top of us."

Ray looked up. He had never considered that possibility.

"Who came down after me?" Larry asked.

"Brad and Brian," Lopez said.

"Well, they're dead now. And I just heard those things down there, so it's now or never. Go on—get!"

Both Lopez and Ray moved slowly, confused at the sudden turn of events. Larry's appearance had happened too fast, had changed things too much, too soon.

"You gotta go quicker than that!" Larry yelled. "I'll give you ten more seconds!"

Then they turned and moved quickly. They had no choice. When they reached the basement, they hurried up the stairs. Just as they reached the door at the top, they heard two explosions that very nearly sounded as one.

* * *

Larry hesitated only a moment after the two officers hurried off. Brad and Brian down in the mine? He smiled. That would be no big loss if they got trapped down there. But Larry was pretty sure they had to be dead. Those two were regularly outsmarted by deer. There was no way they could go down into the dragon's lair and come out alive.

He would start with two, he decided quickly, because he had two in his hands. Halfway in. He pulled the pin on the first and held it loosely in his left hand, then put his pinky finger into the ring of the other pin and pulled the grenade away. The pin came out and both were ready.

He looked into the hole before him and tossed the one in his right hand, letting go of the lever on the other one at the same time. In one smooth motion he transferred the second one to his right hand and threw it, too, into the tunnel.

Then he moved away as quickly as he could, his thumbs jammed tightly over his ears. He wished the damned shaft weren't straight so that he would have a corner to go around, but he had no such luck.

The blasts were almost simultaneous. The force of the explosions themselves wasn't enough to take down the entire shaft, but it was enough to cause the ceiling of the tiny tunnel to collapse. And that collapse was enough to begin a chain reaction in the unstable rock above the tunnel, the rock that had already been blasted once with a much larger explosion six decades ago. Within moments huge chunks of rock were falling into the mine shaft.

One of the first large boulders found Larry, smashing into his shoulder and then pinning him to the ground when he fell. Another boulder hit his head a strong blow, knocking him senseless, and within seconds he was buried quickly and completely. That left no one to witness the complete destruction as fifty feet of mine collapsed in on itself. The way into—and out of—the caverns was completely blocked.

* * *

Lopez and Ray stood on the lawn of Sarah's house, listening in awe to the massive rumbles of the collapse. From where they stood the sound seemed to be coming more from the back of the yard than from the entrance to the shaft in Sarah's house.

As the roar died down, they tried to look at each other, but only ended up blinding each other with their headlamps. They looked away.

"I think he did it," Ray said. "That sure sounded like everything collapsed."

"We have to go check," Lopez said firmly. "We can't assume. We have to make sure it didn't just blast a bigger hole for them to come out of. And Larry didn't come out."

At the entrance to the mine the air was murky and dusty, and it was even thicker in the shaft, but they could still see through it. Lopez led the way into the mine, pulling a handkerchief from her pocket to breathe through. Ray followed, holding his hand over his nose and his mouth.

"It looks like it was pretty solid up there," Lopex said. "There's not nearly as much dirt in the air as I thought there would be. And it's settling fast."

"That's a good thing," Ray said.

It didn't take them long to reach the new wall that blocked their way, completely filling the shaft. The ground around them was littered with rocks of all sizes. Lopez noticed a few snowflakes falling gently in front of her eyes, and she looked up.

"I think we found the other way out," she said.

Above them was a ten-foot-wide hole leading out into the night.

"There's no Larry," Ray said quietly.

"Not unless he went out up there," Lopez said with no hope in her voice at all.

"Damn."

"Let's get out of here."

As they passed through Sarah's house for the last time, Lopez noticed once more just how much blood was everywhere. She was able to look straight at it now.

"Is it over, then?" she asked Ray as they passed Fogel's body. She had avoided looking directly at the body, had avoided thinking about the fact that he was actually gone. Suddenly, though, a feeling of loss overwhelmed her, and the horror of the scene she was walking through registered fully for the first time.

Ray, too, was suddenly feeling different, suddenly feeling the weight of the world slipping off his shoulders. He felt the urge to reach out and take Lopez's arm, but he didn't act on it. They walked across the lawn silently in the darkness and the falling snow, both of them lost in their thoughts, their pistols holstered.

Just as they reached the street, they suddenly heard a high-pitched growl behind them. Both of them whirled, reaching for their pistols, their reaction time slowed by the idea that it was all over. They saw just coming into the limits of their light a creature bearing down on them.

The Noggl was fast and he easily would have reached them before they could fire. Except for the snow. Just eight feet from them his foot slipped and he fell backward onto the street, hitting his head sharply on the ground.

He was stunned for just a pair of seconds, unable to move.

Lopez and Ray froze, staring at the creature before them. It was a shadow of a human being, thin beyond belief with almost no flesh on its bones, skin stretched tightly over its frame, its eyes two macabre black holes in its skull.

"Oh my God," Lopez breathed quietly, seeing for the first time the enemy they had been battling all these hours. It had to be hell to be this creature.

It recovered quickly, though, and suddenly it gave a growl and started to get up. Both Ray and Lopez pulled their triggers and two black spots appeared on its chest, and it was thrown back to the ground.

Lopez stared in disbelief at the creature before them.

"Is that a teddy bear in its hand?" she asked.

Fifty
Au Revoir

Taylor and Henry walked Emily to the helicopter that was on Sarah's lawn. The first chopper had arrived early that morning to find out what was going on. It was manned with just a pair of state troopers looking for Fogel and Lopez. Within two hours, the town had been swarming with law enforcement officers, medical personnel, and television news reporters and camera people. They had even brought in an extra coroner to help with all the work, as well as a pair of medical specialists to examine the Nogglz. The group in Taylor's house had stayed in Taylor's house, not wanting to face the media onslaught, save for Bill the sheriff, who had been airlifted to the hospital early on.

The police had cleared a path of all reporters so that they could get to the chopper unmolested.

"It's been a hell of a night," Henry said, looking around himself at the hustle and bustle. "Now I can finally say that I spent the night at Taylor's."

Emily laughed. You sound just like a dirty old man," Emily said.

"Honey," Taylor said, "you don't know the half of it."

They stopped at the chopper and Emily pulled Taylor close. "Thank you so much for everything," she said. "I'll definitely be in touch. We're staying in touch, right? You'll let me know where you end up?"

"Will do," Taylor replied. "I sure don't think anyone's going to be staying here after this."

Emily turned to Henry and hugged him. "And thank you, too. I appreciate all that you guys did for me."

"And we appreciate all that you're going to do for us," Henry said. "This is a story that really does need to be told." He looked around to see if anyone was within hearing range. "Do you have the journal?"

Emily nodded.

"Good. You're going to need that. Now get out of here. And give your daughter our love."

"I will," Emily replied. "I'm just thankful that I get to see her again. She turned and started to step up into the helicopter.

"Hey, hold the chopper," someone yelled, and they all turned to see Lopez and Ray running towards them.

"They're finally letting us out of here," Lopez said, out of breath from her sprint.

"Good timing," Henry said. "You get to fly out with Emily."

"One minute, people," the pilot yelled back to them.

"I'll tell you what," Lopez said. "As soon as they get that road repaired, I'll be back up to take you both out to dinner, okay?"

"Honey," Taylor replied, "as soon as that road's repaired, we're out of here. There's nothing for us here anymore."

"She's right," Henry said. "I think we've pretty much lost our home. Not the best age to be having that happening to us, but we certainly don't have much choice in the matter. Besides, where in the hell would you take us 'out' to dinner up here?"

"I'd be driving you down to Pine, smart ass," Lopez said.

"Well, wherever I end up, I'd love to have dinner sometime," Henry said, giving Lopez a hug. "You two were great last night. Thank you."

"We'll be in touch," Ray said firmly, avoiding Henry's last comment. "I'll make sure I know where you end up, and we will have that dinner."

"As you wish, deputy," Taylor said with a rueful smile.

"Thank you both," Henry said. "I want to use better words, but I can't find them."

"Thank you, Henry," Ray said, shaking his hand firmly. "I learned a lot from all of you last night. Thank you."

"On or off," the pilot yelled back. Lopez and Ray boarded and Henry and Taylor moved away. In moments the chopper lifted off, and soon it was gone. Taylor and Henry watched it until it passed behind the mountain, then they slowly made their way over Sarah's lawn, across Main Street, and up Taylor's walk. It felt good to be outdoors again, to be walking in the open air. The snow continued to fall softly, and it covered the ground and made everything look clean and pure and beautiful, except where all the people had walked through it and turned it to slush.

"This snow is funny," Henry said quietly. "It's a lie. It's purity. It's beauty in a place where things simply aren't beautiful today. It covers up what's happened here like everyone in the town covered up what happened to Naugle's boys all those years ago."

Taylor smiled. "I don't think it's a lie at all, Henry," she said. "I think it simply is what it is." She paused. "I've got some leftover spaghetti if you'd like an early lunch."

"I'd love one," Henry replied, and he put his arm around her shoulder.

"Watch the arm," she said softly.

Henry pulled his arm back and laughed. It was what it was.

Epilogue

Emily walked slowly down Main Street, holding Taylor's hand loosely. Spring was here and the day was warm, though storm clouds were moving in very quickly in the western sky. They had been here for only half an hour, but they would have to leave soon or face a sure soaking.

Taylor let loose of her hand and ran over to a single red poppy on the lawn next to them, the lawn that had been Sarah's all those years ago. Emily followed her over.

"Look, Grandma—it's pretty!" Taylor said.

"It sure is, sweetheart," Emily said. Taylor reached out to pick it, but Emily gently stopped her.

"Let's leave it here, baby," she said. "Let's leave it so that someone else can enjoy it."

Taylor looked at her as if she were crazy. "But there's nobody in this whole town, Grandma! Who would see it?"

"I don't know," Emily said with a shrug. "But just in case, let's leave it. Okay?"

"Okay," Taylor grudgingly agreed. Then the first raindrops fell.

"Come on, sweetheart," Emily said. "We've got to be going." She held out her hand, then led her granddaughter back to the car. She put Taylor into the child's seat and then stood quietly for a few moments, looking again at Taylor's house, at the pile of rubble that had been Sarah's house, at the car that was parked exactly where she had parked that day so many years ago. These days, the book royalties that still came in allowed her to afford a nicer car, but that fact was bittersweet to her.

Just out of curiosity, she pulled her cell phone from her purse and looked at the screen. She smiled: no signal. Of course. Emily sighed and opened the door, sliding into the driver's seat. It was time to go home and to leave here for the last time.

It was better that they didn't know that they had been watched. It was better that they never saw the creature that stayed hidden among the trees while they had walked the streets of the ghost town that had once been Canyon Bluff.

It had taken him many years to find a way out, to find the exit that the collapse of the mine had created. When he did find it, he had found nothing at all in the town. No life, no memories, no emotions. His mind was long since gone, but his eyes could still tolerate the sunlight as long as he stayed in the shade of the trees.

Though there was nothing in the town but empty houses, he still felt drawn here. He still came up almost every day to sit in the fresh air. None of the other four seemed to share the same urge.

Most of his body mass was gone and he had to go down to feed often, but he felt the town was more a part of him than the caverns were. He didn't know why for he couldn't think of such things—over the last twenty years all ability to think had simply left him.

He watched the car drive away. These were the first people he had seen in years. He slowly shuffled out of the trees and into the now-driving rain, and he made his way over to the poppy that had attracted the small one.

Suddenly he reached out and plucked the flower from the ground, pulling it to his chest and scurrying back towards the entrance to his home. Juan was feeling weak, and he needed to feed.

About the author:

Tom Walsh has spent his life learning and teaching. He's spent 16 years teaching at the college level and seven teaching high school (his favorite thing to do, except for the administrators!). He's also spent four years in the U.S. Army and six years living in Spain and Germany. He currently resides with his wife, Terry, in Bozeman, Montana. Since 1999, he's maintained the website livinglifefully.com, where he shares the words, thoughts, and ideas of people who are trying to help other people with wisdom and advice that can help us to live our lives more fully.

Other books by Tom Walsh:

(If I Should Die) Before I Wake (a novel)
Walker (a novel)
Three Cavaliers (a novel)
Living Life Fully's Daily Meditations
Lay Waste No Power

Coming Soon:

A Universal Guide to Living a Full Life (title subject to change)